D0959239

"They're here..."

Annja felt the breeze that moved her ponytail from in front of her shoulder to her back.

Then she paused.

There was no breeze.

She must have moved, flipped her hair over her shoulder with a jerk of her head. It was the only thing that made sense. Until a strange flutter made her look down.

She didn't know what was causing her sudden nervousness, or making her hear things.

It had to be an insect. It had sounded like that, like wings fluttering.

"Just a bug," she whispered.

A male cry of pain alerted her. She heard a body hit the dirt and the clatter of the plastic-encased camera followed.

"Eric," she whispered.

Footsteps crunched. Those were not Eric's rubber-soled Vans.

Sucking in a deep breath, Annja calmed her racing heartbeat.

She swept out her right hand. Looking into the otherwhere, she opened her fingers and closed them around her battle sword.

Slapping her left hand to the hilt, she prepared to meet whatever was coming around the corner....

Titles in this series:

ROGUE Angel

Alex Archer

THE OTHER CROWD

A GOLD EAGLE BOOK FROM
WORLDWIDE.

TORONTO • NEW YORK • LONDON
AMSTERDAM • PARIS • SYDNEY • HAMBURG
STOCKHOLM • ATHENS • TOKYO • MILAN
MADRID • WARSAW • BUDAPEST • AUCKLAND

If you purchased this book without a cover you should be aware
that this book is stolen property. It was reported as "unsold and
destroyed" to the publisher, and neither the author nor the
publisher has received any payment for this "stripped book."

Recycling programs
for this product may
not exist in your area.

First edition May 2011

ISBN-13: 978-0-373-62149-1

THE OTHER CROWD

Special thanks and acknowledgment to
Michele Hauf for her contribution to this work

Copyright © 2011 by Worldwide Library

All rights reserved. Except for use in any review, the
reproduction or utilization of this work in whole or in part
in any form by any electronic, mechanical or other means,
now known or hereafter invented, including xerography,
photocopying and recording, or in any information storage
or retrieval system, is forbidden without the written permission
of the publisher, Worldwide Library, 225 Duncan Mill Road,
Don Mills, Ontario, Canada M3B 3K9.

This is a work of fiction. Names, characters, places and incidents are
either the product of the author's imagination or are used fictitiously,
and any resemblance to actual persons, living or dead, business
establishments, events or locales is entirely coincidental.

® and TM are trademarks of Harlequin Enterprises Limited.
Trademarks indicated with ® are registered in the United States
Patent and Trademark Office, the Canadian Trade Marks Office
and in other countries.

Printed in U.S.A.

The
LEGEND

...THE ENGLISH COMMANDER TOOK
JOAN'S SWORD AND RAISED IT HIGH.
The broadsword, plain and unadorned,
gleamed in the firelight. He put the tip against
the ground and his foot at the center of the blade.
The broadsword shattered, fragments falling
into the mud. The crowd surged forward,
peasant and soldier, and snatched the shards
from the trampled mud. The commander tossed
the hilt deep into the crowd.
Smoke almost obscured Joan, but she continued
praying till the end, until finally the flames climbed
her body and she sagged against the restraints.

Joan of Arc died that fateful day in France,
but her legend and sword are reborn....

1

Her forged steel battle sword clanked against an iron-plated chest cuirass. The shock of connection had ceased to clatter up her arms and vibrate in her molars. Over the course of the day, she'd become physically numb to violence, to blood.

To her faith.

No, she still clung to faith, to blind trust and humble servitude. It was all she had.

A thunderous warrior's cry from behind her prompted her to spin about. Slick mud made footing unsure. The soles of her laced leather boots had worn thin; she could gauge the rises and fall of earth with a mere flex of foot. She maintained balance.

With no time to deliver an overhand slash of her sword, she plunged it up into the charging soldier's gut. The blade slid under her enemy's bloodied leather cuirass. She felt the soft acceptance as the sword tip sunk into flesh. The soul had been pierced. May God have mercy.

Blood purled down the flat of the blade. Her victim's tri-umphant cry changed to a gurgling requiem. A mace glint-ing with the blood of her fellow soldiers fell from his limp grasp. For a moment he loomed before her in the rain, arms spread, yet hands limp. Mouth open and eyes horrifically wide. Poised between life and death.

As a child she had enjoyed playing in the rain. The world would never again be so carefree.

A heel to his thigh pushed his body off balance. He dropped backward. Mud droplets spattered his face and her leg greaves.

Death proved far too easy.

The violet sky briefly teased at the corner of her eye where mud did not blemish her vision. Too pretty for battle. It prom-ised an end to the abominable weather. A rainbow was swirled in an oily slick before the castle wall.

"Jeanne!"

The familiar voice cut through the cacophony of warfare. Lieutenant Charlier. Just last night his wife had birthed a baby boy who was not breathing. The lieutenant mourned as a black cloud had entered his life. The child had not been baptized before burial, which Jeanne had protested until her throat ached. Now the lieutenant signaled and she followed him. He did not see the English infantryman swinging a deadly halberd behind him.

"No!" She rushed across the battlefield, slick with blood and mud.

A body lay between her and the lieutenant. In the moment Jeanne took to look down and leap over the sprawled enemy corpse, the tip of the armor-piercing halberd poked out from the lieutenant's chest. His arms flung backward as his torso curved unnaturally forward.

She swung madly, utilizing no martial skill save a fierce

determination honed over the past months. Lieutenant Charlier was dead before his palms hit the ground.

Jeanne's sword soughed the air. Impending death held an utterly voiceless tone, yet it sweetened the air as a bird's wings during flight. Her blade connected with the head of the Englishman who had gutted the lieutenant. Because he wore no helmet, the top of his skull was shaved off just above the eyes.

Gulping a surge of acrid bile, Jeanne thrust ferociously following the backswing, but the counterattack wasn't necessary. The man toppled at her feet, his dissected brain oozing out like fresh porridge.

Stumbling backward, metal slapped against metal. Caught by the shoulders, she slammed into an unmoving force. Unable to lift her sword, she struggled, but the man who held her against his armored chest was too strong.

"The Maid of Orléans," he growled. "Does your faith allow forgiveness for murder? You claim power with your sword, vile wench. It is not your power to own. I've never killed a woman, but you are no female. You are a—"

Warm blood spattered her cheek. The man holding her suddenly fell away from her body. She didn't look down and back, because she'd seen too much death. Another man charged at her with a sword to match hers.

The clank of opposing weapons stung her ears. The enemy was right. Who was she to claim power with a battle sword when violence only seemed to beget further violence? Was this truly the path she had intended? How could God command such destruction?

Following a guttural battle cry, a new opponent slashed his bloodied sword toward her. Scrambling to counterattack, her blade tip caught on the screw at her knee greave. She wouldn't be able to deflect the blow. The blade would cut through her skull—

A TRILLING ALARM startled her upright on the bed. Slashing her arms out before her to deflect the blow, Annja Creed cried out, "No!"

When no armored soldier shouted back and she did not feel the agonizing slice of blade to skull, she realized she was sitting in her bed. No English solider stood before her. No mud, or shouts of vengeance, littered the scene. She could not even feel the sting of relentless rain.

The cell phone on her bedside dresser jingled.

She gasped.

The adrenaline rush of the dream did not dissipate. Breathing heavily, she clasped her chest. No wounds. No awkward armor to impede her movements. Not a slick of another's man blood. But it had felt so real. As if she had stood amid the carnage to swing against the enemy.

It is not your power to own.

It was a strange statement she couldn't resist pondering. What power? Had he meant the bloody, yet spiritual, quest that had seen Joan of Arc through countless battles all in the name of faith for her uncrowned king?

Had the people of the times known the Maid of Orléans carried a mystical sword?

Annja possessed that very sword—a sword that had once been wielded by Joan of Arc.

She startled again at the insistent ring, and this time slapped a palm on the cell phone and croaked out a sleep-laced, "Hello?"

"I know it's early, but listen, Annja. I have an assignment for you. It's a really cool segment for the show." The voice on the line jabbered on, but Annja's attention remained divided.

She pressed her hand to her chest. Her heart still beat frantically. It pounded against her palm. She'd had some nasty nightmares about fire before, but not so much the Catholic saint. And never had a dream been so vivid. Almost as if she'd time traveled and acted out the scene herself. Did her forearms ache from swinging the sword as she traversed the muddy battlefield?

"Are you listening, Annja?"

"Yes, go on, Doug. Wait. Did you just say what I think you said?"

"I did."

Annja caught her forehead against her palm. "Doug, I can't believe you asked me to go to Ireland to track…"

She couldn't say the word. Not without laughing. She'd taken on some crazy assignments for her television host job, but this latest suggestion was really out there.

"Faeries," Doug Morrell, the producer of *Chasing History's Monsters,* confirmed.

That's what she thought he'd said.

"Annja, people have disappeared close to a County Cork village called Ballybeag. Rumors report that faeries are stealing them. It's like the legends say when you go wandering on faerie territory, they don't like it and will capture you and make you dance for a hundred years, or something like that. What was the name of that dude? Rip Van Winkle! Wait. He fell asleep—he wasn't dancing."

"Doug. Stop. Please."

"Annja, I'm serious. The report comes from a trustworthy source. The *Irish Times.*"

Ireland's leading newspaper reporting about make-believe creatures? Impossible. But then again, who knew? Faeries were big in Ireland. Or was that leprechauns?

Annja swiped a hand over her face, not wanting to wake up too much, because if she did she'd laugh herself right out of bed. "It was probably a puff piece, Doug. Did you find it in the Entertainment section? Go back to sleep. It's too early."

"I know it's, like, six in the morning. But in Ireland it's

already lunchtime. Do you know they eat blood pudding there? Can you imagine? Anyway, real faeries have been reported kidnapping people. You have to fly to Ireland now. I've already booked the flight for you and the cameraman."

Tapping the cell phone against her chin, Annja exhaled. This was no way to start the day, especially not after her creepy dream. What she needed was another two or three hours of sleep. Not that she hadn't risen early countless times before and been ready for action, but she felt strangely unsettled.

"Doug, I have humiliated myself in more ways than a grown woman should have to endure. All for the sake of the show and its precious ratings."

"And I appreciate your efforts, Annja, you know that. The lost mermaids of Wales episode rocked."

"There were no tails on those women when we filmed them swimming in the ocean. Doug, I'm going to have to revoke your Photoshop license before the FCC catches on to your antics."

"You're kidding me. I thought the tails were realistic. I spent a small fortune on night classes learning how to create water effects."

Annja blew out an annoyed breath. There were much better things to do on a too-new Thursday morning than argue with her producer about an assignment she wouldn't be caught dead taking.

"Get Kristie to do it," she said.

Kristie Chatham, the other host of *Chasing History's Monsters,* would do anything as long as she was allowed to do it in skimpy clothing and suntan lotion was figured into travel expenses. Faeries seemed right up her alley.

"I have two tickets to Ireland in my hands, Annja. One for you, and one for the cameraman. I'll meet you at JFK airport in an hour?"

"I don't believe you heard my emphatic no," Annja said.

Doug never actually connected other people's lives with the fact they did not always sync with his own needs and desires. The kid was young, energetic, and while not exactly a buttoned-up businessman he had put *Chasing History's Monsters* high in the ratings with his quirky style of infusing real history along with legend and myth and making it all somehow work.

Annja grudgingly gave him kudos for that.

"You don't have to believe in faeries to go looking for them, Annja. Besides, when have you ever believed in any of the monsters the show has chased? Dracula? Come on!"

"Believe? Try harboring delusional fantasies," she said. "I could buy into the legend of a Romanian prince killing myriads and spilling so much blood that he was considered a vampire. But little winged creatures? They're fairy tales, Doug. Someone has been pulling your leg."

"Not according to the *Irish Times*. There's a piece about the disappearances in yesterday's Features section. Three people have gone missing in two weeks, the last one just yesterday. Can you imagine how many ways the show would rock if you got footage of faeries?"

"Nope. Not going to happen. I'll stick to Dracula and mermaids, thank you very much. Hell, I've even investigated the chupacabra for you, Doug. But seriously, I think you've been imbibing in too much faerie dust. The tiny critters exist only in kids' movies and, obviously, Doug Morrell's mind."

"Fine."

"Fine?"

She heard the sharp slap of what must have been his palm being slapped against the counter.

"I was saving this part in the event you refused me," he announced tersely.

"What, you're going to actually offer to *pay* my travel

expenses this time? Doug, I'd love to visit Ireland. The country's history gushes up like black gold under every footstep. But stumbling from stone circle to circle in search of magic faerie mushrooms is not my idea—"

"It's on a dig!" he shouted.

Annja paused to recycle what he'd just said through her brain. The man cared little about her profession, and rarely showed interest in the real facts she worked into her hosting segments. She couldn't have heard him right. "As in an *archaeological* dig?"

"What other kinds of digs are there?"

"When you're the man behind the big white curtain, I'm not sure. Seriously, a dig?"

"Yep. Seems student volunteers have disappeared from a dig somewhere in County Cork. No trace of them wandering off or leaving the area. Just vanished. Poof! The locals—and the *Irish Times*—are convinced it's faeries. As am I."

Now he had her interest. Not in the sparkly flying things. *Skeptic* was her middle name. Annja was an archaeologist before TV show host any day. Yet if the opportunity to participate in—or even just hang around—a dig arose, she was so there.

"What's the focus of the dig?" she asked.

"I don't know. They supposedly found some kind of spear. A faerie spear."

"Of course."

"Don't grumble, Annja, you know you want to do this. Your breathing is fast and I can picture you eyeing your hiking boots and boonie hat right now."

"The only reason I'm breathing fast is—"

He didn't need to know about her nightmare. Doug had no clue about her connection to Joan of Arc or that she wielded a mystical sword.

"One hour, and I'll meet you at the airport with tickets in hand."

"Deal." She hung up and shook her head.

She didn't care that she'd just accepted the joke assignment of the century. The opportunity to hang around a dig on Irish soil was not to be missed.

A YELLOW CAB DROPPED Annja off near the departures gate at Terminal 4. She'd packed light. A backpack with laptop and GPS, assorted survival gear and a small suitcase were all she needed. Thanks to both her careers—archaeologist and television host—she was never sure what kind of hotel or living arrangements waited her arrival, and was accustomed to sleeping under the stars—tent or no tent—if need be.

Doug stood on the sidewalk, beaming. His dark curly hair defied the existence of grooming products. Tall and gawky, his jeans hung low on his hips. Though he looked like he'd just jumped off the short bus in front of the high school gym, Annja knew he was just a little younger than her. Men always did come to maturity later than women. She just had to keep repeating that one whenever she spoke with Doug.

Beside Doug, a slender man with pale complexion and a shock of shoulder-length red hair sported an armload of camera equipment and a couple nylon bags slung over a shoulder. He was dressed for adventure in khakis and a long-sleeved shirt.

Annja nodded and received Doug's shoulder-slap man-hug. "Here's your ticket," he said. "I've already arranged for someone to meet you and drive you to Ballybeag. Thanks, Annja, this show is going to rock."

"Uh-huh. Who's this guy?" She cautioned the accusing tone of her voice. She had showered and thought to erase the sleep from her foggy brain, but maybe not so much. "Where's Michael, the usual field cameraman?"

"Sick with strep. This is Eric Kritz." Doug managed a high five with Eric, even though the redhead was loaded down with equipment. "He's the new guy and a buddy of mine."

A buddy of Doug's? That meant he was young, self-involved and one step away from a frat-party bender, Annja thought.

Eric lunged forward with an enthusiastic handshake. Annja had to tug to get her hand back. "I've watched all the episodes of the show," he said. "I'm a huge fan of yours, Miss Creed."

"Thanks. You can call me Annja. How old are you?"

"Twenty." He didn't sound entirely sure of it, though the reply was practiced enough.

Annja swung a disbelieving look at Doug. "Are you serious? Sending me across the sea with a…" The word *boy* stuck on her tongue. Good thing, too. That was no way to start a working relationship. Hell, she just needed to sleep off the aftereffects of the strange dream. "Has he got any experience?"

Doug wrapped an arm around her shoulder and steered her a few paces away from the giddy cameraman. To their left, cabs zoomed by and intermittently deafened Annja. "Not much. But you have to start somewhere, right?"

"I can't believe this. You're sending me across the ocean with Doogie Spielberg? Doug, I'm in no mood to train a new guy. I don't even know how all that camera stuff works. Does he?"

"He does. His father owns QueensMark studios out of Manhattan. They do independent films, documentaries and stuff. Eric has been following in his father's footsteps since he could toddle. He's very good with the camera. He knows the drill and accompanied his father on a stint last summer in Kenya. He's enthusiastic, but more important, he likes you."

Annja rolled her eyes.

"He can take care of himself. He's a big boy."

She glanced back at the guy, who looked like he belonged in the front row of a classroom dodging spitballs from the bully. Not even a shade of five-o'clock shadow.

"You owe me one for accepting this assignment," she muttered.

"Duly noted. You go and do your job. Sleuth out the facts and bring home faerie footage. Like I said, I arranged for a buddy of mine who lives near the dig to meet you and be your guide."

"Another buddy? How old is he? Twelve?"

"Annja." Doug pressed a dramatic hand over his heart. "You wound me. All my twelve-year-old friends are tucked in with their Transformers blankies right now." He winked.

Doug may appear erratic and selfish on the outside, Annja thought, but she could not ignore his savantlike work ethic that had made *Chasing History's Monsters* a success.

"His name is Daniel Collins," he explained. "He's more a friend of Eric's father. Eric spent a couple of weeks at his home a few summers ago during a business trip with his dad. I understand the man's a laidback dude and you'll get along with him, I'm sure. You get along with everyone, Annja."

"Guides are good." Of course, the country was small, about the size of Indiana, but a guide would free her to worry about the assignment.

Missing students. Mystery surrounding an archaeological dig. And…faeries.

Hey, she was a professional. She could handle any assignment Doug lobbed at her. As soon as she got a few more hours of sleep.

"You tell her about Daniel?" Eric asked as he joined them. "Daniel's a bit of an eccentric," he said to Annja, "but more normal than any other person on earth. Trust me on that one.

But whatever you do, don't get him talking about wine unless you've got hours to spare. The man is really into wine."

"I can dig it." She shoved her hands in the front pockets of her cargo pants and eyed Eric. Eager puppy dog waiting for a bone.

"Annja, this story is going to rock!" Doug said.

Her producer's enthusiasm wasn't capable of lifting even a hint of a smile on her face. Assessing her tense muscles and stiff posture, she realized she was anxious. Not only was she voluntarily traveling three thousand miles to chase after Tinkerbell, now she'd acquired puppy-sitting duties, as well.

"First sign of trouble, I'm sending him home," she said as she snatched the tickets from Doug's hands and strode into the airport through the sliding glass doors.

2

His cell phone volume was turned off, yet he'd set it to flash with an incoming call. Garin Braden leaned across the black silk sheets and eyed the caller ID. A familiar, yet unwelcome, name was displayed. He groaned and sat back. A flute of champagne was cradled in his hand, and he ran his fingers through the long blond hair that spilled over his bare chest.

"No bubbly for you?" he asked.

"I'll be up in a bit," she said in a husky drawl seasoned with just the right touch of determination. Her head disappeared beneath the sheets.

The red flashing LED had ceased and now the phone vibrated across the marble nightstand. That indicated someone was leaving a message. He didn't want to talk to the old man at this particular moment.

Slamming back the champagne, Garin set the glass on the nightstand next to the phone that began to blink red again. "Give it up, old man."

Another message vibrated the cell phone dangerously close

to the edge of the nightstand. Just when the phone teetered and threatened to drop to the marble floor, it flashed and Garin snatched it and flipped it open.

"What?" he growled. "This had better be good, Roux."

"It'll surely be more stimulating than whatever it is you're engaged in right now."

"I wouldn't be too sure of that," Garin said, gazing at his companion.

"Mental stimulation oftentimes exceeds that of the physical."

"Doubt it. Why the call? I haven't heard from you in months."

"The Fouquet has resurfaced. Thought you'd want to know about it."

"I'm not particularly concerned about ever seeing that thing again. Too many bad memories. A painting. Is that all?" He clutched the sheets. What the hell was the blonde's name?

"It's being auctioned off at Christie's in New York this afternoon. I want you there. Buy it."

Garin laughed. The blonde popped her head out from under the sheets and grinned at him. He gestured for her to roll to the side. Roux had spoiled the mood.

"I'm not interested in putting that thing on my wall," Garin snapped. He swung his legs over the side of the bed and leaned forward. "Ever."

"It's not for you or myself," Roux explained with castigating patience. "I thought it would make a nice gift for our Annja."

Our Annja. It always startled Garin when Roux referred to her in that manner. It was too possessive.

"Why?"

"Garin, there are more things in life than fast cars,

million-dollar acquisitions and women. You know what month it is?"

"I'm not keen on the late-night quiz show, old man. I'll have you know I was engaged in something far better—"

"Blonde or redhead?"

"Blonde."

"Common. There's always another one around the corner."

True. Garin turned and cast a wink over his shoulder at the pouting female. She got up and lazily wandered into the bathroom. "Why don't you simply call in your bid?" he asked.

"I want you to look at the thing before bidding. I can't be sure this is the actual painting. It's merely attributed to Fouquet and listed as 'in the style of the fifteenth century master.'"

"So why don't you go after the bloody thing?"

"Because you're closer."

"Closer? I'm in Berlin, Roux. And let me guess—you're in…Monaco, reclining under the moonlight on the roof of the yacht surrounded by a blonde, a redhead and a brunette."

"You don't get points for being obvious."

"Technically, you're closer to New York. You go after the thing."

"At the moment, I'm not near any major airport. And there is a time issue. I found out about this just moments ago. And I know you have a collection of private jets and planes and, who knows, maybe even a submarine or two."

"Sold the sub last month."

"I hope it wasn't to the enemy."

"Your definition of enemy is vastly different from mine, old man."

Roux huffed out a breath. Garin loved to tweak at his presumed morals. "No matter. You can get there faster than I, Garin. So you'll do it?"

Garin sighed and shrugged, rubbing a palm over his face. "For Annja?"

"Indeed."

"Fine. Send details, an address and get me set up with a bid number so all I have to do is stroll in and take the thing."

"Done."

3

Rangy and easy in his skin, Daniel Collins was, from outer appearances, quite the character. Long skinny jeans clung to his legs as if glued to the skin. The pants certainly didn't require the white suspenders that hung loosely over a black shirt decorated with gold appliqués across the chest. A red-and-black plaid coat, the sleeves rolled to expose his veiny forearms, hung on his lithe frame. Gold hoop earrings clung to both earlobes and were small enough not to be garish, but added an interesting glint to his narrow face, which was mastered by bushy black brows.

A black fedora capped his head, and he tilted it to Annja as she approached to shake his hand.

"You must be the television host Mr. Morrell asked me to drop everything to come and fetch."

"Sorry about that. Doug tends to think the world moves on his time. So I assume you're as surprised about this assignment as I am?"

"Surprised, but willing. It's not every day I'm given the

opportunity to show a lovely American lady around my neck of the woods." He looked beyond Annja. "Eric?"

"You remember Eric Kritz. He's my cameraman," Annja said.

Eric looked up from his iPod long enough to nod at Daniel. He didn't have the earbuds in. He'd explained to Annja during the flight that he used the music player as a backup hard drive to store still photographs. He must be paging through the aerial photos he'd taken from the plane as they'd landed she thought.

"You're all grown up, Mr. Kritz," Daniel said in acknowledgment. "So, the two of you, have you got some ID so I can be sure you are who you say you are?"

Taken aback by that request, Annja laughed. She was often introduced and accepted merely for her fame and the fact she was associated with the TV show. But a wise man should ask for ID.

She tugged her passport out from her backpack and flashed it for him. "I don't have ID from the show. But I am who I say I am."

Eric did have press credentials for *Chasing History's Monsters,* which he flashed. How he managed a press pass—and she had never been given one—was something Annja intended to discuss with Doug when she returned to the States.

Eric shuffled around in his duffel bag and pulled out a small cigar box. "Mr. Collins," he said, "a gift from my father." He handed over the box.

Daniel sniffed the box, his eyes closing briefly in olfactory satisfaction. "Cigars. Thanks to your father, boy. I do love a Montecristo."

"Inspired by Dumas's story," Annja tossed out. She was an Alexandre Dumas fan.

"Indeed. *The Count of Monte Cristo.* A fine story, if not a wee bit far-fetched." With a wink to her, Daniel tucked the box under an arm without opening it to inspect. He gestured that they follow him to the parking lot outside the airport terminal.

"Doug said you know the dig director and can get us clearance to film on-site?" Annja asked.

"Already done. His name is Wesley Pierce and he expects you. Let's hop in the Jeep and get you settled first. There's a cozy little B and B a few jogs from the dig site at the edge of Ballybeag, and I know the proprietress, Mrs. Riley. Already told her you'd be needing rooms." He winced, noting Eric's general disinterest. "Be sure and take advantage of the breakfast every morning, but with a warning to avoid the black pudding."

"Avoid the black pudding," Annja affirmed as she climbed into the passenger seat of the Jeep. Eric shuffled his equipment into the back and scrambled in. "Would it be all right if we head straight to the dig? After the flight delays and layovers it's late afternoon and I'd hate to lose a day. I want to take a look around, familiarize myself with the area. I may find an opportunity to talk to someone who knew those who disappeared."

"Doug was right about you being focused," Daniel said. "To the dig it is."

Once out of city limits, the regional roads in County Cork—all of Ireland, for that matter—weren't so much roads as pathways carved out of necessity for getting from one place to the other. They weren't well marked, and if so, Annja noticed, the signs sometimes displayed kilometers, and other times mileage—on the same road.

"You have to learn the county quirks," Daniel commented when Annja remarked about the mileage markers. "I've decided it's always best to go by kilometers. But no matter which method of measure you choose, you'll always end up somewhere, sooner or later."

"Somewhere is a better place to be than nowhere at all," Annja agreed. The open-topped Jeep sucked in the country smells as they traversed the rugged road. She tilted her head against the seat and took it all in.

"You feel like you're home?" Daniel asked Eric after they'd been driving awhile.

"Huh?"

"I mean your heritage."

Eric wielded a mini-DV video camera, sweeping it across the horizon.

"Come to recall a conversation with your father," Daniel mused, "I think his pa's grandfather was from around this neighborhood somewhere."

"Cool," Eric said.

Annja caught Daniel's eye. He clearly wasn't impressed with Eric. She had to give the kid credit, though. He was filming, and she liked his focus.

Ireland did take the prize for being green. Though a dusting of fog hung low above the ground, the rolling fields were coated with what looked like tightly packed moss, though she knew it was wild grass. Dark green shrubs pocked the perfect quilt of emerald here and there.

"Is that gorse?" Annja asked of the shrubs spotted with golden blooms.

"When gorse is in flower, kissing is in fashion," Daniel replied. "Or so they say." Again he winked at her, and resumed his attention to the road.

A row of pine trees lined a field where livestock grazed. The cattle were hearty and looked like something out of an old English cottage painting. There were even a couple of sheep.

They careened around a sharp curve that hugged what Annja knew was a rath, a small hill that locals would be keen to avoid because they believed faeries lived beneath the hill.

She had brushed up on the local mythology during the flight. It wasn't in her to resist any kind of mystery, and if that entailed learning more about the history of the land, then she was all for that.

Faeries were definitely integrated into the Irish culture.

"Hang on!"

At Daniel's shout, Annja gripped the handhold above her head and was crushed up against the steel door. A fast-moving white truck barreled toward them. Daniel swerved sharply to the right. The Jeep slid sideways over the rough gravel, the tires clambering for hold.

Thick spumes of road dirt clouded over the open-topped Jeep. From the backseat, Eric cursed and coughed. Annja tucked her face into her elbow but she still inhaled a hearty dose of dust.

"The devil take those lousy bastards!" Daniel gunned the accelerator and managed a remarkable venture over what looked like moss-covered boulders edging the road.

Through the foggy mire, Annja spied something small and white. "Sheep!"

The Jeep veered sharply left. Eric clung to the roll bar and swore.

"Missed the poor bloke," Daniel announced with cheer. "Won't be dining on chops tonight!"

Clinging to the door frame so she wouldn't be bounced out of the car, Annja called back to see if Eric was all right.

"And the equipment?" she hollered after his affirmative grunt.

"Full of dust, but fine."

"Sorry 'bout that." Daniel's grin met Annja's worried glance. She offered him a sheepish smile. The Jeep navigated the road in the wake of the truck that had blown by with so little regard. "The bastards in the new camp have all sorts of macho equipment they're driving back and forth all times of day and night. They've no respect for the land, that's for sure. Fashes me, it does."

"The new camp? I thought this was a single dig? Isn't it just a simple artifact find?" Annja asked.

"Right. Farmer found a spearhead when he was cutting turf on a dried-up blanket bog. NewWorld, the managing outfit, sent in a team to investigate. That team is headed by Mr. Pierce. When Neville took over financing the dig, he split it into two camps to get twice as much work done."

"NewWorld is the company overseeing the dig?"

"Far as I know. Unless Neville has taken the reins and holds sway over the entire operation."

"Who's Neville? I've never heard of a private citizen taking over a dig from a management company. Unless he's with another overseeing outfit?" Annja asked.

"Nope, Neville's private. He's…" Daniel shifted gears and didn't say any more.

Annja suspected he was leery, which struck her as odd. What did he know that he wasn't willing to say?

After a strained silence, Daniel spoke. "He's a very powerful man, let's leave it at that. He's seen something he wants. Now he's going to get it."

A dig separated into two camps was unusual. It was financially prohibitive to operate two complete camps. And Annja knew a management corporation always oversaw any dig operated on Irish soil. No private citizen could simply decide to dig for treasure. It just wasn't done. Annja knew, for a fact, that the average citizen couldn't even buy a metal detector in this country. A person had to have a permit, and had to be either an archaeologist or an ordnance surveyor.

This Neville guy must be very powerful. But what did he

hope to find on a routine dig that had only turned up a spear shard?

"You work on the dig?" she asked Daniel.

"Nope. I'm not a bone kicker. Just stop in every once in a while to chat with friends. It's close to my house." He pointed north and Annja spied a small thatch-roofed stone house across the field. "That's me mum's home. I'm a half mile beyond but you can't see for the hill. The dig site is ahead."

"Time to film some faeries," Eric said enthusiastically from the backseat.

Annja rolled her eyes, but noticed Daniel's lifted brow at her reaction. She was perfectly willing to allow the older villagers and those born and raised in the country their belief in a folk superstition. Folk tales and myth had been bred into them.

But Daniel Collins seemed an educated, modern man. Not one to be placing a bowl of cream out on his back porch at night.

4

"Looks like the rain is going to stay away today." Daniel pulled onto a gravel road edged every twenty feet by head-size boulders. It led to the dig site. "You're in luck."

"The luck of the Irish, eh?" Eric intoned from the backseat.

"Don't try the leprechaun accent, kid," Daniel said. "It'll only get you in trouble around here."

"Sorry."

Annja offered Eric a conciliatory smile from over her shoulder.

They rambled over rough pot-holed gravel and dirt tufted with grass. It wasn't a real road, but had obviously been worn down by the trucks like the one that had run them off the road earlier. Where the truck had come from was a mystery. And though she only got a brief look at it, she could swear it was armored because the windows were narrower than usual.

The field was a compact area, perhaps a half mile long, bookended by a forest on one side and an electric fence on the other, which Annja assumed kept in cattle or sheep, though she didn't spot any four-legged creatures at the moment.

"Is that the farmer's land beyond the fence?" she asked.

"Yes. The dig sits on the river's edge, a bit over half a mile from the shore. The forest separates the two."

The fog had receded but the sky was still gray. Annja spotted eager students at work in the dirt thanks to a tarp canopy erected overhead should foul weather decide to break.

Annja scanned the grounds, excitement brewing. She forced herself not to grip the door handle and run out and start mucking about in the dirt. It didn't matter what they were digging for, she wanted to get her hands in the mix. It had been too many months since she'd been involved on a real dig. Sometimes breathing dirt all day was better than sex.

"The Bandon River is a jog to the west beyond the trees," Daniel noted. "We get some boats, private yachts and the occasional lost barge up the way. Great for fly-fishing."

"Really? And I left my fishing rod at home," Annja replied.

"I can hook you up if you're interested in snagging a salmon or two."

"We'll see if I have a spare moment. I'd love to learn to fly-fish."

Daniel's attention averted sharply. "What the bloody—?"

The Jeep squealed to a stop and Eric groaned. The kid was juggling camera equipment to save it from breaking. He wore a sheen of dust from their near-miss with the truck, but it managed to give his face some color.

"A fight?" Daniel shoved open the driver's door.

Annja pinpointed the scuffle fifty yards ahead, just outside a staked canvas tent. It wasn't a friendly disagreement with shaken fingers and vitriolic words. Fists were flying.

Daniel leaped out from behind the wheel and raced across the muddy grounds.

"Is he going to join in?" Eric said with so much disbelief Annja had to smile.

"Appears so."

"Cool." Aiming his video camera at the scuffle, Eric began filming. "What could they possibly be fighting over on a dig? I mean, this place is boring central. People poking about in the dirt with dental picks?"

They did use dental picks for the finer, detail work. And what was so wrong with that? Annja wondered.

Turning the other cheek to the boy's ignorance, Annja stepped out from the Jeep. "I'm going to check it out. Stay out of everyone's way, but…keep filming."

Much as she didn't approve of the macho posturing, if there was tension between the two camps, as a reporter, she was interested. As an archaeologist, she never overlooked the details. If people were disappearing into thin air, then exposing the differences and arguments between the two camps could be key in learning the truth behind it all.

A crew of six men dressed in cargo pants and T-shirts— standard dig gear—surrounded two struggling men. A tall, sun-bronzed dark-haired man with dusty khakis and no shirt delivered a punch that sent the other black-haired bruiser sprawling into Daniel's arms.

Daniel shoved the fallen man aside and went at the dark-haired one full force. He wasn't necessarily trying to stop the violence. In fact, he assumed the other's position and now pummeled the shirtless one in the gut. The man's abs were well defined, and he took the punches with a grinning challenge and gestured with his fingers to deliver more punishment.

"Boys," Annja muttered, and then smiled despite herself. The one who'd been shoved aside snorted blood and spat as he assumed a bouncing, fighting stance. He wore black khakis and military boots. His black hair was shaved to stubble. Swinging, he lunged for the pair and rejoined the scuffle. All three went down in the wet soil that had once been grassy, but now was being shaved bare by kicking, sliding boots. None seemed to have the upper hand, and if they did, it was quickly lost to another.

The men standing around watching the fight pumped their fists and urged on their man. A few women in T-shirts and shorts, and scarves to tie back their hair, lingered away from the fight near the marked dig. Their interest was more worried than keen.

Hands to hips, Annja wondered how long they'd go at it before someone got seriously hurt. Could be a means to blow off some steam after a long day spent hunched over and digging for nothing more than worthless pot shards. But this was no way to act on a dig. Archaeologists enjoyed a good workout and were not slouches. But they preferred to use their brains not their fists. At least, the ones Annja had worked with followed such moral compasses.

Did she need to whip out her sword and show them who was boss?

Annja crossed her arms firmly, biting her lip. Wouldn't go over too well, and she realized the fight was probably more a means to let off aggression, and if denied that, the men would stew and simmer—over *what* she intended to find out.

She was surprised at Daniel's eagerness to join the fray. He'd come off as laidback and good-natured. Though he had shouted at the truck that had almost run them off the road. But who wouldn't have?

Could the stereotypical belief about the Irish temper hold truth? It was looking pretty plausible.

Someone must have found something valuable. That was Annja's only guess as to the source of their rage. If one camp found something of value, who then did it ultimately belong to?

Then again, she didn't notice any find tables or black rubber buckets with bits and shards of pottery. Must be inside the canvas tent.

The dig was flat and bare and surprisingly clean of spoil dirt. The turf had been cleared away from a forty-by-forty-foot section beside the tent. The second camp was about two hundred yards to the north just over a ridge that was too high to be one of the infamous potato ridges still remarkable from the nineteenth century. It was far enough away so one couldn't shout back and actually hear what had been said, but close enough for curiosity.

Beyond the ridge she spied a truck, similar to the vehicle that had almost driven them off the road. It looked like a delivery truck, though. She figured it must contain supplies or could even function as a mobile office for the dig director.

The situation was odd. Digs didn't split up like this unless they were large and initial investigation proved a major feature had been uncovered like an entire castle wall or even a village.

If they'd only uncovered a spearhead, Annja couldn't imagine why the split. Unless artifacts had been sighted in both locations. Still, it would be difficult to get permission from the county for such a large operation.

A jawbone cracked. A male groan was followed by a litany of Irish oaths and promises to do something nasty to the other guy's mother.

"All right, boys." Annja stepped close enough to feel the wind of one of their punches. "Fun and games is done. Time to get back to work."

"You heard the lady," Daniel growled from his position, bent over one man and clasping him about the waist, while the other twisted his leg to topple the threesome. "Feck!"

The dark-haired man was the first to pop up from the tangle. Hopping from foot to foot, his fists ready for a defensive swing, he smiled a million-dollar blast of white that made Annja do a double take. Relinquishing his fight stance, he smoothed a palm over his muddied abs and gave her the once-over. A preening look. She straightened her shoulders.

The man was not ugly at all. Sometimes her assignments really were easy on the eyes. And she hadn't bothered to check the mirror after arriving at the airport. Her face must be coated with road dirt like Eric's.

"A lady stepping up to the fight?" he volleyed at her. "Fancy a tussle with the boys, then?"

"That was a tussle?" She lifted a brow, noting the scrape on his shoulder. "Was the bloodshed worth it? What were you fighting about?"

The other guy, whose lip was cracked and bleeding, struggled from Daniel's grip, shook himself off and puffed up his chest. He wore a dark blue muscle shirt streaked with dirt. "Ma'am."

He'd apparently taken a clue from the dark-haired man and didn't want to be shown up in manners. Annja discreetly rubbed a hand along her cheek. A fine sheen of dirt smudged her fingers.

"It's Annja," she offered, holding out a hand to shake, and receiving a slap of mud-caked sweaty palm. "Annja Creed."

"Annja's here to do a shoot for her television program," Daniel offered with a swipe of his palm across his sweaty hair. Retrieving his hat from the mud, he placed it on his head and gave it a pat. A chunk of dirt landed his shoulder.

"Absolutely not," the militant one spat out.

"Cool your jets, Slater," the brunette said. "Let's offer Miss Creed our nicest welcome before you start slinging mud at her."

"If I'd known the welcoming committee was going to get rough, I'd have worn my armor," Annja joked.

Then she recalled the nightmarish dream. Fighting in mud? The dream had nothing to do with this situation. Couldn't have. She offered a hand to the dark-haired man, who shook it and held it a little longer than usual.

"Wesley Pierce," he offered. "Director of this camp. You going to put us on the television? Be sure to get my good side, will you?" He turned and offered a beaming smile, face coated with mud.

"This is Michael Slater," Daniel introduced the other, who eased a hand aside his jaw. Annja noticed the empty gun holster strapped under his left arm.

Slater spat to the side and nodded to her. "No filming on location."

"Nice to meet you both," she replied. "And don't worry, it's just a segment for a show on monsters."

Slater looked her up and down. His face was streaked with dirt and sweat. Anger vibrated off him like heat waves in the desert. "Monsters?"

She shrugged. "Faeries, actually."

Slater smirked and disregarded her by turning and slapping the mud from his black khakis.

"You need to sit down," Annja said to Wesley.

She assumed responsibility since it was sorely lacking, and directed Wesley to a bench outside the dig area that was cordoned off with rope and pitons.

"Wanker," she heard Slater mutter. Obviously directed at Wesley. He slapped Daniel across the back. "Good to see you, mate."

She had thought Daniel wasn't an archaeologist, but he seemed to know most in the camp as he waved to some and slapped palms with others. What did the man do? Spend his days visiting the site? Did he have a job? Doug had mentioned he was some sort of collector. And he obviously liked his cigars.

"A friend of yours?" she asked, bending before Wesley Pierce to inspect his damaged shoulder. He sat on an overturned plastic bucket, knees spread and shaking his arms out at his sides to simmer down.

He shook his head. He was obviously in pain, and she didn't want to touch him, or make him appear weak in front his friends for needing attention from a woman, but...

"Your lip is cracked."

"It'll heal," he muttered in tones heavily creamed with an Irish accent. "Bloody Slater. Bastard is walking around with a pistol strapped at his side."

"Is that why you two were fighting? Why the need for weapons at a dig site?"

"Exactly," he said, and flinched.

One of the women arrived with a small plastic tub of clean water and a towel, which Annja took and dabbed at Wesley's face. The cut on his shoulder was merely an abrasion.

"Why don't you tell everyone to clean up their loose," Wesley said to the woman. "Day's shot as it is. Might as well head out." The girl nodded.

"Sorry. Can I do this for you?" Annja asked, holding the towel before him. "Or would you prefer I not?"

"Go ahead. If I get the attention of the prettiest lady on the lot, I'm all for that." He spat to the side and flashed the bird toward Slater's retreating back. "No bloody guns!" he shouted.

Slater dismissed his theatrics with a return flick of the bird.

"Not even for security?" she asked.

Security was not uncommon on a dig, Annja knew, but it usually consisted of a hired guard or a camera set up to keep an eye on possible theft. That was if valued artifacts had been discovered, such as gold, jewels or even centuries-old bones.

"You must have found something important," she tossed out, but Wesley continued to fume, his eyes following Slater's departure to the other camp, flanked by a couple of his own people.

"Ever since Neville took over financing the dig this kind of shite has been happening on a daily basis. First, it's splitting up the camps and shoving us over here away from the peat bog, then it's sending over spies to snoop out what we've found. Like they didn't think to simply ask? And today it's the gun. Don't let him intimidate you, though. He'll try to kick you off his site. He got rid of the BBC yesterday."

"Really? Then I don't think our little show stands a chance if the BBC isn't allowed on-site."

"Don't worry, I'll vouch for you. Besides, you're much prettier than the BBC reporter. He acted like he had a stick up his arse when Slater accused him of sensationalizing the remains of the dead. Ha!"

Eric clattered up with camera equipment hanging from his hip belt. A mesh backpack dangled over one shoulder, a few cords poking out. He twisted at the waist, the video camera recording the surroundings.

"The dig site located two kilometers west of the R605," he narrated into his mic. "Go ahead, Annja, take up my narration. You know more about the landscape than I do. Describe some of this stuff. It's all so cool."

"Eric Kritz, Wesley Pierce. He's my cameraman," Annja said. She dipped the towel in the water, and sat beside Wesley on another bucket. "Not right now, Eric. Go scan the work site. Over where the earth is marked off and you see that big hole?"

"Okay. Whatever you say, Miss Creed." He ambled off.

"Don't step inside the ropes!" she yelled at him.

"He's never done this before?" Wesley asked.

"Not on a dig. But he's got to learn sometime, right?"

"You're not like the other television shows. They come in with lights flashing, scripts girls fluttering their wares and makeup ladies wielding powder-laden brushes."

Annja knew of at least two BBC shows that dealt with history and archaeological digs. "We're American, not British. Our focus is more on…myths and legends."

"That's an interesting twist. How did an American show sniff out this dig, if I can ask?"

"My producer read the *Irish Times*." Which, now that Annja thought about it, couldn't possibly be true. Doug reading the *Irish Times?* He must have been surfing the Net and got lost when trying to drum up information on Irish stout. "Anyway, he learned that people have been disappearing from the dig."

"Three so far. Two men and then Beth Gwillym just yesterday morning. I'm glad Slater chased off the BBC because this is a small, personal situation. The presence of paparazzi is only going to aggravate the brewing tension. I expect utmost respect from you and your cameraman, or it's out of here for the both of you."

"I promise it. I'm sure the families will appreciate a low-key investigation until the truth comes out."

"It's a sad, strange thing."

"Are you sure the missing people didn't just wander off?"

"To where? Look around you, Annja. There's the river right there beyond the trees, and a vast stretch of land to all three sides. Not many places to wander and get lost. Sooner you'll wander right into a pub in Ballybeag, the only village in County Cork that features four corners of pubs."

Impressive, but not relevant at the moment, Annja thought.

"What about that forest? It doesn't look very dense."

"It's more a copse than a forest. You can walk through it in ten minutes and drop directly into the river if you're not paying attention. A man's to be careful of the tides—they'll sweep you downriver faster than you can holler your last words. Besides, I walked through those woods after each disappearance. Nothing but underbrush and magic mushrooms in there."

"Magic mushrooms?"

"You have to know which ones are the right ones because the wrong one will kill you."

"You indulge in mushroom-eating often?"

"Not a once. Though some of the ladies were giggling mightily the other night on the way to the pub after-hours. I had to wonder if their noontime gambol through the woods had netted more than just a few ticks."

He smirked and took the wet cloth from her to press against his bare shoulder. "So you've come all the way from America to investigate? Doesn't feel right."

"I'm not here on an official policelike means. We reporters go anywhere the stories are, most especially on our show." A show that chased monsters like Frankenstein and Dracula and the bat boy. "Have the authorities done a search?"

"Sure, the gardai took a look about. They're a couple of good blokes. Took names and asked all the right questions, but what can they do when people disappear into thin air?"

"Thin air is a remarkable statement. Did anyone actually see them disappear?"

"Nope, happened at night."

"At night? You work at night?"

"No, we head for the village come suppertime, which is right about now. Though some stay until the sun sets. Night is when 'the other crowd' most likely will come out."

Annja winced. Seriously? Did grown men believe that tiny

people with wings existed? Though her research told that the faeries of Ireland were originally human-size. It wasn't until they'd been defeated by mortal warriors that they'd glamorized their shapes smaller and retreated underground for safety.

If a person bought into the whole faerie thing.

Wesley licked his cracked, swollen lip. Stubble lined his jaw and upper lip. A young female in tight T-shirt and shorts wandered up and offered him a pair of black-rimmed sunglasses, which he accepted with a grateful nod.

"I know what you're thinking," he said, "And I won't elaborate, because you won't believe it. You'll have to learn for yourself."

She appreciated his respect for her skepticism. But that she didn't detect a hint of tease in his tone troubled her.

"So have all three disappeared from your dig?" she asked. "Not the other?"

"One from our camp, two from the enemy camp."

That was interesting. And it almost ruled out dirty dealings from the other camp. If they'd had two disappear.

"The enemy camp, eh?"

"I know it's not subtle, but 'camp one' or 'two' is mundane."

"Michael Slater must be the director of that one," Annja said. Wesley nodded. "He doesn't strike me as an archaeologist," she said.

"He's not. Can't be. Hell, I have no clue what he is, but I haven't seen him lift a trowel yet. He just paces their stretch of bog, eyes keen to his surroundings."

"So you two don't get along? Aren't you both working toward the same end?"

"I thought so. But I'm not so sure anymore. The bloke won't provide any information on what they find, nor will they allow my people to cross that imaginary line they've drawn in the grass."

"What *is* the end goal? My producer mentioned something about a spear shard. Doesn't seem like much to go on. Certainly no reason to stretch out the dig into two separate camps. What time period are you dealing with?"

"The spear shard is only seventeenth or eighteenth century. I haven't had it radiocarbon-dated yet, but it's a good guess. Initial excitement spread rumors that it was the spear of Lugh," Wesley said. "I think it was the farmer whose land we're squatting on was responsible for that. Legend says Lugh's spear is one of four gifts the goddess Danu granted the Tuatha Dé Danaan. The spear always makes a kill when thrown, and returns to the thrower's hand. If it doesn't find its target, it kills the thrower."

"Not something I'd ever want to test."

"Come on, Annja, where's your sense of adventure? I know you've got it. You're the real thing, aren't you? You like to dig for the truth."

"And what is the truth here?"

"Nothing spectacular. Like I said, the shard is only a few centuries old, and was found too near the surface. Since arriving three weeks ago, we've only uncovered some tin pieces and pottery shards that date to the nineteenth century. I'm going to have the soil tested. There was a lot going on in Ireland mid-nineteenth century."

"You mean the potato famine?"

"Indeed. I think we've uncovered a homestead from the period. Well, there was an obvious stone wall jutting about a foot out of the earth. The farmer had been dismantling it over the years, using the stones to plug up holes in his yard dug by a dog. No bodies, though, which is either a damned blessing or a strange misnomer. Lots of people perished during the famine. Unless this homestead was abandoned, I'd expect to find bones."

"Could have been buried in a mass grave closer to a village," Annja said.

"True."

"Why the secrecy from the other camp?" Annja asked. "And what prompted the other camp at all? Daniel said it's been a few weeks since the split?"

"Like I said, Neville has taken over the reins from my employer, NewWorld. I haven't received any information from them since about a week after my arrival. And I have called and left messages."

"NewWorld being the overseeing company?"

"It's a relatively new outfit. I think they're getting their bearings. That's why it was so easy for Neville to sneak in. And Slater treats me as if he has to tolerate my presence."

"So officially you're working for whom?"

"NewWorld."

"So the digs are managed by two separate companies?"

"Far as I know. Haven't a clue what Neville's outfit is called."

"That's out of the ordinary. You know this Neville guy?"

"Frank Neville. Never met him, and don't think I want to. I'm just here to do a job and report my findings. So long as Slater keeps his gun in the holster we'll all be fine."

"He was waving it around? He wasn't wearing it just now."

"Handed it to a buddy before we got in the scuffle. He was shooting coots. Idiot. It scared the women on my crew something fierce. This job doesn't pay well, as you should know. It's not worth the angst of having to endure a loose cannon."

"It certainly isn't. You have any theories on the disappearances beyond…well…?" *Faeries.*

"Nope. Haven't had time to think about it much. I know that sounds callous. I'm losing crew and I don't know how much longer before Slater scares them all off. Someone goes missing, or decides this work isn't for them, and leaves without warning, I just gotta let it go."

"You think any of the three wandered off because they didn't like the work?"

"Possible."

"What were the two men's names?"

"Brian Ford, he was from Kansas. I've worked on a dig previously with him in Africa. He's a curious sort, but easily distracted. If he hooked up with a looker one night in Cork, well, yes, he could have just wandered off without notice. The other guy is Richard something-or-other. Didn't know him. He joined us the day the camps split and ended up on the enemy side, so I didn't get to know him at all."

"Did you ask around Ballybeag for Brian?"

"Annja, I said I've been busy."

His lack of concern disturbed her. Had he reneged all responsibility for his crew when the sites had split? He didn't seem like a man to do so. And could frustration be a reason for lack of interest? Doubtful.

If Wesley had something to do with the disappearances he would be less concerned than if he had not, she thought.

"I'll want to poke about the other camp, as well."

"I'd watch your back around Slater. He's tough, coiled tight as a spring. He's no bone kicker. Looks like some kind of corporate thug hired to keep the lessers in line, if you ask me. I don't like him one bit."

"So he was the one to physically ensure the camps split?"

"Yep, packed our tent and supplies up one night. Next

morning we arrive over at the bog, only to find our stuff sitting over here. Thinks he's going to get to the prize before we do and then he'll hand it over to Neville."

"What could the prize possibly be if the spear of Lugh has been ruled out?"

"Fungus." Wesley chuckled and shook his head. "I don't know, Annja. What I do know is that Slater charged in two weeks ago all generous and 'let's find the treasure,' ensuring me I had the financing to hire a few more hands. But since he's added the additional camp, he's no longer providing for our side. I've had to scramble for funds to keep it going."

"Why continue without the support?"

He turned a look on her that Annja knew she had given many a doubter over the years. She answered her own question before he could. "Because something *could* be there."

"You never know what will turn up from the depths of history. And if someone wanted so desperately in on the other dig, then there must be something worth finding, eh?"

"Exactly."

"What's your focus, Annja? You spend any amount of time in the field when you're not filming?"

"Whenever I get the chance. Medieval studies are my specialty, but I'd never pass up a chance to help on a dig. Can you use an extra hand?"

"Hell, yes. You won't be too busy with the television show?"

"I won't get in your way. Just want to dig about a bit, get my hands dirty. And yes, I'll be filming segments. Okay, here's the truth. My producer wants me to track faeries."

"Seems to be the consensus on the disappearances." Wesley shrugged. "Be difficult getting the other crowd on film."

Could someone please be on her skeptical side? she thought. "I'm sure. But maybe I can help solve the disappearances. If someone is kidnapping people who are generous

enough to volunteer their time for such grueling digs, I want
to find out who that someone is."

"I like you, Annja. You're a flash of sunlight on this sorry
camp. If it's not the weather giving us headaches it's Slater.
You want me to show you around?"

"I'd love that—"

Shouting from across the way alerted Annja. Slater was
stabbing a finger into Eric's chest. Eric had wandered too
close to the enemy line.

5

Daniel had wandered off somewhere. A sweep of the camp's periphery did not reveal the eccentric plaid-clad Irishman. Wouldn't a guide have explained the lay of the land to Eric? That he probably shouldn't wander onto the other camp, which was headed by a pistol-packing director? On the other hand, Annja was already taking sides and she hadn't begun to learn the real facts. It wasn't like her to make off-the-cuff judgments.

She insinuated herself between Eric and Michael Slater, and asked Slater, "Now what? Your bloodthirst not satisfied yet?"

Slater stepped back and smirked a slimy grin. Wesley was right; he did look too polished to be an archaeologist. And a bit too much with the angry, tight neck muscles.

"You have no fear, do you," he countered, "stepping in the middle of a confrontation like that?"

"I doubt it was a mutual confrontation. Are you okay, Eric?"

"No problem," he said. He clutched the camera to his chest and didn't look fine. His face was flushed as red as his hair.

"Don't worry, he's a trooper," Slater said. "I was just blustering with him. Seems you're the lady in charge, so I best direct my concerns toward you. No cameras on the grounds," Slater barked. "You were not granted permission to film here."

"Mr. Pierce already gave me approval," Annja said. "Don't tell me the two camps are like two separate countries. Do I need a visa to access your dig?"

Slapping a palm over the gun holster, not as a means to pull it on her but perhaps just a security reassurance, Slater shook his head.

"Does Frank Neville have say over Pierce's camp?" she challenged.

Slater crossed his arms high across his chest. "How do you know Neville?"

"I don't, but I'm learning more and more each minute. Like the camp was split right after Mr. Neville's men showed up." Aware Eric was filming over her shoulder, she raised a hand and blocked his view. "Take a break, Eric. This isn't necessary for the show."

"But it shows the volatile mood on the dig," he protested. "A mood probably created by the presence of the otherworldly."

Slater's brows waggled. He smirked and spat to the side. "Lookin' for faeries, then, are you?"

"No. Erm…" This assignment was so lacking in credibility. But she'd never let that stop her before, or make her look bad. "I'm here to investigate the disappearances."

"That'd be the fair folk," Slater offered. "Good luck with that."

He turned and stomped off, delivering her a smirking sneer over his shoulder.

"Good luck with that," she mocked at his back. "This is hopeless, Eric. No one will take me seriously if they think I'm tracking faeries."

"You won't be saying that when we have them on film. I can feel the eerie mystical presence in the air." He scanned his camera around to her face.

"Can you?" She sighed. "Good for you, Eric. The land *is* steeped in the mystical. I guess I need to relax and let it take hold of me, too."

"Want to do the introduction now?"

"Save it. I want to walk the area with Wesley and see what's what."

"I'll be right behind you."

"No, you are not my shadow—at least, not right now. You can film the countryside and get some pretty shots of the green rolling hills. The sunset is really enhancing the vivid greens and the sky as amazing. That'll look great on film. Then skip down to the river and scan for mermaids if the mood takes you. But I don't need you until I need you. Got that?"

He tilted his head aside from the viewfinder to eye her. "You see? There *is* an aggressive mood hanging over us all."

She opened her mouth to protest, but thought better of it. Annja stalked off, wondering if there was something to what Eric had said. When normal people became aware of danger such as a gun-wielding dig director, they went on guard without realizing it. It was simply an innate reaction to the feeling of uncertainty. Who wanted to work a dig with that kind of menace in the air?

No matter. She shouldn't allow the volatile mood to creep into her psyche so easily, and would not.

A fine mist veiled the camp, dulling the air, but not Annja's determined attitude. Surely, if faeries did exist, they would be here in bonny Éire. The green was so intense it hurt her eyes. Rolling soft grass, untouched by dig tools or rut-forming tires, undulated up a distant hill and was topped by a scatter of scraggly pine trees.

Breathing deeply, she concentrated on centering herself. She had let anxiety get the better of her. A deep inhale scented salty and fresh, mixed with earth and gasoline fumes.

"Petrol," she muttered, correcting her language for the country.

"This way." Daniel appeared, muddy fedora tilted to shadow his eyes. "I'll show you about the camp. You've already met both dig directors."

"Yes, and Wesley offered to show me around."

"He's nursing his wounds and letting the females fuss over him. This won't take long. You've seen most of the layout already."

His footsteps were fun to follow. Toes pointed forty-five degrees outward, Annja tried to fit her steps into his prints in the drying mud but her balance wavered from the task.

The sight of a little old lady in her peripheral view intrigued her. One was never too old to work a dig as long as they were eager. But Annja suspected perhaps the woman was a local who brought food to the crews, which was always a blessing when that happened.

She caught up to Daniel's long strides. "Who is that?"

"Ah? Me mum. She visits digs on occasion. We get a lot in the area. Wanders the countryside and riverbank endlessly. Always looking for geegaws and collectibles, she is."

"Collectibles? But whatever is dug up on-site is an artifact. She doesn't try to buy things from the dig, does she?"

"Buy? Oh, no. You'd be amazed what an apple pie and a string of fresh blood sausage can get you."

"You're kidding me."

"It's how I learned to barter, watching me mum. She's an avid collector. Her cottage is filled overflowing with all sorts of things. You'll have to pay her a visit while you're here."

"I think I'd like that." The idea of the old woman bartering for things found on digs—items that should normally belong to the landowner or government—stirred Annja's curiosity. And her sense for protecting history.

"She'd be pleased if you would stop in for supper one night. I'll arrange it, then."

"So you have an interest in archaeology, Daniel?"

"Nope."

"But you know the dig directors?"

"Yep."

"What about this Neville guy?"

"Frank Neville. He's an…acquaintance. I met him a few years ago and traded him a bottle of Lafite."

Eric had referred to wine as being Daniel's passion.

Bartering was a way of life for some people. They lived off the land, didn't consume anything that could not be recycled and basically existed off the electronic grid. She suspected Daniel was the sort, and perhaps got by on very little, save for what he obviously bartered for.

"I know everyone in the area and most of West Cork, too, it seems," he said. "Hear they believe they found some kind of faerie spear on this particular dig."

"Allegedly. The spear of Lugh. It's connected to the Tuatha Dé Danaan."

"The tribe of the goddess Danu. I know the story. Don't know much about the spear."

"One of four magical gifts brought by the Danaan from

four island cities of Tír na nÓg. It's supposed to never miss
its target and always return to the hand that threw it."

He nodded, and shrugged. "Me mum's probably already
got it, then."

WHILE THREE WOMEN and one man went about cleaning up
their loose dirt and packing away their tools for the night,
Wesley was still working when Annja returned to the dig
square.

He waved her over and showed her the strata trench. Dug
down about two feet, this trench was preserved to study the
stratigraphy and gauge the year for each level of earth dug.
Photographic records were usually kept nowadays, but Wesley
explained he'd given Theresa a drawing frame and set her to
work recording the north corner of the dig where a few pot
fragments had been partially uncovered.

"Everyone should learn how to do it the old-fashioned
way," he said.

Annja sensed he enjoyed teaching and the satisfying
tedium of the old-fashioned way. She would never go against
a director's methods, and didn't mind the old-fashioned way
so much herself.

He handed her a trowel, and Annja squatted next to him.

In this quadrant, the crew had dug down to about the mid-
nineteenth century, according to a small matchstick tin they'd
found two days earlier. Wesley suspected they'd tapped into a
farmhouse that may have held victims of the potato famine.
He planned to bring in soil samples to a lab in Cork for
verification.

"I suspect we'll find the pathogen that destroyed the crops,"
he commented. "As I told you, we haven't found any bones
yet. Perhaps this farmstead was lucky and the family found
their way to Liverpool or even America."

Neither of which option would have been preferred, Annja

mused. The Irish immigrants arriving in America had been treated as second-class citizens, if they made the trip successfully. The emigrants crossing the ocean to find prosperity in America were usually struck down with disease and fever during the long journey on the so-called coffin ships. And if they did set foot in New York, they were discriminated against, cheated and treated cruelly.

In England they'd received no better treatment. As soon as they'd arrived in Liverpool most of the Irish riffraff had been deported directly back to Cork.

With the open dig plan, the entire squared-off area was dug down, and baulks, or aisles of dirt marked in a grid and not dug, were not utilized.

Annja preferred the open-dig method. It was well enough that the walls of the open area served as a stratigraphy to measure their progress. One stone wall had been unearthed, and Wesley's crew had earlier uncovered a fireplace.

"Was that feature apparent before digging began?" she asked Wesley.

"Yes, the entire stretch of wall and the stones of the hearth. The farmer removed the turf and found it. We've got dirt here, though, not peat like the other camp. I'm guessing the enemy camp is looking at the end of a farm plot, perhaps animal stables and a pond."

Wesley pointed out an area he was working on and she moved beside him to inspect.

"A wall feature, yes?" He traced the outline of an oblong mound with the tip of his trowel. "Probably another two or three feet into the earth. Puts us back another few centuries. I just wish we had the time to go at this slowly. Yesterday one of my crew destroyed a wood feature, could have been a table or part of a chair. Can't blame her, though."

Annja teased the dirt with her trowel and worked efficiently next to Wesley. "Why the rush?"

"Slater's been pushing to get us all to leave. I managed to negotiate another week."

"What have they found that they want to keep you off the entire dig so badly? Have you gone over and taken a look around?"

He swiped a hand over his hair and lifted his face to worship the setting sun. "Tried, but there's security at night. Only one guard I've noticed, but I'm sure that's a machine gun slung across his shoulder. Couple of nights ago they drove a truck in and something was going on."

"You camp on-site?"

"Not usually, but I'd been tooling around with this feature, wanted to get deeper. You know how that goes."

"You love the work," Annja guessed.

"As much as I bet you love it. I gotta ask, and I hope you don't mind."

"Go ahead."

"How did you ever get involved in a TV show that chases after stories like the other crowd?"

"We chase all sorts, actually. Werewolves, vampires, yeti." Annja smirked. "We're an equal-opportunity monster-hunting show."

"Well, now, you ever talk to a vampire?"

"No. You?"

He cast her that sexy grin that Annja was beginning to realize must work as a sort of lodestone to any women within stumble-over-her-feet range. "Nope, but wouldn't mind the conversation over roast pheasant with Vlad the Impaler."

"He's dead." She lifted a trowel of displaced dirt and emptied it into a nearby bucket. "And so is Frankenstein's monster and Dr. Jekyll. Not dead, actually, never existed."

"Skeptic, eh? So why this assignment?"

"It got me here, sitting in a pile of ancient rubble, with trowel in hand. Couldn't be happier. Well, I could."

"How so?"

"Earlier, you mentioned the men who disappeared, but we were interrupted before I could ask more. Can you tell me anything about the girl who disappeared from this dig? Description? Was she friends with everyone here? Anyone have something against her? Was she native to the area?"

"Whoa, the detective is overtaking the archaeologist."

"It's what we do, isn't it? Play detective. Search for clues and piece them together to create a story."

Wesley tapped the trowel against his boot to shake off the dirt and sat back, wrists resting on his knees. "I wish I could help you, Annja." He scanned the sky, yet Annja sensed his sudden lack of ease from the tapping of his fingers on his knee.

"Beth Gwillym was spending the summer here on the dig. She came from England, though haven't a clue whereabouts. I don't do background checks. Basically, if you're willing and not stupid, you're hired. She was pretty, young and amiable. I know it sounds awful, but I've been preoccupied with that other damned site lately. While I had in heart to keep my people protected from loose cannons like Slater, I should have been paying more attention to my own site. Beth was friendly with everyone, I do know that, didn't have any enemies."

"What about boyfriends? Anyone she was seeing? That she might have had a fight with?"

She couldn't catch his facial movements because he'd tilted his head down, perhaps away from the sun. Annja suspected it was something less to do with the light than a need to keep secrets. Interesting.

"You're not going to accept the well-agreed-upon fact that the other crowd snatched her away?"

Annja sighed. "Wesley, I know the Irish hold great reverence for…the fair folk. And sure, faeries like to steal humans, or trick them into their circles and make them dance for years and years."

"They steal babies, too," he added, more seriously than she wished. "Leave behind changelings, sometimes nothing more than a dried old stump sitting in the cradle."

"Right. I don't wish to challenge anyone's pagan beliefs—"

"Ooh, the Catholic chick is challenging my beliefs."

"What makes you say I'm Catholic?"

"A guess. Almost twenty percent of the world is. And I'm not a pagan, just a believer in what feels right."

"Little people with wings feels right to you in this situation?"

He smirked. "No. But if you've read anything about the Irish legends of the Tuatha Dé Danaan, they're not so little. Our size, actually."

"I did do research on the flight here. They were warriors who landed in Ireland around 1470 BC."

"Right," Wesley said. "And after many battles against the original Irish, or Fir Bolgs and Milesians, they were finally defeated and went to live underground with the Sidhe. They never reveal themselves to humans, unless you're one of the old folk who do put credence in the myth. I bet every other farmhouse in the county still puts a bowl of cream out on their back step before turning in, to appease the other crowd."

"Bet the feral cats love that," Annja said.

"Meow," Wesley said snidely. "So I'm guessing I'll never see Annja Creed's name connected with astro-archaeology?"

"You got that right."

Some astro-archaeologists believed humans on earth were descended from aliens, or at the least, they'd been given alien technology to create some of the amazing architecture throughout history. A person had to possess a certain degree of belief in the unbelievable. No skeptics allowed.

"Ever been to Puma Punku?" Wesley asked. "That site will make you wonder."

"I have, and it did."

The ruins in Bolivia were rumored to be seventeen thousand years old, yet they possessed remarkable stone technology. Some of the construction blocks were estimated at four hundred and forty tons. There was no known technology at the time that could have transported those blocks the distance from the quarry. The precisely cut stones stirred rumors of alien involvement in the creation.

"You know anyone with the other dig who might talk? Someone friendly and not packing a Walther?" Annja asked.

The sun beamed across Wesley's face as he thought about it. Annja loved the rugged, adventurer look. He was a man of her kin. Happy under the open sky, and always with dirt under his fingernails, and a question that needed answering.

"Nope, not a one. They're mostly new since the camps have split. Don't really know any other than Slater. He's a Brit, you know."

"Got a problem with Brits?"

"As a matter of fact, they don't know how to dig correctly." He tapped her trowel, which she had been absentmindedly scraping across the surface, and now realized she'd nicked a piece of something white. "What do you have there?"

"Looks like a bone. Excellent. Let me show you how well I can dig."

"All right, American. Hey, what's that?"

Looking up from the find, Annja squinted and scanned the horizon. A crowd was gathering at the field edge where the grass grew high and both camps joined.

"Let's go take a look." Wesley left her behind, but not for long.

"Annja!" Eric appeared, gestured toward the commotion and took off, camera at the ready.

The cause of the excitement wandered onto the dirt area in front of a parked vehicle. A woman about twenty-two. Surrounded by curious people, she held out her hands as if to ask for space, or maybe just to keep her bearings.

"Beth," Annja heard Wesley say.

The missing girl? She quickened her steps to join the gathering. The crowd was keeping its distance, not blocking her in, yet one woman took Beth's arm and led her to a stop.

"Beth?" Wesley approached her. "Where have you been?"

The bedraggled woman stared blindly at Wesley. A few leaves were tucked in the dirty blond strands of her tangled hair. Her fingers and palms were dirty, as well as the knees of her khaki pants. All in all, though, she looked healthy; maybe she'd just taken a stumble in the dirt.

Annja recalled what Daniel had said about her disappearance. She had been missing a little over thirty-six hours.

"Who took you?" someone called out from the crowd.

"Yes." Annja stepped forward and addressed the woman. "Do you know what happened? Who took you? Or did you get lost?"

Beth looked up and when Annja thought the frail, shaking woman was looking into her eyes she realized she was focused just over her shoulder—where Eric stood with the camera.

"The fair folk," the woman said.

The crowd nodded, muttering that they knew it. Didn't want to believe it, but now it was a sure thing.

Annja turned to Eric and rolled her eyes at the camera. "Cut," she said.

6

Garin left the details of landing at the airport to his pilot. The man had never failed him, and always managed to land within minutes of his estimated arrival time.

Garin planned to send his luggage directly to his Manhattan penthouse because he was headed straight for the auction house.

Strolling toward customs, Garin mused over why he'd jumped so quickly at the snap of Roux's fingers. He didn't usually allow the old man to order him about. Hell, for more than five hundred years the two of them had embraced a sort of unavoidable acceptance of the other. Because they were the only five-hundred-year-old men walking the earth these days. They had a connection that neither would deny, and when one truly needed the other, all petty disagreements were overlooked.

And if Roux thought Annja would appreciate the Fouquet, then Garin could see that—much as he never wanted to look at that painting again. Obtaining it would be no problem. So long as he made the auction in time.

He checked his watch. Bidding didn't start for another hour and a half. The limo could have him there in forty-five minutes.

Annja Creed. Now there was a remarkable woman. She put the woman Garin had left in his bed to shame. There was simply no comparison between the two.

Annja was a breed apart from the sort of women with whom Garin surrounded himself. She would never allow any man to push her around, to make assumptions regarding her willingness to please and/or serve him. Smart, sexy and adventurous, she also owned the one thing that kept Garin up some nights.

The sword once wielded by Joan of Arc.

It was a sword Garin had seen in use by the sainted young woman, for he had been apprentice to Roux when the man had been appointed to guard Jeanne d'Arc. For some reason, after the sword had been wrested away from the Maid of Orléans and shattered, Garin and Roux had become immortal. He didn't know why, but he'd accepted the gift for what it was. Who wouldn't accept immortality?

But now that the sword had been put together and Annja wielded it as if a mystical extension of Jeanne's will—what then?

Garin couldn't be sure if his immortality had been lost. He didn't feel older. It had only been a few years since Annja had taken possession of the sword. And Lord knows he'd tried to take it from her, to smash it, and put things back the way they should be. But he couldn't.

Out of Annja's hands the sword would not remain solid, unless she willed it so. She could hand it to him to look over, if she wished—and she had. But she did not trust him to do anything more than quickly inspect the thing. And she shouldn't.

But would he really break the thing should he again be given the opportunity? Some days he wasn't so sure. Gaining Annja's respect overwhelmed any desire to push her away as a result of stealing from her. He sincerely wanted to know her. To experience her in ways that not only included the flesh, but the mind and soul, as well. She fascinated him.

Very few women did so.

With a smile on his face, and his thoughts on the limber body of Annja Creed, Garin handed his passport to the customs official behind the counter.

He'd romanced Annja. He'd attempted to seduce her with fine things. She played along, but only so far. She wasn't stupid, rather leery at times, and then at other times he could almost believe she was as interested in him as he her.

But to win her completely would end the wanting, the yearning, to learn more. And did he really want to spoil that anticipation?

"Did you have your passport, Mr. Braden?"

"Huh?" He steered his focus to the woman holding his wallet. He'd handed her his wallet by mistake? How one's mind could get distracted when it was focused on a gorgeous woman. "Sorry." He reached inside his inner suit coat pocket. "I have it…somewhere."

Where was the damned thing? He'd had it on the jet. Had he dropped it after disembarking? "I seem to have misplaced it. I'm sure it's on my private jet. I'll just give the pilot a call—"

"If you'll just step aside, Mr. Braden, we can work this out."

Garin stroked his fingers down the lapel of his Armani suit and delivered his best sexy grin to the woman, who looked like she was serving the end of a thirty-hour shift and desperately needed a kind word. "I've got an appointment. If we can make this quick? I know it's in the jet."

The daggers in her look pricked his confidence. "Your jet just taxied for takeoff, Mr. Braden."

"What?" He looked aside, as if to search for the jet, but he was too far from any window overlooking the runway. "We've only been on the ground twenty minutes. He couldn't have refueled so quickly. Where is the man headed?"

"I have no idea, Mr. Braden. Please, if you'll come with me."

Garin slammed a fist on the counter, but refrained from swearing.

This was not going as smoothly as he'd anticipated.

7

Annja watched keenly as Michael Slater argued with Wesley over who would give Beth a ride to a hospital in Cork. Beth had disappeared from the good camp—as Annja had come to already consider Wesley's camp—so why Slater cared was beyond her.

They didn't argue for long. One of the women caught Beth as she fainted, and barked at Wesley to start up the Jeep. Slater conceded with a shake of his head and a glance to Annja. He'd obviously decided to blame her for things that went wrong.

"Quite the commotion, eh?" Daniel joined Annja as she turned to pace back to the tented area for a respite from the sudden mist. The saying was true: if you don't like the weather in Ireland, just wait five minutes. She'd give it ten.

"Beth's been missing for almost two days," she said. "I can't imagine what she must be feeling right now. Or thinking. She must be out of her head. At the very least, hungry and in need of a shower." And so mentally traumatized as to believe she had actually been taken by faeries. "Is the hospital far?"

"It's a bit over an hour's drive into Cork."

She would have liked to ride along with Beth and Wesley, asking questions as they made their way to Cork, but Annja did have a sense of compassion. And she had promised Wesley she would respect the situation. She was not a paparazzo desperate to get a photo of a wide-eyed innocent. Yet she must talk to her. Whatever Beth had been through could lead Annja to discovering the other men who had disappeared, and who was behind it.

"I might drive to Cork tomorrow, see if she's coherent," she said. "I don't think she needs too much fuss right now. Wesley will ensure she gets the proper care. I suppose not much will get done on the dig now. I should head to my B and B. I've got some research to do."

On hospitals in Cork and Beth Gwillym, she thought.

"You fancy that meal at my mother's?" Daniel's attention focused on the retreating vehicle, a strand of grass twitching at the corner of his mouth.

"A home-cooked meal sounds great, but there's Eric, too."

"He can come along. Mum always makes a feast on Fridays. She expects me to bring over friends. Girlfriends mostly, but I haven't been a good son about that lately."

He cast her a wink and marched off.

Had that been flirtation? The man had to be twenty years her senior. Not that he wasn't attractive, albeit eccentric.

MICHAEL SLATER MARCHED across the trampled grass to the edge of the excavation site where the dried peat cushion made his footsteps feel as though he were walking on a strange planet.

The chief archaeologist, Maxwell Alexandre, was packing

up his shovels, buckets and other equipment. He ran an efficient dig and was meticulous about putting things away at the end of the day. Slater appreciated anyone with a fastidious bone. Maxwell did what he was told, with little argument.

Rain rolled down his temples. Slater did not like the weather in this country; it was much worse than his native London, and that was saying a lot.

He gripped the handle of his Walther P99, still in its holster. It was something he did probably a dozen times a day. His training buddies had given him shit for his attachment to the thing. Bugger them. Some guys stroked their bollocks every now and then; he stroked his gun.

Alexandre popped his head up from the area marked off with pitons and ropes. "What was the commotion over there?"

"The girl is back," Slater spat out. "The one the captain grabbed the other day."

"How the hell did that happen?" Alexandre kicked the base of a black bucket, toppling it over. It was empty. "How'd she get free?"

"I don't know, but heads will roll." Twisting his neck against the tight muscle tugging along his jaw and throat, Slater nodded toward the black SUV that transported the crew into town each night. "You packing up?"

"It'll be dark soon."

"I thought you understood we are on a time crunch? I want to be out of here within the week."

Everything else Frank Neville had his hands in was scheduled to come down to the week's deadline. This wasted nonsense of digging in the dirt twisted his knickers the wrong way. He had not signed on for kicking about bones.

"I know that." Alexandre stood before Slater. He was taller by three inches, but both men were aware that when push came to shove Slater held the upper hand. "I've uncovered the entire skeleton." He gestured behind him and Slater eyed the ground. "She's a beauty thanks to the peat. Preserves bones and bits of fabric real nice like. But not sure I'm going to find any more rocks."

"Give it another few days. Don't things tend to…move around over the years?"

"Erosion does tend to do that, though not so much in these conditions. We'll strip the area for sure. Won't leave a single pebble unscrutinized."

"You think it could have spread as far as the other camp?" Slater asked.

"Unlikely. Such a contained cache is probably going to be within the marked area we've pitoned off. I think it would be next to impossible for the rocks to move from the bog to the dirt the other camp is working in. Unless an animal did it? That's always possible. When's the next truck come in?"

Slater tucked his hand under an arm over the pistol. "Not that it's any of your concern, but tomorrow night."

"Just want to know to get the crew out on time. Settle your britches, Slater, the operation is going well."

"This operation is a joke." Slater harnessed his anger. "The girl—Beth—should have never gotten away. I'm going to check on the guys down by the river."

8

"We moved them." Reggie Marks, the captain of the officious little barge that camped down by the river, scratched his belly, and slapped his grungy felt cap back onto his bald head.

"And in the process you managed to lose one helpless woman?" Slater fisted his palms. "I can't believe your ineptitude. Who hired you?"

"Your boss, that Neville bloke." The captain sniffed, drawing far too much phlegm into his nasal cavities for Slater's liking. He hacked and spat a globule over the starboard side of the barge. "Ain't gettin' paid to babysit or mollycoddle. You want we should keep some woman fancy and entertained, then you're looking at the wrong crew. Just be thankful I didn't let Smelly Joe get his hands on her. That man breaks his women."

Despite his managing to keep a handle on all the operations Frank Neville had set into place since arriving in Ireland, Slater hadn't been quick enough on the draw when hiring the barge crew. Good men were few and far. Neville trusted

Slater to oversee this operation and as a right-hand man for his business deals, yet he still did a lot of work on his own. He was too determined, and far too controlling, to sit back and let it all happen.

"What you standing there for?"

Slater winced as the captain snorted again. "Nothing at all." He turned and strode off.

To CLAIM THE OFFICIAL title of *village* in Ireland, the settlement had to have a church, a post office and a pub. No other buildings required. These three things met, you have got yourself a village, Annja thought.

Remarkably, the village of Ballybeag boasted the Four Corners. Each corner featured a pub, though for all proper purposes the east corner was more a grocery store/petrol station that sold diner food and poured Guinness, as well.

O'Shanley's sat on the west corner and Annja chose it for its smiling pink pig painted on the window. Daniel had dropped her and Eric off at a quaint bed and breakfast and they'd dumped their gear in their respective rooms. They'd missed the supper call, but the proprietress had offered to make cold beef sandwiches for them. They had dinner plans, but she left Eric behind to gobble down a few.

She sat down at the bar next to an older gentleman and ordered a Guinness. The bartender nodded and went to work. She knew a properly poured pint was all about patience.

Eric ambled in while she was waiting. He set his video camera on the warped wooden bar, ordered a Coke and winked at her. "No drinking while on the job," he said. "A man's gotta stay sharp."

"Did you get footage of Beth coming out from the forest?" she asked.

"Yep, and it rocks. Her face was all 'Hey, what's going on?

Who are you people?' and she was stumbling and looked like she'd been through hell."

"But no faerie dust, eh?"

"Faerie dust? Damn, I wasn't looking for any. It should have sparkled in the sunlight, right?"

"I'm kidding you, Eric."

"But seriously." He leaned in, spreading a hand between them on the bar. "Maybe when I run the video through the threshold the faerie dust will show up like a black light seeking…er, well, you know."

She did. And that image made her hope the sheets in her room had been changed since the last guests had stayed there.

"You up for a home-cooked meal in a bit or did you fill up on Mrs. Riley's sandwiches? Daniel Collins invited us over to his mother's this evening."

"I'm full. Mrs. Riley made me eat three sandwiches and a huge bowl of cole slaw. It was good, but by no means could her cooking compete with a Big Mac."

"If that's what you want you'll have to drive into Cork."

"Don't tempt me," he said. "I may love to travel but I am a fries and burger guy all the way. I think I'll pass on the invite. I want to check out the local music scene tonight."

"Really? How much of a local scene is possible in a village this size? The population is less than two hundred."

"You'd be surprised, Annja. On the way here, I saw musicians with guitars and flutes walking the street. I think they're playing at the Hollow Bog across the way tonight."

The south corner pub.

"It's interesting that you're into Celtic stuff, Eric. Good for you."

"Celtic? Sure." He tilted back the mug of soda, and Annja had to smirk. The kid hadn't a clue what the local music was like. The Metallica T-shirt he wore promised he'd be more than a little disappointed upon hearing flutes and fiddles.

"You got enough money?" she asked, then inwardly cringed. She wasn't the guy's mother. But she did feel protective of him. She had traveled to dozens of countries and knew being abroad could be overwhelming. Away from his family, he had to feel vulnerable.

Annja hadn't any family to claim, save for a few friends back in Brooklyn. She didn't need family. Well, she tried to put it out of her thoughts. She'd been orphaned when she was very young. Family wasn't necessary to survive.

"I'm cool, Annja. Do you think a video of the music would be good to insert into our piece? I mean, it would be like a montage of the culture."

"That's clever, Eric. I like it. Film away. I'll catch up with you in the morning."

He held up a palm and Annja answered by high-fiving him. Pleased, Eric gathered his equipment and left.

Annja wished the bartender would hurry, but noted her pint was only three-quarters full, and sat there waiting for the final top-off.

"Beautiful day," she said to the man next to her. He nursed his own half-full pint.

"You folks from the dig?" His craggy voice was the closest Annja felt she'd get to leprechaun-speak.

"Yes. We're filming for a television program that broadcasts in America."

He nodded, his focus on the glasses lining the shelf behind the bar. Most had names written on them with a fancy scrawl and white pen. Not a big talker, she decided, but amiable enough that she might get something from him.

"I'm looking into the disappearances from the dig. Three people. Did you hear about that?"

He nodded again, and then sucked down a long swallow. "'Twould be the other crowd."

"No offense, but—"

He chuckled as if his mouth were full of pebbles. "Ah, anytime a person starts a sentence with no offense means they are out to offend."

"No, I—" The pint of Guinness was set before her. Liquid black gold captured in a glass. Annja dipped a finger into the thick creamy head and licked it. "If I may ask, when was the last time you saw the other crowd?"

The man made a show of turning toward her and propping an elbow on the bar. His salt-and-pepper beard had been stroked to a point. Age spots battled with bright blue veins across his cheeks. "Lassie, you need to know the other crowd are never seen, only felt."

All righty, then. "Has this happened before? People gone missing? And the suspicion is that…er, the other crowd is involved?"

He swallowed back another tug, and took his time before answering. "I recall two decades ago Certainly Jones went missing for three months."

"And?"

"He was found in a mud hole near the Bandon River. Broken leg."

"He was in the hole three months?"

"No, he slipped and fell after the other crowd allowed him to go home. Had to promise them he'd never drive the Hightow Road again or cut the ash tree at the north end of his property."

Annja knew that certain trees and bushes were revered as faerie trees. Oak, ash and the hawthorn bush, being the few she recalled from her research. It was thought the Sidhe, or faeries, lived beneath them in their tangled roots. Entire freeway systems were built around centuries-old trees for fear of messing with the faerie mojo. Same with faerie raths, like they'd passed on their drive out to the dig. The grass-covered hills were believed to house faeries beneath. It all related to the earliest inhabitants of the Island of Éire, the Tuatha Dé Danaan, as Wesley had confirmed her research.

"Tell me about the Tuatha Dé Danaan," she asked. "If you wouldn't mind."

The man sized her up a moment, long strands in his eyebrows dancing as his forehead creased. Determining if she were worthy of his tale? With a slight nod, he splayed open his hand and began. "It all happened so long ago, in the BC times that you bone kickers like to dig about for."

"BC means Before Christ, or Ante Christum."

She caught the sharp cut in his glance and decided to remain silent for the rest of his story.

"A race of giants called the Fir Bolg were overtaken by the supernatural tribe Danaan. The tribe was reputed to be magicians and wield remarkable powers no man could explain. They battled against the Fir Bolg up by Cong, northwest of here. I've been there a time or two. The air broods still."

He paused for a dramatic sip of Guinness. Annja found herself sipping just as carefully.

"It was the Celts who defeated the Tuatha Dé Danaan. It is said the battle was so bloody the sea turned red for an entire year. But when the Tuatha Dé Danaan knew their end was near they turned themselves into wee folk and fled underground to live among the Sidhe. You ever see a faerie rath?"

"The hills across the countryside? Yes. They are mystical." She could go there. For the sake of his story.

"You best watch how you go about those raths and sacred ruins, my girl. The fair folk don't give favor to those who tread their grounds with malicious intent."

"Would they go so far as to kidnap a person who was making them angry?"

"Oh, yes."

"What about someone who wandered onto their grounds without ill intent?"

"You keep asking stupid questions, you'll go missing, too," the man snapped, and turned back to his pint. Then she caught his grin before he quickly hid it by taking another swallow.

"Thanks for that encouraging vote of confidence. Stop asking questions and keep an eye out for things you can't see. I'll see what I can do about that," she said.

"Make sure that you do."

Annja relaxed as the thick froth trickled down her throat and was washed deeper with the cool beer. She'd have to tell Bart about this pint. He'd enjoy hearing every slow, creamy detail. She'd seen her dear friend Bart McGilley enjoy his fair share of Guinness.

"Heard Beth Gwillym wandered in from wherever she'd gone missing," the man tossed out.

"Yes, little over an hour ago, actually. Did you know her?"

"I've heard of her."

"Wesley Pierce drove her to Cork to have her checked out by a doctor."

"Ah, Pierce is the bloke who winks at all the girls and flashes his unnaturally white teeth at 'em. He and Beth had a thing, you know."

She'd suspected Wesley hadn't told her everything. "How do you know?"

"Whole town knows. We know everything that's up with everybody."

She believed that. It probably wasn't that easy to hide an affair, drinking problem or addiction when the center of town boasted the Four Corners.

"They had a spat, they did," the old man said. "You might want to question loverboy if you're intent on finding the real answers."

"I'll do that." She believed the old man wasn't trying to throw her off. He had no reason to.

"You talk to Mrs. Collins up the way?" the man asked. "You want to know about the other crowd, she'll have what you need."

Interesting. Daniel hadn't mentioned his mother's knowledge of faeries. "Thanks. I'm having dinner with her this evening."

"Then you'll see her collection. That lady does have a pack rat in her. Blessed Rachel."

9

Garin raced to the curb where his limousine waited. The driver already had directions to the auction house. He slid inside and grumbled about the delay. "I had to get a passport waiver. This is obviously not my day."

He settled in and reached for a bottle of Evian water as the car drove away from the airport. That hit the spot. They'd grilled him on his overseas travels. It was as if they'd suspected him of third-world espionage.

Although he could claim a certain amount of notorious dealings, he covered his tracks well. And he'd kept his cool while sitting in the customs office. He knew when to bow to authority and when it was best to make a fuss and start threatening subordinates.

To his credit, the man who'd contacted the German consulate to verify his passport had been polite and efficient. He'd wanted to get Garin through customs as quickly as he could, and Garin appreciated that.

"What time have you got?" he asked the driver.

"Ten after three, Mr. Braden. I'll try my best, but the auction started at three."

"Damn it."

Roux had called while he'd been crossing the Atlantic Ocean to let him know his bidding paddle would be waiting. He wasn't sure of the order of items to be auctioned off. He might still make it, unless the Fouquet went first.

"I can call in my bid. I'll have to. Roux wanted me to take a look at it first, but it's got to be the painting," he mumbled to himself.

He slapped his suit coat, mining for his cell phone. "Hell!"

"You have a phone up there, Stephan?"

"Sorry, Mr. Braden. My daughter dropped it in the toilet this morning. Did you forget yours?"

"It's back at the airport." He turned, assessing which would be faster—making the turn and getting back on the ring road that surrounded the airport, or driving straight on and crossing his fingers this limo could fly.

Neither seemed a viable option.

"You have any painkillers up there, Stephan?"

REMARKABLY, HE ARRIVED at the doors to Christie's at twenty minutes to four. Garin rushed through the entrance, his presence and sheer size keeping most from questioning his determined path toward the auction room. He stopped at the reception desk and showed ID to get his bid paddle. At least he still had his wallet.

"Has the Fouquet been offered yet?"

The woman in thin, black-rimmed spectacles drew up the auction list on her computer and scanned it. "You mean the painting in the style of Jean Fouquet? Yes, Mr. Braden. That was just purchased. Is it what you've come for? I'm very sorry. We are offering a Parker, which is similar in style."

"Not interested. Can you tell me who did win the Fouquet?"

"That information is private, Mr. Braden."

Beyond the glasses, the woman's eyes gleamed brightly. Her skin was pale and flawless. Her features were delicate, even disguised beneath the stiff and proper gray suit. A butterfly struggling to explode from her cocoon.

Garin leaned across the marble desk, lowering his voice and tendering it softly. "Would you deny the winning bidder the opportunity to double their money from someone who is interested in obtaining the work?"

"Well…" She looked over her shoulder, checking all corners and the closed office door.

Garin followed her finger as she trailed it across a line detailing the buyer's name and address. He read upside down, and committed the information to memory.

"Thank you, Miss…"

"Haversham."

"A lovely name," he said. "But not so lovely as you."

"Oh." She glanced aside without the expected blush. "It's a pity you missed the bidding."

"It is. But I'm not a man accustomed to being denied anything he wants."

She lowered her gaze and now she did blush. "I guessed that about you."

"Good afternoon, Miss Haversham. It was a pleasure." He winked and turned to stroll out, controlling his need to punch the wall as he did so.

So close. And the damned painting had gone for five hundred thousand. Was he willing to lay down a cool million for something he'd hoped would be burned and never again see the light of day?

"Not if I can take it for free," he said.

10

Somewhere in the thatched cottage half a mile north of the dig site, a clock chimed 10:00 p.m. Annja noted that it was difficult to track each chime for the ambient noise of smaller clocks ticking, infinity balls clicking one steel ball against the other, alarms chirping and one small wooden stick man climbing up a ladder.

Mrs. Collins's home, which much resembled a hobbit's cottage on the outside, was a virtual museum of oddities and geegaws. Pack rat, indeed.

"Daniel tells me you already own the spear of Lugh?" Annja tossed that out there. She was in a fine mood. Visiting and shooting the breeze had made her forget all about Beth's return to camp. Okay, not forgotten, but she realized there was no sense worrying about her. She was safe and Annja intended to visit her tomorrow.

Rachel Collins clasped her hands before her face. Crepe-thin skin did not conceal the faint blue veins beneath, nor did the twinkle in her eye master her bright green irises. "I've had the spear for decades. Come see."

Daniel stayed behind in the kitchen, drying the supper dishes. Mrs. Collins had served up a feast of raspberry lamb chops, basil-seasoned small potatoes and two different kinds of homemade bread rolls. The shortbread cookies for dessert must had been bathed in butter. They'd slid down Annja's throat like a dream.

So maybe family *was* all it was cracked up to be. If she'd had a mother to cook like that for her every night, Annja might be twenty pounds heavier and less of a world traveler.

Led down the hallway that was narrower for the shelving from floor to ceiling, Annja noted the more interesting trinkets. A blue plastic, poseable Aquaman figure, minus one hand. A copy of a Fabergé egg, only thumb-size and very likely decorated with rhinestones. A few fist-size clods of dirt. Maybe they were imagined meteorites. She spotted what looked like an alicorn, twisted bone and all—as if unicorns existed. A perfect yellow rose was amazingly preserved in a bowl of clear marbles. It wasn't silk, either; Annja touched it gently to be sure.

They entered a small living room and Annja felt her vision go crossed from the utter cacophony of stuff. Everywhere things hung on the walls, inhabited the corners, dangled from the ceiling. There was a television, which she wouldn't have immediately picked out were the sound not on and had the flash of a toothpaste model's teeth not caught her eye. Yet another chord to the cacophony of whimsy.

"An amazing collection," she said, then managed to save herself from tripping over a small fluffy thing that could be a real dog, though the way it was sprawled on the white bearskin rug, she couldn't be sure it wasn't a large black stain. "Where did you get all this stuff, Mrs. Collins?"

"Oh, I've been a collector since I was a wee lass. Always

picking up bits and bobs wherever I go. I never spend much on any single piece. Most people give me things, or I find them. The digs are great places to walk after-hours. All kinds of interesting baubles to be found there."

Things a legitimate archaeologist, and the country of Ireland, would consider stolen.

Annja winced. She crossed her fingers there were no real artifacts in here. She wasn't sure how she'd react, much as Rachel was the sweetest little old lady she had ever met. And man, did she make a mean shortbread.

"Here it is." Rachel turned and displayed a small spear upon both hands. It was two feet long, made of wood and decorated with faded red paint that had obviously been stripped by sun and age. The head looked bronze for the green patina that tipped the base where it was fitted into the shaft. "The spear of Lugh."

She presented her find so grandly Annja found herself nodding in acceptance as the woman handed it to her. It was aged, but not centuries old. Certainly not an artifact. She wondered if the woman would be offended if she saw Annja search for the Made in China marking.

"Interesting." Annja tilted it in one hand.

"Oh, no, dear, mustn't attempt to hold it as if you intended to throw it toward your prey."

Annja smirked at the woman's real fear. Okay, then. She'd have to get Eric to film a segment with Rachel talking about the other crowd. If anyone believed, it had to be this woman.

"I understand the legend says that the spear of Lugh, when thrown, always makes a kill," Annja said. "Then it returns to the owner's hand."

"Exactly. And if it misses the target, it returns and kills the owner. Not a pretty outcome for you, dear."

"Nope." She studied the tip, sliding a fingernail under the

patina. It was bronze. So that ruled out China. "Those faeries certainly are a vicious bunch."

"Mustn't speak of them so, dear. They don't appreciate being named so bluntly. I prefer 'the wee folk.'"

"Wee folk, eh? And yet, weren't the Tuatha Dé Danaan, who gave this spear to Lugh, great and mighty warriors?"

"That they were."

"And they were man-size, not small."

"Yes, indeed. The folk come in all sizes, dear. I tend to the wee ones, I do."

"And how do you tend to them? Milk offerings on the back stoop?"

"Can't be doing that, the cats will get into it." Rachel offered Annja a pitying once-over. She wasn't about to waste her time explaining her beliefs to someone she guessed could care very little. "I'll take that, then."

Annja relinquished the spear. Rachel held it reverently as she placed it on a shelf above the television. She had to give the lady credit for exercising her imagination. And honestly, if a child were brought up in an environment that revered the other crowd as real, then it wasn't even right to argue with her.

"That's a pretty piece of quartz," Annja noted of the stone above the spear's shelf. "So clear and defined. You find that near your home?"

Rachel handed her the cool piece of stone. About the size of an acorn, one side was roughed and curved, while the other had defined crystal facets.

"Right where the newer dig camp has set up at the bog's edge, actually. But it's not quartz, dear, it's a rough diamond."

Annja lifted a brow at that, but didn't challenge Rachel's statement. Faerie spears and Fabergé eggs, so why not real diamonds? She had never heard of diamonds being found in

Ireland. The country was overflowing with gold and uranium, but not the sparkly bling.

"That bit of rock seems to fascinate many," Rachel continued. "That Mr. Neville Danny brought over a while back wanted to buy it from me."

Frank Neville, the supposed leader of the bad camp that had wrestled control from a major management company? Annja studied the quartz more fiercely. What would Neville want with a bit of crystal? "How much did he offer you?"

"A thousand pounds," Rachel declared with as much amazement as she must have felt to receive the initial offer. "Can you believe?"

"And you didn't sell?"

"Dear, a diamond that size is worth hundreds of thousands pounds sterling."

Annja clutched the stone. She had no training in discerning a real diamond from quartz. Geology was not top of her studies, but she knew enough. It was possible it could be diamond.

"And yet you keep it on a shelf."

"Oh, I don't need the money, dear. It's just a pretty trinket I enjoy owning."

Annja sought a light source, but the only thing in the room was the TV. She didn't know rocks. It could be common quartz. It could be something more valuable. Only someone in the know could determine. Like Frank Neville? Had to be if the man had offered her that much for it, and yet so little if it were real.

"You know it's illegal to keep items found from a dig site."

"It wasn't a dig site when I found it, dear." Rachel held out her hand. Two bends of her fingers demanded she return her prize.

Annja handed the stone to the woman, who polished it against her sleeve before replacing it on the shelf.

"Danny says I've not to worry about the things I find on my property."

Annja did the map work in her head, and figured she couldn't have possibly found it on her property—the dig was set on property owned by a farmer who had let his crops go years ago—but she wasn't prepared to push the argument.

The stone was quartz, nothing more. And to find a rough diamond? That would indicate a diamond pipe in the vicinity. She wasn't up on the mineral rights of Ireland, but felt sure it had to have been scoured for diamonds by now.

"So you met Mr. Neville?"

"I didn't much care for the man," Rachel commented as she touched the pink-furred head of a goggle-eyed alien. "He didn't even try my blood pudding."

Much as the idea of eating blood pudding had made Annja's stomach twist, she had to admit Rachel's version with oatmeal and barley mixed in with the pork fat and blood had been delicious. Whew. She'd cleared that culinary hurdle. She guessed she wouldn't get out of Ireland without running into tripe sooner or later.

"He was missing something incredible," Annja commented.

"You ladies plotting ways to take over the world with mum's arsenal?" Daniel tapped a cracked tin shield that Annja placed circa 1970s.

"Your girl is very smart," Rachel said. "I like her."

Annja caught Rachel's beaming eye and decided it was time to nip this premarital fantasy in the bud. "It's getting late. I left Eric to himself in a village with four pubs. I'd hate to have to explain that one to his family. It was a lovely meal, Mrs. Collins."

"You'll come back soon, dear."

It was stated, not a question. Daniel offered Annja a shrug and led her outside. The night was still and the stars were out full force in the black sky.

"She's a marvel," Annja commented.

"Don't worry, she's not picking brides."

"Are you sure?"

"Well…" He let that one hang.

Annja had no intention of encouraging a romance. Something about Daniel appealed to her, and his age didn't bother her at all. But long-distance relationships were deal breakers in her book. And one-night stands, while she entertained them on occasion, she had to be in the mood.

"Thanks for the meal, Daniel. Uh, you're not at all concerned about some of the stuff your mother picks up in fields and dig sites?"

"You mean things that would have archaeological value? No. It's all junk, Annja. You saw the plastic alligator with the pink glass eyes?"

"I did. I also got a good look at her so-called diamond. She said Frank Neville offered to buy it from her. Why would someone offer so much money to buy a chunk of quartz?"

"I wasn't aware of the offer. How much is so much?"

"A thousand pounds."

"Ah, well, then, I imagine me mum didn't sell. Neville was probably humoring her. Mum gets so few visitors nowadays. And a handsome man comes to visit? Well." He strode down the cobbled pathway to the white-painted gate before his mother's home. "Care to walk a bit? I could show you my stones."

"Your…stones?" She didn't even want to go where her mind was tugging her to go.

"Big ones," he said with a smile. "Just beyond the ridge. Come along. An archaeologist won't want to miss this."

After a brisk amble across the field and over a hill capped

by hawthorn and heather, Annja and Daniel descended a slope to a grassy field.

"Not exactly Stonehenge, but it is a treasure all the same," he announced.

Annja stopped beside Daniel. Halfway between them and the river's edge stood a circle of stones. A remarkable circle that sported three—no, four—standing stones twice as high as her.

"It's amazing. What's the name of it? Is this cataloged as a monument?"

"It is. And it's called GrayStone Circle. Their history is that the devil tried to throw them in the Bandon River, but his reach wasn't so good."

Annja smirked. "The devil threw a lot of stones about the country."

"Indeed, every other legend of standing stones involves the Old Lad. But it's on Collins land so we've the right to allow or disallow people from visiting it. I get a lot of hikers passing by, but like to keep visitors to a minimum. Destroys the land to have vehicles driving through. Want to walk closer?"

Annja didn't answer. She took off down the slope, her pace increasing to a jog.

Three pillars of roughly rectangular shape stood spaced about ten feet apart. The third pillar tilted at a forty-five-degree angle. One stone lay on its side and it rose as high as her waist.

Daniel joined her and sat upon the fallen stone. She prowled the upright stones, spreading a palm across the cold, pocked surfaces as she marveled.

"Ever do any excavations?" she asked.

"There was one in the 1920s, and then later in the sixties my grandpa allowed an archaeological team a go at it. Found some bones in ceremonial ceramic pots and a bunch of useless shards. They're all in me mum's collection now."

"Even the bones?"

"Aye." Daniel lay on the recumbent stone and Annja leaned against the tilted standing stone. He crossed his hands at his stomach and closed his eyes. "When I was a lad, me and my friends used to come here and romp about. We'd play theater and this stone was the stage. Or we'd trick the lasses into laying down on this one and we'd play the doctor."

He opened an eye to catch her raised brow.

"Ah, but we'd play sacrificial victim, too. Certainly Jones used to be the priest with the knife. He'd cut out our gizzards and offer them to the gods under the full moon."

"Wow, you must have had a lot of gizzards to spare."

"That we did." He sat up and faced her in the moonlit darkness. "They're magical gizzards, capable of regeneration under the full moon. Sacrifices were only done under the full moon, you understand."

"Of course."

"See there?" He pointed to the tallest stone, notched along the top. "On the winter solstice you can view the sunset through that notch. Only day of the year that happens."

According to popular belief, druids had been lured to use these stone circles—crafted well before their time—as a means to tell time and season by carefully using notches and holes in the actual stone and aligning them with the sun and various planets.

Daniel jumped down and stood before her, his face even with hers. "So what do you think? Do the stones bring out your inner pagan? Do you believe the Tuatha Dé Danaan may have once used this very circle for something?"

"Possible."

"You're lying through your teeth, Annja Creed. You are a skeptic."

"Someone has to be." She leaned against the stone next to him and scanned the dark sky, sprinkled with star flashes.

"I won't dismiss their use for astrological time telling and calendars. And sure, sacrificial offerings can't be disregarded. But as meeting places for faeries?"

He stroked her cheek, brushing aside her hair with a forefinger. The touch was warm and it startled her, but not enough to want to move away. So maybe she could be put in the mood.

"You New York City types have lost all imagination," he said.

"So I'm a type? I have a very healthy imagination. Sitting under the moonlight on this amazing monument to history stirs up all sorts of images of druids, Vikings and Celtic warriors. I'd love to have witnessed the creation of a site like this. Can you imagine the ingenuity? The planning? We think our technology is so remarkable, and yet, we can still only make conjectures as to how these stones were moved and what their uses were thousands of years ago."

"So you aren't all about the bones and textbooks."

"Give me some credit. I *am* here looking for faeries."

"Indeed." Daniel leaned in and kissed her.

Annja leaned forward to accept the kiss. It was warm. Nice. He stroked a hand along her back and moved her closer.

Moonlight kisses beat standing stone circles any night. And Daniel Collins knew how to kiss.

Daniel nudged his nose alongside her ear, and whispered, "You're a fine New York City woman, Annja." He pressed his forehead to hers.

She sensed the kiss had ended, and that there wasn't going to be any more this evening. But she didn't need it, because this kiss would last her awhile.

"I'd try to convince you to take off your clothes for the doctor," he said, "but I guess you'd be on to me with that one."

"You got it. I think sacrificial victim would kind of spoil

the mood, too. What say you get me started on my walk back to Ballybeag?"

"You in the mood for some wine?"

"Are you trying to seduce me, Daniel?"

"I was, until I mentioned wine. You probably don't want to get me started talking about that."

"Eric mentioned the same thing. You like your wine?"

"It's a hobby."

"It is late. I was serious about keeping an eye on Eric."

"If he's fortunate, he stopped at O'Shanley's where Mary-Margaret filled him up with sausages and a bland ale. If he's lucky, he wandered into O'Leary's and well…perhaps you should hurry. If the Guinness doesn't put him under the table, Lisa McGinley's flirtations will. See you tomorrow, Annja."

She waved him off and picked up her pace.

11

He'd had the Manhattan penthouse only a short time, but he used it often. Garin Braden traveled extensively. It was more wanderlust than anything, though he did have varied business interests that saw him flying from country to country. Staying in one spot for more than a week was not something he managed well. And he'd only negotiated a forty-eight-hour stay in the country with the waiver, so this trip was par for the course.

The first thing he did upon entering the penthouse was walk straight to the refrigerator. It was stocked with beer and bottled water. He took out a Faust, an elite Bavarian beer, twisted off the cap and tilted back half in one swallow.

Next, he rummaged for a spare cell phone in his office. There was enough charge to make a quick call.

"I had thought to hear from you sooner," Roux said without the niceties of a greeting. "How did it go?"

"Is today April 1?" Garin asked, only half joking. "I've

had a hell of a day, which I won't detail for you. Suffice, I did not get the painting."

"It wasn't that difficult an assignment. You had plenty of time to make the auction. Don't tell me you finished off with the woman before leaving?"

"I won't dignify that one with a reply. There was a delay at the airport. I arrived twenty minutes after the Fouquet went. But I have the buyer's address. I intend to case the home this evening."

"Case it? Garin, do not, by any means, steal the thing."

"Since when are you so averse to acquiring things by any means necessary?"

"Since this is a gift. A gift that will lose all meaning should it be obtained through nefarious means."

"That's a big word, old man."

He did not like it when Roux went all responsible on him. Hadn't he and the man shared more than a few adventures in *acquiring* over the centuries? He knew for a fact that some of Roux's prized possessions had cost him no more than the seduction required to distract or the skills utilized to slip it out of view.

"Listen, she won't know how the painting was acquired," Garin said. "So the point is moot."

"I'll know," Roux growled.

"Do you even know where she is?"

"You haven't stopped by her loft to see if she's home?"

"Haven't had time. I've been racing the clock. You think she's in New York?" She could be. Or she could be trekking the world on some fantastic adventure. Which didn't change the fact he had not gotten his hands on the painting. "I'll give her a call."

"After you charm the buyer into *selling* you the painting," Roux said.

Garin opened the fridge again, not searching for food. His

eye fell on the 9 mm pistol in the vegetable crisper. "Don't press me, old man."

"You're as old as I am. Can you have it in hand by tomorrow afternoon?"

"Are you writing up party invitations? I thought this was going to be a small to-do?"

"It is. I'm just…I want to make everything right."

The concern in Roux's voice made Garin uneasy. Garin knew Roux had a weird sort of father-daughter relationship with Annja. He protected her when he could, and had taught her the fighting skills she now used brilliantly.

"Since I'm doing all the legwork, then I'm sure you won't mind funding this little venture."

"I'll give you my credit card number."

Garin found a pen and wrote down the number. "That'll work. I'll call you back after I've acquired the thing without use of nefarious means."

He clicked off and slammed the fridge door. "I hope she appreciates this."

12

"Wake up."

Annja expected to find a hungover young man buried beneath the sheets. Hell, Eric hadn't had time for a hangover, he was probably still riding his drunk.

Annja had stopped into O'Leary's and the bartender confirmed feeding him supper, then serving him countless rounds of Guinness as she watched Eric cozy up to the flute player with curly blond ringlets.

A tuft of red hair disappeared beneath the sheets. Annja pinched Eric's shoulder.

"Ouch. Ma, I'm sleeping."

"I am not your mother."

"Huh? Oh, Annja. Wh-what are you doing in my bedroom? Did we—" He lifted the sheet to inspect for missing clothing. "I thought I was with Bridget."

"Oh, please. Get dressed. We're going out."

"Out?" He sat up. The room was dark but Annja saw him

pat his chest as if checking to see if he wore clothes. The boy could only dream. "What time is it?"

"Two in the morning. You wanted to film exciting scenes for the show?"

"Heck, yeah. Oh, man, my head."

"Take a couple of aspirin and splash your face with cold water. You did bring your night-vision lens, yes?"

"I did. Two in the morning? Is this normal? I don't recall seeing any episodes that featured you all bleary-eyed and whispering in the dark."

"You must not have seen the Transylvanian episode. We spent a lot of time lurking around graveyards and dark castles for that one. You want to come along or sleep off that drunk?"

His feet hit the floor. His body swayed, but he maintained equilibrium. He redirected the tousle of hair hanging in his eyes. "Give me five minutes."

"I'll meet you out front. Dress for a hike and sneaking about."

"Cool. Stealth filming in the wilds of Ireland."

To HIS CREDIT, Eric was ready and dressed all in black in four minutes flat. Camera in hand, he tugged down his misbuttoned shirt and gave Annja a thumbs-up and a wink.

Men had it easy. Just tug on any old wrinkled bit of clothing and they were good to go.

Annja couldn't complain. She'd tugged her hair into a ponytail, donned jeans and a T-shirt and never worried about makeup. It wasn't something she used during a dig, just a bit for filming. But filming at night would make her face too eerie. Makeup would just increase the horror level.

"We headed to the dig?" Eric asked as he strode alongside her in the quiet darkness. His running shoes crunched the loose gravel. He hadn't complained about his aching head, nor had he slurred his speech. It was always the young males who could hold their liquor the best.

"Yep. I want to take a look at Slater's dig."

"So that's why the sneak. Annja, you do the dare."

"We won't get any opportunity to look around during the day if Slater is ambling around with a pistol. Who knows how many guards he has posted. And why is that? Since when is muscle needed to protect a dig site from fellow archaeologists?"

"You tell me. I'm just the guy with the camera."

"There's something weird going on at the site, and I want to dig deeper."

"Dig deeper." Eric laughed. "Good one."

Annja rolled her eyes and headed off the main road and toward the dig, which was about five kilometers away. The hike was pleasant. The clear black sky twinkled with bright stars. The air smelled so fresh she wanted to bottle it and sneak it back home with her.

Crickets chirruped loudly in the long grasses. Annja didn't care for crickets after having to eat them in the wilds of the Serengeti to survive a night without supplies. They were too crunchy and the hind legs tended to get stuck in her teeth.

"I can't see the site," Eric said.

"It's a couple kilometers ahead. And so you know, when we get closer, we're doing stealth tonight. Sneaky quiet, don't-let-anyone-hear-us kind of work, okay?"

"Cool."

"Whatever you do, no matter what you see, keep your mouth shut, got it?"

"Chill, Annja, I can do the stealth."

That had yet to be determined—and only too late—Annja felt sure.

"You feeling better?"

"I only had four or five pints. I am so good, Annja."

"Are your parents aware you drink?"

"Annja, you are so not with the program."

She suspected more young people drank than their parents were aware. And he was a college guy, so it should come with the territory.

"My mom's dead. Three years ago. Breast cancer," he said. "And dad doesn't care much as long as I don't do something to embarrass him and his company."

"I'm sorry," she said. "Is it just you and your dad, then? Any brothers or sisters?"

"No siblings. Can't you tell I'm a spoiled-rotten only child? What about you?"

"No family," she said, and quickly dismissed the burgeoning conversation.

THE DIG SITE WAS DARK. No artificial lighting was strung along the camp tents. There was one small tent, which could be the director's office, and a larger tent that must be the central cache for finds and perhaps to keep tools.

It didn't appear as though anyone was about, but Annja knew better. If Slater had been packing a gun yesterday, there had to be a reason. She wasn't about to let down her guard.

Annja was only half as curious about the actual dig area as she was about the truck parked behind the main tent. It was likely the supply truck that had driven in the tents and work equipment, but she could have sworn it was smaller and white the day she'd first arrived.

Positioned behind a thick fence post that must have been dug in at the demarcation where peat stopped and dirt began, she tugged Eric's sleeve so the kid would not step out into the open and reveal their presence.

"Stay behind me," she warned. "You got your camera rolling?"

"Sure, but what are we looking for in the night?"

"Anything suspicious. You want faeries?"

He nodded eagerly.

"It's not going to happen. There's something real and very likely human kidnapping people from the dig, and we're going to find out who that is."

"You think someone from this camp—"

"Haven't a clue. I wanted to talk to Beth earlier but she was distraught."

"I would be, too, if I'd escaped from people with wings."

"Eric." She gritted her teeth. "Do you know it's not wise to talk about them or to name them with anything other than a euphemism? They can hear you. And they don't like it."

"Really?" His eyes searched the darkness.

Annja felt sure that would not nip his determination to find the fair folk in the bud.

"You going to talk to Beth tomorrow?"

"First thing in the morning. Now come on, let's look around. Keep to the camp perimeter. Don't step out into the open—your silhouette might be seen against the sky. And stay low."

"You're very good at this, Annja."

"This is my signal for you to film." She made a V of her first two fingers, then pointed downward. "I'll point toward what I want filmed. Got it?"

She put a finger to her lips before Eric could reply, then whispered, "Stealth mode from here on. No talking."

Annja knew it wasn't wise taking an inexperienced man into the field. And if there was something illegal going on in this camp, they would have night security, and she felt positive Eric would not react as she hoped—calmly and quietly.

This would be a quick, in-and-out reconnaissance. But she did want to get anything curious on film for later study. Her eyes would miss a lot in the darkness that a camera could record.

Bending low and scampering across the grass, she headed for a mound of dirt dug up from the dig square. The spoil heap, which would eventually be sifted and sorted through before using it to backfill the site. The rich peat combined with abundant heather growing around the camp perimeter stirred a gorgeous perfume in the air.

To his credit, Eric followed silently. He scanned the camera across the grounds.

That gave her an idea.

Kneeling behind the spoil heap, Annja held out her hand. "Let me take a look with that, will you?"

He handed her the camera, and she scanned it across the site, noting the corded-off area where the diggers had cleared a surprising amount of turf and soil for the four weeks they had been there. They were using a grid to dig, unlike the other camp's open square. Interesting.

Across the way, the camera marked out the tents and a makeshift trestle table with various shovels and brushes and a few artifacts scattered on it. There was no movement in any of the tents, but she felt sure someone slept inside. Whether security, or Michael Slater, she couldn't know.

The truck was parked beyond the tent. It was about the size of a delivery truck, but had no company name or discernible markings on the sides. A small flashing green light inside the cab caught her attention.

Annja moved the camera from her eyes and squinted to see it was actually a red LED light. Must be on a stereo or GPS system. Another look through the camera found no movement in the cab. A scan along the bottom of the truck bed didn't spy any boots casing the perimeter.

The camp was locked down for the night. And her scan didn't spot any hidden cameras. Not that she would find something that had been cleverly hidden.

She handed the camera to Eric and gestured that they

should creep over the spoil heap. She landed in the dig area beside the taut cord line that marked off one side.

Eric slid down the dirt and with a muffled grunt he stumbled deeper.

Annja clasped his wrist as he let out an abbreviated exhale. "Got you," she whispered.

She held all his weight. He hung over a tarped-off section. If she let him go, he'd slide onto the tarp, make a lot of noise and possibly damage whatever find had been protected beneath the tarp.

In the dark her sense of depth didn't exist. Annja felt about with the heel of her boot for leverage, found a sure footing, then leaned back to pull Eric up. He stumbled not so gracefully across her body and rolled onto his back, without making a sound. The camera he held above him, which had remarkably been spared.

Points for him for not sprawling on top of her. But she was worried they were destroying the site, and didn't want to leave evidence they'd been here.

Grabbing the camera from his fierce clutch, she swung it toward where he had just been. Leaning forward, Annja lifted the tarp and scanned the grounds. "Nice."

"There's something in there?"

She handed the camera to Eric and gestured for him to film. She knelt before the artifact and dug in her pocket for her Maglite. Cautious to keep the tarp over the find, but lifting it so she could look inside and shine the light without the beam being noticed, she looked over the skeleton.

It had been dug out completely. It was likely the team would lift it from the ground and begin to label and mark the bones in the morning. It looked complete, sprawled on her side—yes, a female, for the flatter and proportionately larger pelvic bone. One arm had disconnected and lay a foot away, above the skull. Earth erosion tended to move skeletons all over the place. This one was remarkably well preserved and intact. She knew they could attribute that to the humid conditions of the peat bog.

Anna switched off the light. With a glance toward the tents to confirm no movement, she then turned it back on and flashed the beam across the wall of the square to survey the strata. It appeared to be about as far down as Wesley's camp, which would put this skeleton mid-nineteenth century.

It was a guess. It could be older, having been pushed up by erosion, or much younger even, having been buried in a shallow grave. Unless she could study the bones under good light it was all a guessing game.

Much as she wanted to investigate further, Annja couldn't risk spending too much time bent over the dirt when she hadn't secured the area.

She felt Eric move beside her, and pressed a hand to his knee to stay him.

"Thanks," he murmured.

She made the signal to film and lifted the tarp. As he carefully leaned forward, she hooked her fingers through a belt loop on his jeans. He understood what she was doing and dared to lean farther.

Annja held firmly while Eric filmed, starting from the foot bones and all the way up and along the extended arm. When he slapped her ankle, she tugged him back.

She should have brought along a plastic bag to collect a soil sample, but this had been a spur of the moment decision to come here. She always carried one in her backpack for such an occurrence. Watching the periphery, she determined all was still quiet. She gestured for Eric to follow her back over the mound of dirt where she paused.

Taking the camera from Eric, she then looked over their tracks. Not so messy, and the dig grounds were not clean and smooth. This area was used a lot. Maybe no one would notice the extra footprints.

With a signal to follow, Annja put her light in her pocket. She then crept along toward the tent. Without clear sight of the ground she had to be cautious of stones or ruts in the dirt that might trip her. Or a stray tool. She worked slowly and scanned the horizon as she did so. The moon was half-full and the air was clear and bright. If anything moved, she'd notice the silhouette against the blue-gray sky.

Keeping her distance five feet from the tent, she straightened and insinuated herself alongside one wall. Ears keenly perked she heard snoring from within. One single snore. It didn't mean only one person was inside, only one who snored.

Would Slater stay overnight at the camp? Possible. Did that mean *he* was the security? Pretty lax, if he was snoring.

She moved onward. Eric kept filming. The man had a remarkable sense of his surroundings and did not trip. He must be an athlete; grace came naturally.

The truck was parked ahead. Taking a straight line because there was nothing to hide behind, Annja swiped at the breeze that moved her ponytail from in front of her shoulder to the back. Then she paused.

There was no breeze. And she hadn't moved her head.

"Annja?" Eric whispered.

She must have moved her hair, flipped it over her shoulder with a jerk of her head. It was the only thing that made sense. Until a strange flutter made her look down.

"I hear it," Eric whispered. "They're here."

"Nothing is…" For some reason the protest didn't feel right. She didn't know what was causing her sudden nervousness, or making her hear things.

It had to be an insect. Beetles were noisy, their carapaces

clattering against wings in flight. It had sounded like that, like…a fluttering.

"Just a bug," she whispered, and signaled they continue.

There were scads of colorful beetles native to Ireland. And if not that, it could have been a wasp or some big insect she was glad she hadn't seen.

Gripping her ponytail to pull it forward over her shoulder, Annja let go of the guessing games and focused.

She reached the truck, pressed a palm along the metal side and walked the length of the bed toward the back. Something clanked behind her.

That was no insect.

Eric swore and slapped a palm to the truck bed. Annja's heart pounded. The muscles in her neck and shoulders tightened. For a moment she stood like a statue, as did Eric. He'd tripped on something metal. So much for grace.

When alert, her senses heightened, picking up breaths and footsteps more easily than most. Both of them glanced west. No noise came from within the tent. The snoring had stopped, or else she was too far away to hear it.

Moving around to the back of the truck bed, she gestured for Eric to follow. Testing the back doors with her fingers, she was surprised to feel them give. They were not locked.

A male cry of pain alerted her. She heard a body hit the ground and the clatter of the plastic-encased camera followed.

"Eric," she whispered slowly.

Footsteps crunched the dirt. Those were not Eric's rubber-soled Vans.

Sucking in a breath through her nose, Annja calmed. At times like this, she had nothing to fear because she wasn't a lone woman without protection.

She swept out her right hand. Tapping into the otherwhere

she opened her fingers and closed them about the hilt of her battle sword. Slapping her left hand to the hilt, she prepared to meet whatever swung around the corner of the truck.

13

Bright light flashed, causing Annja's pupils to constrict and reducing her ability to see in the darkness. She didn't need to see who held the flashlight. Now that she had marked his position, she swung her arms out wide, twisting at the waist. The blade landed at his throat.

"Drop it," she demanded. The flashlight beam wobbled and landed on the ground. "What's in the other hand, too."

The clatter of a pistol barrel hit the ground. The man was big; she had to look up to feel his breath on her face. Salty anxiety wafted from him.

"Who are you?" he growled in a British accent similar to Slater's.

"I could ask the same. Anyone else out here tonight?" She pressed the blade into his flesh. It hadn't cut, but she could change that quick enough.

"Hey!" His knuckles hit the truck bed behind him as he raised his hands in placation. "Watch it!"

"Bring the volume down. Or are you alerting your

buddies?" Annja maintained a keen sense for her surroundings, especially any footsteps approaching from behind.

"I'm the only bloke on security tonight."

"No one else? The tents are empty?"

"Yes, they all leave at nightfall."

"I thought I heard someone snoring in the main tent."

"I'm the only one. Trust me, duck."

That would never happen. Annja twisted the blade to press the flat of it under his jaw, prompting him to lift his chin. "What did you do to my man?"

"Tranq dart," he said. "It will knock him out for a couple hours."

"Eric?" she called.

She heard a groan.

"You must have missed," she said to the security guard. "Step aside."

She followed his careful sideways steps with the blade of her sword, wedging it firmly against his neck. When he stood against the open sky his silhouette, imposing as it was, showed her he was barrel-shaped and probably more brawn than physically agile. That could either work to his advantage or, if she was quick, to hers.

Bending and performing a sinuous move, she snapped up the dart gun from the ground with her left hand. That moment of inattention got her a boot to the side of her shoulder. Her body collided with the rear truck tire. Yet she maintained her hold on both the gun and sword.

The security guard ran around to the other side of the truck.

Scrambling to her feet, Annja skipped over Eric's fallen body. "Be right back. Stay there."

"My leg," he said, and groaned.

Stopping to listen, she heard heels scuff across rubble.

Annja tracked the man to the truck cab. He could hop in and drive away, but not on her watch.

She dashed around the front of the truck and slashed her sword across his thigh as he took the first step up into the truck. With a yelp, he released his grip on the steering wheel and landed on the ground, arms splayed.

Pinioning him with the sword tip directly over his heart, Annja loomed over him. With her other hand she teased the dart gun's trigger. It was spring-loaded, ready to fire.

"What's in the truck?" she asked.

"Nothing but supplies." His heavy accent was difficult to understand, but she got the hint. "Bloody trespasser," he said.

Yes, she was. Thankful for the darkness, she felt sure if this guy reported a woman sneaking about camp with a cameraman in tow, it wouldn't take long for anyone to put two and two together.

"Why don't you let me take a look inside?"

"It's shovels and buckets!" He finally decided to play along.

"Just a peek, then, to verify. Stay."

Holding aim on him with the pistol, she backtracked to the end of the truck. Releasing the sword into the otherwhere gave her a free hand to dig out her Maglite. A flash of it inside the truck bed found it was empty save for, indeed, a stack of empty black buckets.

Did Slater's camp believe security was necessary to protect a few supplies and a skeleton? She'd heard of rivalry at dig sites, but this was pushing it a bit far.

She thought she should have a look inside the tents, but as the man had stated, she was the trespasser. She didn't need to cross any more lines tonight, especially since her original plan to sneak in unnoticed had gone haywire.

"We'll be leaving, then, nice and quick," she said.

Pulling the trigger, she aimed for the guard's arm, and was pleased when he grunted as the dart pierced flesh. A good shot should put him out completely within fifteen to thirty seconds.

"Ah-ah." She nudged his arm with her toe. "Just let that rush through your system. Good boy."

His body relaxed under her foot. With a nudge of her boot toe to the side of his head, she verified he was out.

Slater would hear all about it in the morning, which gave her a few hours to come up with a good reason for scouting his camp in the middle of the night.

Rushing around the side of the truck, she expected to find Eric out cold, too. He sat with his shoulders braced against a tire. Annja knelt before him.

"Some kind of dart," he muttered, huffing as if his breaths pained him. "I tugged it out of my thigh as soon as I felt the hit. It just cut through some skin but didn't go deep, but I can't feel my leg now, Annja. I'm paralyzed." Panic eddied his voice up an octave. "I can't lose my leg. I'm young. Girls don't go for guys in wheelchairs. Well, some do, but those chicks are whacked. Annja!"

"It's a tranquilizer. Your leg is asleep. The more you move, the more the adrenaline pushes it through your system. Though, perhaps it didn't hit the bloodstream with the shallow cut. I think you lucked out, Eric. Just give me one minute."

She retrieved the video camera and swept it across the camp one last time, including taking in the fallen guard's face.

"Annja!"

Eric must be falling asleep. Or there could be others who had been alerted by their noise. The guard had no reason to lie about being the only one on-site, and every reason if he were protecting something valuable.

Annja shut off the camera, and raced back to Eric's side.

"It stings," Eric said as she went to help him stand.

"You're going to have to hop along beside me," she directed. "We have to move fast before anyone else discovers us. Put your arm around my shoulder and let's go."

"You got the camera?"

"Yep." She helped him to stand and hop on one foot.

"How'd you get away from that dude? He was huge. And he had that gun."

"Used my feminine wiles."

"Wiles?"

"Quiet now. We'll talk when we get back."

Passing the truck and tents, she thought briefly about the strange feeling she'd had before finding the guard. That someone or some*thing* had been near her. Something she could not see, yet it had felt as if wings had moved the air about her.

With a careful scan of her surroundings, Annja led Eric into the dark countryside. If there were faeries out here, she'd try her best to avoid any raths or hawthorn bushes, anything the other crowd deemed their own.

Just to be safe.

14

They arrived back at the B and B around 5:00 a.m. After Annja inspected Eric's thigh and declared it a superficial wound—the dart had torn his jeans and abraded the skin—he fell immediately to sleep.

She decided to view the video of the enemy camp in the morning. She'd managed three hours of sleep when the proprietress knocked on her room door, announcing breakfast below.

Eric's knock followed shortly after that. He popped his head in the doorway as Annja was sliding from under the covers. She tugged the sheet up to her chest. She wore the same T-shirt she'd been wearing last night but below that it was just her underwear.

"You coming?" he asked.

Annja marveled that he was bright and shiny after so little sleep. Was she really getting old enough that she admired the resilience of youth?

"Of course I am. Nothing can keep me away from black pudding. How are you feeling?" she asked.

"You were right, it's just a nick. I think it was more shock at actually being shot at than actual injury, you know? But I'm tough." He flexed his biceps. "This is turning out to be way more exciting than following my dad around on documentary gigs." He gave her a thumbs-up, then closed her door.

Fifteen minutes later, after some amazing luck at finding the bathroom empty and the shower stocked with towels, Annja sat at a table perusing the black pudding. It wasn't mushy or in any sort of form she associated with pudding. It was actually sliced blood sausage that was then fried. Although there was nothing keeping her away from the delicacy, she changed her mind, and went with double the rashers and eggs. An extra helping of beans was served, too.

Mrs. Riley and her son joined her, along with Eric, who was very focused when he ate. He'd criticized the local cuisine, but he certainly had no problem putting it down when it was available.

"What's that, honey?" Mrs. Riley asked as her husband entered, coddling something close to his chest. He headed for the refrigerator and opened it up.

"Wine from Mr. Collins."

Annja saw Mr. Riley slide a dark wine bottle into the fridge. "Daniel Collins?" she asked.

"Yes, he's got the nicest wines," the man said as he wandered into the dining room. "He barters, did you know?"

"What did you trade this time, honey?" his wife asked.

"Ah? Oh, er, nothing of much import. Something I found in one of the delivery trucks." Annja had been told the husband delivered auto parts to various repair shops in County Cork. "Never you mind much, it's all in the goblet, don't you know. That's what Collins told me. Something about allowing the wine to breathe, and the width of the goblet opening. Nice to meet you, Miss Creed. My wife tells me you're with the dig up yonder?"

"Actually, I'm here to film a segment about the people gone missing from the dig."

"Ah, that'd be the fair folk, then." Mr. Riley sat down and tucked a napkin in at his collar and began to murder the runny eggs on the plate before him. "You don't expect to catch the wee things on film, do you?"

She caught his gleeful wink.

"Not at all. I've been told the fair folk are not seen but rather experienced."

"It would bring a disaster upon you to attempt such shenanigans with your filming equipment. I was quite relieved when the BBC was shuffled out of town, don't you know."

"My crew is small, just myself and Eric. And I hope to explore the more…human aspects of the story while I'm here."

The husband and wife exchanged glances. Did everyone believe in faeries except her?

"You know, Rachel Collins owns a genuine faerie spear," Mrs. Riley said as she offered Annja another pour of paint-peeling coffee. "And Certainly Jones, well, he's always sauced so we can never be sure what truths he speaks or if they are faerie tales. It's all tales of faeries, then, isn't it?"

Annja offered a closemouthed smile.

"To think it all started with Farmer Gentry's arthritis," Mr. Riley said around a mouthful of beans.

"Is that the name of the farmer whose land we're digging on?" Annja asked.

"Indeed. He found the spear fragment when he was cutting turf to soak in."

Annja lifted a brow. "Soak in what?"

"Himself. Peat is good for the muscles and bones," he explained. "Gentry soaks every other day and swears he's much more spry for it. Good for the arthritis, don't you know. You tell me you haven't seen those fancy salons in the United States that sell the peat baths for restoration and beauty for thousands of your American dollars?"

"I don't really go to spas," Annja replied. "It makes sense, though. The peat would retain vital minerals and carbon that could have a healing effect on the body."

Mr. Riley nodded, pleased with the information he'd bestowed, and his wife patted his forearm.

Annja would have to remember that silver lining the next time she found herself mucking about in a fresh, deep bog.

MR. RILEY OFFERED Annja and Eric a vintage black Mini Cooper to use for the day if they'd stop by the market and pick him up some cigars. Annja was ready to tell him he could probably barter with Daniel for those, too, but it was the least she could do in response to his generous offer.

More rust than paint coated the body of the compact road hazard. But after a few stops and starts Eric got a handle on the stick shift.

On the passenger side, Annja reviewed the night's footage that she'd transferred to her laptop. Even enhancing the video and altering the brightness didn't allow for much clarity. It had been a dark dig. But the skeleton did show quite nicely, which pleased her.

She was able to confirm the pelvic bone was female from the wide sciatic notch nicely revealed on film.

She couldn't be sure, but the pale gray smudges along the femur looked like fabric. It was very unlikely that fabric would have survived so long in regular dirt, but not impossible when buried in a peat bog. Peat retained moisture well, which preserved things like skin, bone and some fabrics. Heck, it even cured arthritis, according to Mr. Riley. A sample of the thread strands could be dated with the proper lab equipment.

Wesley Pierce had contacts in Cork. They'd be able to learn a lot about the corpse if they could test the fabric.

She much preferred to do things on the up-and-up. She wondered if Michael Slater would be open to her testing the fabric strands if she asked nicely.

Plugging in the satellite card, she then went online and searched for information about the area along the Bandon River. That brought up a surveyor's map. The forest and bog were noted, but the makeshift road to the river was not.

Next she researched nineteenth-century Ireland.

The first few pages of hits detailed the potato famine and the incredible trials and struggle the Irish people—and countries including Belgium and Prussia—endured for that period in the mid-century when their most prized and fruitful crop had been blighted by a fungus, leaving a quarter of the population starving, unable to pay rents and seeking mass emigration. The loss of crops—a way of life—had killed millions within a five-year period. To this day, the country's population was still less than it had been in the nineteenth century.

It was very interesting, but she still couldn't figure how that would make the one skeleton worth protecting with security and why people were disappearing. Anything left behind from the famine period could not be particularly valuable.

And to consider Mrs. Collins's makeshift diamond, Annja could only shake her head. She decided to let the information brew.

Eric reported the town was just ahead, beyond a field of grazing sheep.

It was time to find Beth Gwillym and hear her story.

ERIC LET ANNJA OFF at the door to West County General Hospital, then drove off, looking for a parking space.

What the hospital offered was standard issue. Drab green

walls enclosed the sick and their caregivers in a dreary environment. The smell of antiseptic and bodily discharges permeated the air. Fluorescent lighting cast over the staff, who were clad in more drab green and looking as downtrodden as the sick.

Annja walked with purpose. She bypassed admissions, knowing she'd be asked if she was family. After determining the entire first floor was for emergency and outpatient services, she took the stairs to the second floor.

Would Beth's family know their daughter had been admitted to the hospital? she wondered. Wesley had seemed a little too clueless when it came to information about his employees. He should have files with addresses and emergency contact information.

Reading the charts fitted sideways into metal holders outside each door, Annja finally located Beth Gwillym. Just as she touched the door marked See Front Desk for Visiting Regulations, a stern voice stopped her in her tracks.

FIVE MINUTES LATER Eric found Annja wandering the hall some distance from Beth's room. He'd left his camera equipment in the Mini, which was smart. No need to draw more attention to what they were doing. "No luck? Is she sleeping?" he asked.

"I've been firmly told by a nurse that I'm not allowed to visit unless I'm a relative."

"That rules out questioning her."

Annja took the measure of the hallway. The nurse's station stood four doors down from Beth's room. The receptionist was out of sight. Annja had noted the woman wore thick glasses and had to lean in close to read the computer monitor. It would be easy to slip past her. But nurses came and went from all directions, including the occasional nun. She could risk slipping in and waking Beth, but would she even speak to her? She may not remember seeing her yesterday afternoon after coming out of the forest in her ravaged state.

And if she did, that didn't guarantee she'd speak to a stranger about her experience.

She needed a friendly face to ease Beth's possible distrust.

"Why don't you take a peek at her chart?" Eric suggested, gesturing to the metal file holder near Annja's head. "I have a digital camera in my pocket. If we're sneaky we can take shots of the whole thing, then duck out and read them."

"Eric, that's illegal."

But beyond dressing up as a nun, Annja was out of ideas. She only wanted to help Beth, and learning anything about her condition could lead to who had done this in the first place.

"In there." Annja gestured to the men's bathroom across the hall. Sneaking down the hall and slipping the chart from the rack, she pushed open the bathroom door. Eric was waiting in the handicapped stall. "Hurry."

Obviously shocked at her daring, he clutched his digital camera near his chest and gaped.

"This freaks you out?" she said as she opened the file and held it for him to snap a shot. Page after page they worked. "You're the one who suggested it."

"Everything about you freaks me out, Annja. Turn." He was snapping faster than she could turn. "I was just kidding. Sort of. Maybe. My leg still aches from last night. And you dispatched that behemoth security guard with your bare hands. This is cool, in a freaky kind of way, you know?"

"Make sure you get a clear, high-resolution shot."

"I am the cameraman. Don't worry about my work. You just hurry. I think I hear someone coming."

"Turn and face the door." Annja stood on the toilet seat

and crouched so it would appear that only Eric's feet were inside the stall.

The door creaked open. Someone came in and used the urinals, then left.

"He didn't wash his hands," she said, and jumped down. "I think we've got it all. Let's go."

OUT IN THE CAR, Eric moaned about his wound tingling but Annja didn't offer sympathy. She scanned the hospital records on her laptop. Eric's handiwork had produced clear and readable images; it was as if she held the actual records in hand. Medical terminology was not her thing. It read like hieroglyphics—yet hieroglyphics she could decipher after some study.

"Anything?" Eric asked.

"Not sure. She's diabetic. I wonder if she might have missed an insulin dose, got disoriented and wandered off?"

It was possible, but Annja felt sure Beth would have been in much rougher shape upon her return. And diabetics always carried an emergency kit on them, didn't they?

Then she read something she understood.

"It wasn't lack of insulin. Overdose on lysergic acid diethylamide."

"LSD?"

She narrowed her brows at Eric. "I don't want to know how you know that."

"Come on, Annja, everyone who's been through high school knows that. And look at you, acting all Goody Two-Shoes when you just stole private hospital records."

"Don't remind me."

"So she was on LSD?" he asked.

"Sounds like it. And she overdosed."

"Is that the same thing as magic mushrooms?"

"No. They would have made a notation if they'd suspected

as much. I think you'd have to eat a lot of mushrooms to actually overdo it, anyway. A drug overdose may have led her to
wander away from the site and get lost."

"Sure," Eric said. "But I didn't pick up any 'hey, you want
to get high?' vibes from anyone in the camp."

"Neither did I. And it feels wrong. Wesley mentioned
magic mushrooms, and insinuated that maybe a few of the
crew members had eaten them, but this is different." She
tapped the laptop with the tips of her fingernails, thinking. "Maybe it wasn't voluntary but administered? If Beth
had been kidnapped, and taken forcibly from the site, then
drugged—that would explain her thinking she'd been taken
by the other crowd, don't you think?"

He shrugged. "It's not as cool as the real thing—captured
by faeries—but I can dig it. But she was gone, like, what?
Almost two days? And would they have kept her high on LSD
that whole time? That's one hell of a trip."

"No kidding. I'm missing something here, and I'm not sure
I'll have it until I can talk to Beth and get the truth. I wonder
what the residual effects of an overdose are?"

"Do you think we should go for a hike through the forest
edging the dig?"

"That's not a bad idea. It's where Beth emerged. She had
to have come from somewhere."

"Maybe down by the river?"

"Yes, but what's down there?"

"We won't know until we look."

Impressed by Eric's dedication, Annja closed her laptop.
"All right. I think we should wander down during the day,
though. Makes for easier sleuthing with the sun out. I'm going
to talk to Wesley first when we get back to camp and see if
he has any more information about Beth and…"

"Magic mushrooms?" Eric winked.

"Right. Magic mushrooms. Remind me why I agreed to this crazy assignment?"

"Because you are a professional with the ability to maintain decorum even in the most bizarre of situations. And you always uncover the truth."

"I'm really starting to like you, Eric."

"Cool. Wanna make out?"

She shot him a look.

"Psyche. You're way too old for me." He grinned and turned onto the gravel road.

SLATER SLAPPED his cell phone shut and shoved it in his front pocket. A call from Frank Neville was never pleasant. The bloke was not rational, by any means, but he disguised it with alarming calm. With him threatening to come out to the site, Slater had to cool down Neville's ire before he thought to step foot behind the wheel.

He thought he had things under control. Then random dig workers had stumbled onto Frank Neville's private business. And he felt he'd taken control of that problem, as well. Until that woman from the American television show had arrived all perky and snooping about.

One wrong move and this operation could go up in flames.

Striding into the cool shadows of the supply tent, Slater located the security guard he'd found that morning sprawled by the truck. At first, he'd thought Peter Donovan was sleeping on the job, but closer inspection determined he'd taken a beating. The man had whined about some woman with a sword sneaking up on him in the middle of the night.

Slater pulled out his pistol and pressed it to the guard's neck. The man startled from a snooze on the cot.

"Whoa, mate, what did I do? I told you everything I know."

"A feeble woman came creeping about the site late last night and beat you up. Did she have wings, too? You know the whole faerie story is just a front. They're not real, idiot."

The guard nodded, but his eyes shifted as he considered the statement. "One of the fair folk? No. She was big—I mean, normal size. She was smaller than me, so that makes her feeble."

Slater shoved the pistol barrel deeper into flesh.

"Wait!"

Slater recited the guard's idiot confession from the morning, "And she had a three-foot-long battle sword, which explains the cut on your neck."

The guard nodded frantically.

Slater tilted the guard's chin up with the pistol barrel, none too gently. "You sure you didn't cut yourself shaving last night, Donovan?"

"I'm telling the truth, boss."

"So why'd you go and call Neville about it after I thought we'd cleared things up? You know I run this camp. You got a problem or concern, or someone trespasses, you come directly to me. What, about those simple rules, don't you comprehend, Donovan?"

"I'm sorry, boss, I forgot. Neville's number came up first in my phone and I thought he should know."

"Yeah? Well, that's my job now, isn't it? Communicating with Neville. Yours is to guard the camp and keep out trespassers. Good work, Donovan. Bang-up job. You fell asleep last night and woke up in the middle of one of your sex fantasies to battle the metal-bikini-wearing warrior woman."

"No, uh, it wasn't like that." Donovan eyed Slater's trigger finger. "She was real. And she had a kid with her. He was filming, like with a movie camera."

Now that was new information. Slater tilted the gun barrel to point straight up. If he pulled the trigger now it would go through the bottom of Donovan's mouth and come out through his nose, shattering cartilage and gifting him with a permanent hole in the center of his maw—if he was lucky.

"Keep your eyes on the site and your hand on your gun, not your phone, got that?"

Donovan nodded profusely.

"I'll need you to be on top of things tonight, Donovan. We have another midnight run. I don't want any witnesses."

"No problem, boss. If I see that woman again, I'll shoot her."

"No, I don't want you drawing attention to what we're doing here. Detain and secure her, but do not injure her. Just like the others. Got that?"

"Uh, sure."

"Good boy." He patted the man's cheek with the gun's barrel, then turned and strode from the tent. "Idiot."

15

Despite wielding the sixteen-digit credit card number that Roux should have been more careful giving to him, Garin couldn't resist the compulsion to walk the sidewalk before the brownstone. After looking over the four-story walk-up, sandwiched between two equally bland, brick-fronted brownstones, he scanned the houses across the street.

It was midmorning. The nine-to-fivers had left hours earlier in their pursuit of another dollar, another pat on the back, another missed subway train. A few dog walkers pranced the sidewalks, but most of the residences appeared unoccupied.

The best vantage point for his target was the red house across the street and to the south. The third-floor window was shielded with white lace. Little old lady must live there, he thought. Which meant she was likely home.

Garin noted digital security pads on all the buildings near the front doors. Old wrought-ironwork screen doors preceded most of the entry doors. No doubt, the neighborhood was populated by geriatrics who kept a tight fist on their fortunes. But that never dissuaded a determined thief.

He knew little about Mrs. Banyon, who had purchased the painting via a proxy yesterday afternoon. There had been but a few mentions about her on the internet, although he did find generous donations had been made to the Metropolitan Opera and half a dozen libraries in the various boroughs in her name. To Garin, that meant she was either very generous, charitable or she needed a tax write-off.

Unfortunately, he hadn't managed to obtain Banyon's phone number. Garin knew approaching without a call could be risky. And door-to-door salesmen probably didn't go over at all in this neighborhood. The delivery-man act was beneath him, so a direct approach it would be.

Buttoning his suit coat so his movement would not reveal the Glock holstered under his arm, he took the steps to Mrs. Banyon's residence and rang the buzzer. It was immediately answered by a man's cough crackling through the ancient intercom.

"Excuse me. Who is it?"

"Mr. Garin Braden. I don't have an appointment, so please forgive me. Mrs. Banyon acquired a painting yesterday at Christie's that I am keen to discuss with her. If I could have but a few minutes of her time?"

"She's not seeing anyone."

The intercom static abruptly ceased, leaving Garin staring at the bronze-slotted cover. He raised a hand to knock, but relented. He buzzed again.

"Mrs. Banyon has no interest," the voice intoned gruffly. Another cough followed.

"I understand," Garin said. "And I certainly do not wish to be a bother, but I've been authorized to double the price she paid for it if she is interested in letting it go."

Hell, it wasn't *his* money.

Long moments passed. Garin was almost ready to buzz again, when the front door opened. An emaciated yet tall man in butler's livery managed an ingratiating smile.

Money always talked.

16

Annja strode into the cool shade the canvas tent offered. The sun was high and bright. But rain could arrive on the Emerald Isle at any moment. It offered a dream scenario for a dig. Lots of sun during the day with light rain in the evening to keep the work area moist and workable.

She'd decided to use the opportunity that found everyone out enjoying the weather to snoop about the camp base. A clue linked to Beth, or even that the crew was imbibing in magic mushrooms, was what she hoped to find.

Wesley's field notes were scattered on a table in a couple of hardback notebooks. Various pieces of wood, pottery and metal had been sorted into black buckets. A few larger samples lay on the table. Annja had been told that one of the girls had unearthed a carriage wheel rim and had been so excited she'd tripped and bent the frame.

Annja recalled a few of her first digs. She must have driven the dig director nuts with her constant, "Is this a find? Is this anything? Should I keep this?" questions.

She touched a plumb bob and measured its solid weight in her palm. It was used to dig level stratigraphy into the earth and for squaring up drawing grids.

"No faerie spears. Yet," she said with a bemused tone, and set down the tear-shaped lead bob.

It wasn't as if she expected the dig to *not* find a faerie spear. They might find any means of ancient weapon under the dirt and peat. That wouldn't surprise her one bit.

But a *magical* spear once wielded by a race of people believed to be faeries? That would take some doing.

On the other hand, Mrs. Collins supposedly already owned the spear of Lugh, and kept it above her television right next to a Doctor Who tin lunch box and a mint-condition 1972 Kennedy silver dollar.

And who was she to question the existence of an ancient magical weapon capable of appearing when needed?

Once, she'd thought it strange that she, of all people, had managed to take possession of Joan of Arc's sword, and could utilize it to fight the good fight. She'd initially dreaded needing to use it because that meant something bad was happening, and usually to people who didn't deserve the aforesaid something bad.

Now, she had grown into ownership of the sword. The sword was hers. She was comfortable swinging it at enemies and liked seeing their initial reactions. A chick with a sword? Seriously?

She never got too cocky with the power she wielded. Okay, ninety percent of the time she avoided cockiness. The sword was there for a purpose and she wouldn't abuse that power.

So why did the funky dream about the sword not being her power to own bother her so much?

Perhaps her subconscious was checking her pride, making sure she did not go over the edge with it all. And although she was confident owning it, she also knew she'd never completely understand any of it.

Especially the pair of five-hundred-year-old immortals who had happened into her life along with the sword.

She wondered what Roux and Garin were up to. Roux was likely sunning himself off the coast of France, surrounded by a couple of supermodel types with tans as deep as their cleavage—and not apologizing for his playboy lifestyle.

And Garin, well, Annja could never be sure if the man was up to something no good, or downright evil. Sure, he had occasions to good, but deception and betrayal came easily to the man who wanted to get his hands on her sword and shatter it. And if he wasn't trying to trick her, he was trying to kiss her.

Suddenly swung about by the shoulder and shoved against a hard plastic packing case, Annja felt the barrel of a pistol against her temple at the same time she processed the fact that Michael Slater stood before her.

"What the hell are you up to, Creed?"

She was not intimidated. Only angry that Mr. Slick had managed to sneak up on her.

"Taking a look around," she offered. Admittedly, feeling the barrel of a gun pressed to any part of her did make her nervous. "Any rule against that? This isn't even your camp. What happened to staying on your own side?"

He slid off the safety.

"You don't want to start this argument with me, Creed. I don't like you. And you can't convince me you're here only to record a few video clips and push around some dirt."

"Don't forget the part about the faeries," she said.

"Creed, I have a loaded gun pressed against your temple."

"I noticed. Your people skills suck. Anyone ever tell you that?"

He glowered. She was pushing it, but for some reason she didn't sense that he would actually harm her. Not with a loud gunshot, within fifty feet of half a dozen workers.

"I don't care whether or not you do like me," she said. "And I can film where I want. You don't make the rules about that. And yet, when I look over all the people working both digs and involved on the site, one of those things is not like the other. That would be you. You're no archaeologist. What are you? Security? Military? You're some kind of soldier, aren't you?"

"Soldier?" He smirked. The gun stayed at her temple. The scent of gunpowder and cleaning oil stung her eyes. "You're making assumptions. I'm security. Nothing more."

"Yeah? Why the need for such intense security? Most digs I've been on provide a flashlight and walkie-talkie to the security guards. What have you found over there in your little corner of the dig? Something valuable? Gold? Jewels? Diamonds?"

"I want to know what the hell you and your camera boy are doing traipsing through private property in the middle of the night?"

It wasn't as though she'd thought the security guard would keep their adventure a secret. But she did not appreciate Slater's brusque manner.

"You're not going to shoot me," she said. "Because then you'd have to get rid of my blood-dripping body in broad daylight."

"There are places on a body that'll take a bullet without producing excess blood loss," he said. Delivered with cold detachment.

"All right, then, where would you put my not-bleeding-so-much body? Oh, wait, you can stuff me in the back of that truck with all the empty buckets. What, are you mining for something?"

"I'm not in the mood for jokes, Creed. You're just lucky you missed the booby traps."

"Booby traps?" He was kidding. Maybe. "Now you're scaring me. What? A trip wire? Explosives?"

Slater smirked and snapped the pistol away from her head. He clicked the safety back on. "Explosives?" He chuckled. "Been there. Done that. Got the T-shirt."

His snark didn't work as well as it might from, say, a normal human being. But then, she shouldn't be kidding around with a man who held a gun.

Slater strode about the tent and turned toward her, but maintained a few paces of distance. The tension, which had held his jaw tight, was now gone. It relieved Annja only a little to see him holding the pistol pointing down near his thigh. Definitely military. He didn't drop his shoulders and he remained alert, ready for whatever leaped his way.

"What is your story, Creed?" he asked. "You come marching onto a private dig like you own the place and can do whatever you want."

"I was invited here."

"By whom?"

That wasn't exactly true. She was here following a lead. The fact Daniel had offered to show her around did not constitute an invitation. But Wesley had certainly extended one, spoken or merely implied.

"I'm gathering research for a television program. But I'm not the BBC, so chill."

"Research on faeries. Right. Go scamper about the woods, why don't you, and leave us to our work here."

"And what, exactly, is that work? The camps have split for a reason. And I'm guessing that reason is you don't want anyone to know what you're up to over there. You've got something to hide. Is it two bodies? How is it Beth managed to find her way back to camp while the other men are still AWOL?"

Slater cocked the pistol again but didn't aim it at her. Annja sensed his anger rise by the tightening of his neck muscles and his increased breathing. His tell was that pulse in his jaw. "Man holding a gun here. Why is it you're not afraid?"

"Afraid?" Maybe a little, she thought. But never let them see you sweat. "A charging mountain lion would invoke my fear. Terrorists wielding C-14 makes me afraid. A thug with a gun? Been there. Done that. Shredded the T-shirt."

That got an angry chuckle out of him. He crossed his arms, which ended up aiming the pistol out the door. Lips compressed, he studied her through narrowed eyes because the sun had burnished his face and made it look as though *squint* was his only possible expression.

Annja studied him back. Handsome, in a rugged, burned-by-the-sun way, and rough with a military cut and manner. His accent was British, but there were so many variations she couldn't place it precisely. Which didn't matter much. The camp was populated with people from all over.

There was something a little too slick about him. Prepared. He knew how to hold a gun. It fit his hand as if an extension of muscle, flesh and bone—much like the sword fit her grip.

The man was not a bone digger. He was trained. Militant. He'd performed security detail before, and probably not on a dig. She still couldn't abandon her guess that he was some kind of soldier.

"If I find out you've been treading on our dig layout again," he said, "I won't hesitate to use this." He made show of waving the gun before tucking it under his arm in the holster.

"Big man, threatening a woman," she said.

"Something tells me that kind of threat is nothing new to you, Creed. Call it intuition. Am I right?"

He'd been reading her as effectively as she'd been reading him. That made him an even more frustrating opponent.

"Thought so," he said when she didn't respond.

Annja let out her held breath. "Back to the question about what you're mining—"

"Mining? Apparently you missed the memo about requiring large equipment and drills and automated machinery. We've got a little hole, Creed. I'm sure you saw the skeleton sitting on top of the earth. What scares you about that?"

"Like I said, I don't scare easily. But I do know you weren't pleased to see Beth Gwillym come wandering out of the forest yesterday. What's that about?"

"You have no clue what I think about or what concerns me."

"Not for lack of trying."

"I'm not a man who shows emotion. You probably read my surprise wrong." After a pause and a wince, he asked, "Is Beth okay?"

He didn't care for the girl. The question was forced, Annja thought.

She shrugged. "Recovering." Revealing it was a drug overdose didn't feel right. She didn't want to give him the easy comeback. "It's not faeries."

"Who'd a'thought?" Slater crossed his arms and eyed her carefully. "Are we the only two people in both camps who believe that?"

He was siding with her now? Hmm…

"I sure as hell hope not," she said. "Why don't we start over, huh? If I come over this afternoon, during daylight, and ask for a tour around the dig, would you oblige me?"

"Can't do that, sweetie. We're on a time crunch. Don't think I can find anyone with the free time to cater to your whims."

"What's so urgent?"

Slater ran his fingertips along the table as he strode away. "It's just business, Creed. Any other time, any other place—"

"So that means you'll have a pint with me in the pub later?" she called.

He paused at the tent opening, the blinding sun behind him. "Rain check."

17

The room at the end of the second-floor hallway was so humid Garin felt as if he'd entered a tropical rain forest. Black shades were drawn and the air smelled like lilacs and menthol. The weight of the scent clogged at the back of his throat.

He winced at the underlying smell of sickness. If the old man had told him Mrs. Banyon was sick, he might have walked away.

No, he would not have.

"She's just woken from a rest," the butler explained. "She's quite sound of mind, yet age tends to work havoc on her frail bones."

"So she's not sick?" Garin asked quietly.

"Oh, yes, two feet in the grave and clinging to life with but a fingerhold, to be sure."

Garin took that comment as rather odd, and a bit too gleeful. Perhaps the butler was aware of a sizable inheritance attributed to him in her will. The old lady had better kick soon, then, because the butler had to be pushing ninety if he were a day.

"You may be seated beside the bed," the butler instructed. "Madam, this is Mr. Braden, as I've explained. I'll leave the door open and stand outside in the hallway."

A withered hand waved the butler away.

Garin pulled the hard-backed chair around so he could sit facing the woman lying in the bed. Describing her as frail was putting her condition lightly. She looked a ghost of a ghost. Long silver hair streamed across the white satin pillowcase. One would guess her a child swallowed up by the lace-trimmed bedsheets. But when she smiled at him, Garin felt her joy touch his heart and warm it ever so slightly.

"Such a treat," she said in a little girl's voice to match her appearance. "Are you an angel come to take me away?"

"Sorry, Mrs. Banyon, but I am the farthest thing from an angel."

"That makes things so much more interesting, doesn't it?"

Garin chuckled. He liked her too much already.

He wasn't averse to the elderly. Hell, he'd had a few lovers he still visited on occasion. Lovers he'd taken during the forties and fifties who were now treading their graves. It was a sentimental quirk he'd kill for if anyone found out. Roux would never stop heckling him for it, surely.

"My name is Ruth," she said. "You've come about my painting?"

She referred to it possessively already. And Garin sensed flirtation might not prove effective, in this situation.

He followed Ruth's gaze down the bed and to the wall facing it. There it hung. Remarkable evidence that detailed a devastating moment from history. It had been a long time since he'd seen the work.

Garin stood and approached the painting. He almost

touched it, but did not. That Fouquet had sketched this scene at the moment of its occurrence, and then retained such a vivid memory of it to paint decades later, did not cease to stun him.

He bowed his head, and clasped his elbows, suddenly feeling exposed. Like he didn't want the world, or even one sweet old lady, to discover his truths. There were so many truths that he flaunted, and yet twice as many that he guarded carefully.

"I was late to the auction yesterday," he said, pacing the room. Aware the butler stood outside the open door, he continued. "I had wanted to acquire the Fouquet. It's very…" Blatant? Shocking? Truthful? "…speculative. It is a reclusive piece, though. It's never been a part of Fouquet's known works."

"Which makes it all the more valuable. I've wanted it for years," Ruth said in yearning tones. "You should know, I've got a connection to it."

Hell. That would make obtaining it more difficult. He still had gloves and lock-pick tools at his penthouse. Overpowering Jeeves outside would be like pushing over a kid.

"A connection?" he said. "Tell me about it."

He sat again and leaned an elbow onto the bed. It felt right to clasp her hand, and he almost dropped it for her skin was cold and the bones felt as thin as bird's limbs. He imagined she might have once been a dancer, petite and airy, dazzling audiences with her grace and pale beauty.

"I've always had an interest in the saint," she said. "Ever since I first wrote a report on her in high school. She was so determined, unwilling to accept defeat. I modeled my life after her. Striding forward with grace and determination."

"Remarkable." He wondered how long she had left for this world. And would he have to wait it out until that fingerhold the butler had so gleefully mentioned finally let go? He didn't have time or the inclination to sit about.

"I've got a connection, as well," he offered. "I don't wish to be rude, Ruth, but I wonder how much longer you'll have to enjoy it?"

"Days, surely," she said.

It was said the dying knew within six months of their demise that death was imminent. That they began to put their lives in order before they even realized for what reason. And often, when they were but days from their final breath, they could choose to simply go, or to hang on as loved ones selfishly begged them to remain.

Of all the deathbeds Garin had sat beside, he had never asked a dying person to stay merely for his own gratification. It was not his right to bind them to this mortal coil.

Ruth's eyes were still bright. The light had not yet gone out. "What is your connection?" she asked softly.

"My great-great-great—" he wasn't quite sure how many greats to use "—many more countless greats,-grandfather actually posed in that painting."

"Ah? But how is that possible?"

He slipped his hand from hers and walked over to the painting. It was a risk, but he guessed her eyesight wouldn't be sharp. Standing beside the Fouquet he waited as she looked at both him and it.

"I see," she said softly. "It is true. And you wish to deny a dying woman a few final days of happiness by taking away the one thing that means the most to her?"

"How can it have acquired so much meaning to you in so little time?" He grasped the bedpost and scanned the bedroom. So many trinkets, and baubles and silver mirrors. A girlie-girl even so old. "As I told your butler, I can offer you twice what was paid for it."

"I've no need for money now, Mr. Braden. What do

you think I will do with a million dollars if I have but two days?"

She had him there. Although…

"Charity. You seem like a generous woman, Ruth. An endowment to the Metropolitan Museum of Art in your name, perhaps?"

She closed her eyes, tapping her fingers upon her chest. Garin couldn't know what she was thinking. Had he lost her by being too forward?

He could take out the butler with a chop to his throat, and snatch the painting. The old woman might have a heart attack before he even made it out the front door.

Ruth's eyes opened wide. "Any charity?"

"Just name the organization, and it will be done."

She smiled, and it was wicked. "Come closer, Mr. Braden. There may be something you can do for me, after all."

18

Annja set up her laptop under the canopy next to the dig. Nearby Wesley was explaining to one of the young women about the intricacies of dry stone walling. She'd uncovered a skull and was so excited she'd tripped over the ropes and had crushed the east wall of the feature.

Annja could only smirk. Digs were still wrought with excitement and eagerness, but she'd lost the clumsy stumbling bit years ago.

Actually, since she'd taken the sword in hand, her physicality had improved markedly. Graceful was not a word she'd have ever labeled herself a few years ago; now she embodied it, and wasn't ashamed to think so.

Swinging the sword had given her some nice moves and she knew her body had lengthened and her muscles had streamlined as if she'd been doing some serious Pilates. There wasn't an ounce of excess fat on her frame, despite her indulgent meals with Bart at her favorite local restaurant, Tito's. Roux had ensured she learned the various martial arts, and she loved to box in the gym with a trainer.

She liked feeling powerful. So few women really embraced their power, be it physical or emotional. They accepted lower pay in equal position to men merely to have the opportunity to climb the cooperate ladder. They demurred to their professional colleagues. They held back tears and assumed caretaker positions when no others would step forward to the task.

And they rarely stood up for the innocents—save for on paper and in court—by swinging a battle sword in the faces of evil. Someone needed to do that, because the world was stepping up and shoving those evil faces out in mockery.

She did have a right to wield the sword. No dream was going to make her think otherwise.

Thanks to a satellite card she could grab an internet connection even in the middle of rural Ireland. Eric had uploaded the segments he'd filmed of the landscape and scenery for her to proof. She'd check those later.

Now she searched *Frank Neville* to see what she could find. Three search results produced websites, but she suspected Neville's Nutritious Nuts was probably not the organization funding this dig. Nor did twelve-year-old Frank and his collection of vacuum cleaners hit the target.

The other Frank was mentioned in a federal case concerning drug trafficking. That could be her man, but it appeared as though that Frank was sitting in San Quentin at the moment, and he had to be eighty.

Typing in *Michael Slater* brought up another scatter of sites and unlikely professions.

"Can you look up a map for me, Annja?"

Wesley appeared by her side. Annja noticed the woman he'd been teaching now carefully brushed at the skull, and no longer leaned on the stone wall for support. Good for

Wesley for not admonishing her too hard, and allowing her to continue with her find. Hands-on was the only way she would ever learn.

"Let me guess," she said. "Ireland, nineteenth century?"

"I'm interested in the survey of land during the potato famine. NewWorld is being slower than molasses to answer my requests. Actually, I think I'm on my own."

"No problem. I've got satellite." She typed in a search. "You get lab results back on the soil sample?"

"Later today. I'm driving to Cork. You want to come along?"

"I might, thank you. I stopped at the hospital yesterday but they are only allowing relatives."

"Maybe I can get you in to see her."

"How is that possible if they're only allowing relatives? You and Beth were close?"

"Like I said—"

She wasn't going to fish around and risk him holding back information again, not in a situation like this. "Before you answer that, a man I met in one of Ballybeag's pubs told me—and supposedly it's a well-known rumor—that you and Beth had a thing."

Wesley bowed his head and raked his fingers through his hair. He cast her a you-caught-me smirk. "It was a one-night thing, Annja. I didn't think my sex life was important to your investigation."

"It's not, but did you and Beth have an argument? Did she have any reason to wander off?"

"Because of me? Hell, no."

"So why didn't you tell me?"

"Because that's exactly what I thought people would think, that I did something to put her in danger. Slater said as much."

"Slater?"

"He threatened me to keep quiet about it all or he'd tell everyone I hit Beth."

"That's why you two were fighting when I arrived."

"Yes. I was protecting Beth's reputation more than mine. She's just a kid, Annja. Well, you know, she's legal, but only twenty. I was glad Slater got rid of the BBC because the last thing Beth needs now is lights and cameras and nosy reporters. You aren't going to film Beth in the hospital?"

"I…" It seemed necessary for the story, but also intrusive, as he implied. "I'm not sure. I'd never force her to do an interview unless she was of sound mind and knew exactly what she was agreeing to. I have compassion, Wesley. I would never harass someone just for a sensational story." She tapped a few keys and brought up a site of historical maps.

"Did I see you and Slater chatting earlier?" he asked.

Chatting? With a gun pressed to her temple. That was a good one.

"He's not exactly the chatty sort. More of a what-the-hell-are-you-doing-in-my-air kind of guy, you know?"

"Yeah, he's an arsehole."

She couldn't have put it better herself.

"My goal is to keep the terms between us good," Wesley said. "He does have the gun."

"And, obviously, the upper hand. Is he trying to push you off the dig completely?"

Wesley leaned in to command the keyboard and scrolled through the list of maps the geological site brought up. "I don't intimidate easily, Annja. And I will not be chased away with my tail between my legs. I'm here on behalf of New-World, no matter who supposedly runs the dig now. And until NewWorld tells me to back off, I'm staying. But I feel as though they've abandoned me."

"The company hasn't been in contact with you? To give directions as to whether to stay or pack up?"

"Nope."

She glanced over to the opposing camp. Slater's stick-straight profile was nowhere in sight, but the camp had erected a canvas tarp with rope run through grommets along the east side of the dig that basically served as a wall to keep the other camp from seeing what was going on.

"I'm not sure why you're so curious about that British arsehole, but I like it," Wesley said. "Feisty women turn me on."

What to say to that? She wasn't the classiest chick when it came to flirting with the opposite sex. In fact, she tended to slip into goof mode too often when the need to be something more than a television host or archaeologist arose. Fortunately, no one was aware of her flirtations at Daniel's stones the other night.

Wesley tapped the screen. "Here's what I need. A land survey dated 1851. I have a printer in the back of the Jeep. Can we make a connection?"

"Connection?" Annja dropped her lower jaw. The man's eyes were so blue. Blue set against suntanned flesh and underlined by a movie star's smile. "Uh…"

His smile tilted and his eyes narrowed. "Earth to Annja." A snap of his fingers startled her out of her silly stare. "Where were you right now?"

She most definitely was not going to tell him that she'd taken a dive into his baby blues. "Uh…the printer. Just wondering if—yes, we can make that connection. Let's go see what we need to do."

He chuckled as she grabbed the laptop and marched toward the Jeep.

A moment later, Wesley strode alongside her. "You want to see Slater at his finest?"

"What does that mean?"

"It's Saturday night. You can find him, myself and a few

others from the dig in Cork at the Bones Club. It's bare-fists night."

"Bare fists? A fight club?" She studied Wesley's face. "You've still got a cut lip from the other day."

"Yeah, but I think that was from Collins. Slater's a gut puncher. If you lose against him you'll be walking bent over for days and won't be able to keep food down. I ate groats for four days in a row after my first match against him a few weeks back."

"So let me get this straight. You all are enemies, mastering your individual digs and spearing each other with the evil eye during the week. Then on the weekend…?"

"The gloves come off." He smacked a fist into his palm. "It's good-natured, though. We shake beforehand and after. A man shouldn't enter the fight with anger, only the need to test his own skills."

"After the fight I witnessed upon arriving I have to wonder if you and Slater *can* go at it good-naturedly."

"Well, then, you'll have to stop in for a look. You come along, I'll buy you a pint afterward."

Annja thought about it. A night at a bloody fistfight wasn't going to further her research for the show, or the personal desire to find those missing people. Yet after her encounter with Slater and his gun, she did want a closer look at the man, to see what made him tick. She wanted to see him with his neatly laced boots and militant posture loosened.

"Deal. I think I'll pass on the ride to Cork, though. I'm going to head into town early. I'll meet you there?"

"Sure. Here's the address." He explained how to find the clubhouse, which was more of a gym than a fancy club. "Ten of the clock. Tell the bruiser at the door you're with me."

19

"The Emerald Isle has long been known for gorgeous land-scapes, mysterious and mystical rock formations and even a leprechaun or two."

Annja paused and shook her head. "This isn't working." The sun hit her eyes and not squinting made them water.

"It's working, Annja," Eric coached. "Just go with it. We need an opening segment."

"Right." She had a lot on her mind, but reminded herself she was getting paid for this. Assuming professional TV host mode, she pasted on a smile and repeated the opening mono-logue to the *Chasing History's Monsters* episode.

They finished ten minutes later, and Annja felt drained. She was the one who bolstered the show's fantasy and high-jinks with facts and knowledge. It was Kristie Chatham's job to do the puff pieces and attract the viewing public with her silicone smile.

"It's people, not faeries," she said to Eric as they hiked to the Mini Cooper. "People with guns, I'm sure."

"Just because the guy wants to protect himself doesn't mean he's capping people, Annja. Slater's cool."

"Really?" She waited for Eric to slide his equipment into the hatchback. He was careful with his equipment, which went a long way in endearing him to her. He was young, yet he did want to learn. And he was skilled with the equipment. She shouldn't have prejudged him so harshly. "I saw him yelling at you yesterday. Is it his Rolex or his smart-ass attitude that impresses you so much?"

"Annja, he's just doing his job. Obviously whatever they're digging for is valuable."

"Any artifact can prove of value. But most of the time that value isn't proven until much later, after the dig has been backfilled and the artifacts have been studied in a lab. We saw a skeleton less than a foot under the topsoil, Eric. That doesn't make it old. For all we know, it could have been a hiker who went missing ten years ago."

"That's callous."

"But it's a possibility, and we have to examine all possibilities before arriving at a truth. There's no reason for security unless it's been proven items of value have been uncovered. I want to know what Slater's team has uncovered."

Eric slid into the passenger seat and buckled up. "Do you always use company time to go off on your own and do side projects, Annja?"

"I'm going to forget you just said that."

"Sorry."

She did not do that. It so happened that the side projects followed her, no matter where she traveled.

"But seriously," Eric continued, "you're on Doug's dollar. Or rather, my father's."

"Your father?"

Eric shifted on the seat. He scanned the horizon, avoiding her eyes. The sky was gray and promised imminent rain.

"I'm not following," she prompted. "What does your father have to do with this trip to Ireland? I thought it was just a box of cigars he'd sent along for Daniel?"

Eric rubbed the heel of his palm against his jaw. Nervous. And so he should be if he was hiding something.

"Eric?"

"My dad is financing this trip. He provided the tickets here and is paying for room and board for me. He wanted me to get a good start in the business, and *Chasing History's Monsters* is my favorite show."

"So Doug was bribed? Why does that sound so believable?"

Doug Morrell was a great guy, had unique and oftentimes insane visions for the show, and at times Annja considered him her friend.

As far as possessing a moral compass, Doug was all over the map. He wasn't beyond Photoshopping fangs on Transylvanian villagers to up the ratings, and Annja felt sure he was behind the incident last year that saw her head pasted on a nude body and circulated on all the online celebrity skin sites.

"Was the other cameraman even sick?"

"I don't know. You'll have to ask Doug about that. I wanted to do an amazing project for my final exam," Eric said. "My media teacher is going to love this stuff."

"Are you a college freshman?"

He shrugged and still didn't meet her eyes. What was so wrong that he'd suddenly clammed up? There wasn't a secret the guy could harbor that would top her secret. Unless…

Annja dropped her head against the headrest. "Don't tell me."

"All right, I won't. But it would so rock if you'd come to my high school graduation, Annja. My friends would get such a kick out of meeting you."

His *high school* graduation. She was sitting in a foreign country with a high school student determined to ace his finals with a complex study in faeries, and who had begun to idolize a man who liked to caress his gun and bully reporters.

"Are you telling me the truth that your father knows all about this?"

"Definitely."

"And he's cool with his son taking time off from school to do this project?"

"It's spring break, Annja, if you haven't noticed."

She had missed that one. Must be the lacking beachfront and bikini-clad girls gone wild. "Next time we hit the pub," she said, "you are drinking soda."

"Come on, Annja. I'm eighteen."

"The drinking age is twenty-one."

"It's eighteen in Ireland. My father raised me with European esthetics. I've been drinking beer for years."

"Whatever. I am not your mother." As he'd so snidely pointed out already.

Annja drove the next forty-five minutes with the radio turned up loud.

Though Cork was the third largest city in Ireland, and was a major seaport, it was easy enough to navigate, if you didn't have to cross the river Lee. The river spread through the city in two channels, forming an island of the city's center much like Paris, and Annja guessed if you had to go anywhere fast, you'd have to constantly cross bridges.

The hospital Beth had been admitted to was on the west edge, so she needn't venture too far into the city. After she'd wrapped filming, she intended to finagle a day of sightseeing here before returning to the States.

But tonight was all about the fight club.

She still hadn't decided what to do with Eric. He shouldn't be allowed to watch. On the other hand, he was a guy; this was probably his kind of thing. On the other hand, he was only eighteen. On the other hand, if she tried to tell him he wasn't old enough, he'd flip.

And on the final hand, she wasn't his mother. And she had run out of hands long ago.

The whole parenting thing must be the toughest job out there. Annja had been raised in an orphanage. She had no idea what it was like to have parents, let alone be a parent.

She parked in the shade and asked Eric to remain by the car while she went in to see if there was a chance of catching Beth coherent, and not surrounded by militant nuns.

"LEARN ANYTHING?" Eric asked when she returned to the car.

"I managed to peek in her room, but she's still out of it. She's listed as serious condition. That's very odd. I never thought LSD could be so dangerous."

But then, any kind of recreational drug had devastating effects if used in large dosages.

Annja navigated an intersection and noted the white van that had been following for a couple blocks turned the same direction. There were no plates, and the windows were blacked out.

If that wasn't suspicious, she'd eat Mrs. Riley's black pudding for breakfast tomorrow without complaint.

20

Checking the rearview mirror, Annja verified that the white van still followed them. She turned right. The van turned right. She kept pace with the minimal traffic and eyed an alleyway set between a closed automotive shop and a music store. With her turn, the van also turned.

They were not being covert at all. It was as if they wanted her to know they were following. That made them either stupid or looking to talk.

Eric looked up from his camera. He'd been reviewing video. "What's up?"

"Nothing."

"Your knuckles are white, and you keep checking the mirrors."

Points for the cameraman. "We're being followed."

"Followed?"

She slapped an arm across his chest before he could completely turn in his seat to look out the rear window.

"By who?" he asked.

"I don't know, but don't be so obvious. Stay calm. And… can you film the van covertly?"

"Covert? Oh, yeah, no problem." He positioned the camera between the seats. "Dude, there's no plates on the van. Is this normal for the show segments?" he asked. "All this stealth and covert sneaking about?"

"To a degree. Depends on who you talk to and if you ask the wrong questions." And whether or not your name was Annja Creed. "But honestly, no, this is not normal."

Two men sat in the front of the van. Annja had no idea if there were others in the back. She didn't spot weapons, but that didn't mean there weren't any. She had the sword to hand whenever she needed it, but sword fighting required close contact. A girl couldn't toss a three-foot sword from the car and expect it to meet its target, then return to her.

Although, that was kind of how Mrs. Collins had explained the spear of Lugh worked. Okay, so she wouldn't dismiss the possibility such a spear existed just by principle, but if it did exist, it was not presently hanging on Mrs. Collins's wall.

"Gotta try that move sometime," she muttered, and slammed on the brakes to avoid a bicycle crossing against a red light.

"Try what?" Eric asked, bent low in the middle of the seats and filming.

"Biking with a death wish," she muttered.

The geriatric cyclist didn't even glance at the vehicle that had almost killed him. Steady and straight on, he continued his lethargic crossing. How he even maintained balance fascinated Annja.

"I can see you doing that. BMX would be right up your alley, Annja."

She could handle the rugged mountain trails with the right bike and equipment. But flying through the air and doing loop-de-loops for the sporting entertainment of it? Not so much.

"All right, enough filming. Time for you to buckle up. They're getting aggressive."

Annja turned away from the main streets and aimed for what she hoped would be a less populated neighborhood. She should drive out of the city but she hadn't got her bearings and with the unfamiliar roads she just wanted to keep Eric safe.

She missed a stop sign, and Eric directed her left. She turned right.

She saw the glint of a pistol jut out the passenger window of the van. "Here we go. Head down!"

She slapped her palm against the back of Eric's head as a bullet pierced the rear window.

Eric swore and slid down as far as the seat belt would allow. "They're shooting at us? What did we do? Is this about filming on the dig?"

"It had better be." If there were thugs after her for other reasons, they could take a number because she only had time right now to deal with this situation. "Hold on."

Swerving sharply, the Mini's tires thudded against the curb as she entered a tight alley. The tarmac was loose and potholes shook the tiny car.

Too late, Annja saw her mistake. The alley was a dead end sided by brick walls. Laundry hung across three or four lines from the second floor up to the fourth.

The white van barreled up behind them and braked to a stop.

"Now what?" Eric had forgotten her suggestion to keep his head down. He eyed the shattered window, which provided no good view of the van. "This isn't cool anymore. They have guns!"

"I don't want to do this with you," Annja said. "I can't risk you being hurt. Sorry about this, Eric."

She punched him under the jaw. The sharp angle rocked his skull and pinched off his oxygen. A knockout punch. He slumped on the seat. Annja shoved him farther down so his head was below the window level and out of risk for catching a bullet aimed at her.

Kicking open the driver's door, she stepped out. A bullet hit the brick wall three feet from her and sprayed the rubble of brick against her shoulder and cheek. She ducked behind the open car door and summoned her sword to hand.

"Watch it, idiot!" a man shouted from near the van. "He said not to kill them."

The door slammed against Annja's shoulder. Someone had kicked it from the other side. Wanting to get the attackers as far from Eric as possible, she climbed onto the hood, ran over the car's roof and jumped off.

One thug was behind her, and one stepped out from the driver's side of the van. Only two. But one was armed. And though she'd heard the order to keep her alive, Annja knew from experience that thugs weren't always good at following orders during the heat of the moment.

Proof pinged the van's hood. The bullet ricocheted and more brick wall exploded next to the driver's head.

"That's me bloody van, idjit!" the driver shouted.

Hearing the shooter's heavy breaths come up behind her, Annja ducked and swung out her sword, cutting it through the air. The blade connected with nylon jacket and flesh and blood.

"What the hell?" the shooter cried. "She's got a bloody sword!"

Following the swing, Annja put the driver in sight. He bent and lunged, going for her legs. She leaped, higher.

One foot landed on the hood of the van. She pushed off

and flipped backward in the air. The gun went off again. Landing behind the shooter, she sliced the sword across the thick part of his thighs, dragging it through flesh. The wound felled him. He rolled to his side, clutching his legs.

She kicked his gun under the Mini Cooper. The clearance was too low for anyone to snake out something from underneath.

The driver wisely put up his hands and pressed his back to the brick wall. "Who the bloody hell are you?" he demanded more shakily than assuredly. "You're starkers, you are."

"You don't even know who you're following?" Annja swept the sword out wide, sending blood spraying from the blade and across the front of the white van. A samurai move. "I get to ask the questions."

With a flick of her wrist, she pressed the blade under his chin. "Who sent you?"

"I don't rightly know," he mumbled. "I didn't get a name."

"Liar."

"I'm a feckin' freelancer!" he protested. "Watch the blade, will you, luv? I think you killed me partner."

"He's not dead. He passed out from the pain. Pain I promise *you,* if you don't start talking. Now you'll have me believe you don't know the name of the guy signing your paycheck?"

"It's all cash now, isn't it?"

"What was the order?"

"To follow the American woman and make sure she gets out of town. Oh." He shrugged and offered a sheepish, blood-spattered grimace. "Get out of town, luv."

"You first."

Slamming the sword hilt against his jaw, Annja knocked him out. He fell in a graceless heap. Checking the other thug to ensure he'd passed out, as well, she bent to pat down the driver's pockets. She found a wallet full of pound notes but no ID.

Turning, she patted down the other guy. He moaned as she dug in his shirt pocket and pulled out a business card. The card stock was thick and edged in gold.

"Wine," she read the single word. Below that was a phone number. "Wine?" Wouldn't a liquor store have a grander name?

"Annja?"

She'd forgotten about Eric. Thrusting her right hand out, Annja released the sword to the otherwhere. She hoped he hadn't seen her pin the thug to the wall with the sword.

"We should hurry," she called out. She told Eric to grab his equipment from the hatchback and follow her out from the alleyway. "They'll come to soon."

The redhead staggered out from the Mini, rubbing his jaw. "You punched me!"

The sight of the fallen men had him sputtering and giving Annja a double take. At the signal, shaking her head negatively, he didn't ask. She could tell he wanted to, but he earned points for discretion.

If he didn't get an A for this project, she'd talk to his teacher personally.

21

"Did you find her?"

"No, she's not in Brooklyn. Listen, Roux, I have to take off. There's a business matter I need to look into overseas. And New York isn't too pleased to have me as a guest, as it is."

"Why the hell not?"

"I misplaced my passport. I'm here on a waiver. I'd feel more comfortable getting out of Dodge. I'll bring the painting to Berlin. We can rendezvous there, yes?"

"Yes, but it won't do much good without Annja there," Roux said.

"Have you spent any time looking for her? Or did the sun fry your thought process?"

"I've tried her cell, but she isn't answering. Have you given her a call?"

"No, but I'll do that. Bet she answers my call first time out."

"You and your inflated ego can go right ahead and try."
Roux clicked off.

Garin handed the baggage claim ticket to the flight at-
tendant and directed her toward his private jet. She'd been
quite open to the idea of jetting over to Europe with him for a
day or two. A little champagne, very little talk, and the flight
would be a dream.

22

Annja knew from experience that the sound of a fist hitting flesh is never as titillating as it is in the movies. Movie sound crews could enhance the sound, change it or mix it to make the viewer wince when the smack reverberated with the flesh and muscle that was just punched.

Most movies didn't show the moment after impact when the flesh is compressed and the muscles tense and flinch. And the sound came more from the fighter's throat—a gasp—upon impact.

Two men Annja didn't know shifted about the makeshift ring. She'd foregone betting; she wasn't a gambler unless it was out in the field and required a split-second life or death decision.

The venue was much cleaner than she'd expected. No back room, basement or warehouse clandestine dive. It looked like an old school gym that had been converted for boxing. The men used the boxing ring, though they didn't wear gloves, and while no rules seemed apparent, they did respect the referee's calls.

After defeating the men in the alleyway she'd considered going to the gardai. They'd been strangely absent from the scene of the disappearances, though. Her intuition told her she wouldn't get much more interest now. She and Eric had watched as their pursuers came to and took off in a hurry in their van. Returning to the car, Annja and Eric headed for the fight night. The one man she had the most questions for was fighting that night, so she sat watching and waiting.

The smoke curling from a cigar enticed her to study the man sitting at the end of the bench five feet to her right. He wore a yellow-and-blue plaid suit coat and ankle-high leather boots. A black fedora concealed the side of his face, but she immediately figured him out.

"Daniel?" she called over the shouting and cheers.

He looked to her, smiled and got up to join her. He offered a toke from his cigar, which she refused with a polite shake of her head. His gesture revealed a black thumb.

"What happened?" she asked.

He examined the side of his thumb. "Bad pen," he said. "Always such a bloody mess. Which one you bet on?" he asked over the din.

"Neither. You?"

"Aye? My money is on Wesley Pierce. Slater's too cocky. He'll blow all his energy at the beginning and won't be able to maintain."

"You come to these fights often?"

"Every Saturday night. I am a betting man."

She held back the comment *I bet you are.* It was always the quiet ones.

"Ma would love to see you for dinner again soon," he said.

"Thanks. I may take her up on that. The food at the bed and breakfast is good but your mother's is out of this world."

"Sunday morning is always rashers and toast at me mum's."

"Sounds far too simple compared to the buffet she served up the other night."

"Why don't we make a date of it? Besides, I can't let you leave the country without showing you my wine cellar."

"Wine?" She thought of the gold-edged business card she'd found on the thug earlier. "Do you sell it?"

"Mostly just a collector. I do barter on occasion. Watch. Slater and Pierce are up."

With fascination, and very little disgust, Annja focused as the fight began with a smack of fists and a call from the referee. Wesley and Slater bandied fists, a few kicks and the occasional elbow.

Both men wore jeans, bare feet and fists. Their chests quickly became slick with sweat and grew red from tenderizing knuckles. Sweat sprayed the air, flying from their hair as a fist connected with jawbone or skull.

The best way to win a fight is to exude confidence, and both men had that mastered. They didn't step down, nor did either come on too aggressively. They were judging their opponent, feeling him out.

Slater seemed the calmer of the two, taking a punch to the jaw or chest and coming right back at Wesley with the follow-through. He showed a firm stance, knees slightly bent. His strong foot was the left one, which allowed him to swing a hard right fist. But even there, he didn't use a closed fist, but engaged more often the heel of his hand, which delivered more force and prevented the broken fingers a closed fist might risk.

Wesley was more aggressive, guarding his face with his right, his left hand tucked near his chest and close to his chin.

He kept his elbows hugged to his ribs, but swung them out when advancing, which widened his approach.

Neither man fought dirty. No spleen shots or knees to the groin. Annja was waiting, though. She expected it from Slater.

To enhance the experience, the room was filled with shouting Irish- and Englishmen. A few that she recognized from the dig stood around the ring. Most Annja didn't know.

Eric hung out by the door. The bouncer had absolutely refused to allow any camera equipment inside, and Eric was worried about leaving his stuff out in the Mini with the shattered back window, so he kept a keen eye out. That surprised Annja, but then Eric did a lot to surprise her.

The kid was no fighter. That was apparent from his winces, and occasionally he'd duck his head into his hands and close his eyes when blood spattered the air and the entire crowd groaned in reaction to the imagined pain.

"Nice kidney jab," Daniel commented.

She had to grin at that. "You ever step in the ring?"

"Don't need to," he said around the cigar. "As you saw, I can pick up a little rage-release now and then simply by joining the fray. It's in the Irish blood, don't you know." He aimed a sly wink at her.

Was it the Irish blood or merely male blood? Annja wondered.

Men liked to beat the snot out of one another any chance they got. It was nothing personal. Aggression and the need to let it out were encoded in their DNA. Most men's DNA, that is. Some simply preferred watching, which seemed to provide as much of an adrenaline high as the actual fight.

Annja glanced to Eric. Having lost his aversion to the violence, he made a jab with his right fist. There was that primal instinct kicking in. She chuckled and scanned across the crowd.

Wesley had promised they'd get a bite to eat after this, and she was hungry. He probably wouldn't mind if she invited Daniel along. But she did also want opportunity to talk to Slater. It had to have been his men after her and Eric earlier. Who else even knew her in this country?

Focusing on the fight, she narrowed in on Slater. His body was sleek and lean and muscles wrapped his frame like efficient body armor. He had guns that she wouldn't want to stand the brunt of.

He reminded her a little of Bart McGilley, her NYPD detective friend in New York. She occasionally sparred with him in the boxing ring at the gym close to her loft. Bart's moves were smooth and spare, as were Slater's. He never dropped his guard, and would sooner take a punch to the gut than expose his chin. He was very still, and took everything that came at him rather than bouncing out of reach and risking letting down his strength base.

On the obverse, Wesley's moves were all over. He shuffled left and right, but didn't lift his feet. He was loose but not stupid, yet obviously untrained. His movements were erratic, effectively keeping Slater alert and on his toes. He couldn't judge what Wesley would do next.

Slater stuck with straight jabs and punches. Occasionally he'd wrap his fingers into a fist and deliver a blow, but more often than not he kept an open palm and worked on Wesley's soft spots like the face, throat and gut.

If he stuck with simple punches like that, Slater would win, Annja decided. Though the match was pretty even, and she much preferred to see Wesley walk away victorious, she figured he'd had less experience in a fight than Slater. His punches were wide and slower, connecting all over Slater's body.

Slater took those wild punches by stepping into them. He minimized the distance between connection and thus reduced the impact. Wesley dodged and tried to avoid Slater's moves. Of the two, Wesley was already huffing and drawing in gasps.

Slater exhaled as Wesley's fist smashed his solar plexus. He turned into the punch and was barely moved from his feet. He returned a punch up under Wesley's jaw that sent a spurt of blood soaring overhead.

Restraining her need to join in the shouting and to throw out a few encouraging cheers for Wesley, Annja glanced to Eric. He'd moved forward, leaving the door.

His father may never forgive Annja for this. But he obviously trusted his son wouldn't get into trouble. What a gift, sending his son off to Ireland to film video for his high school project.

Slater went for an elbow jab, which removed his guard and allowed Wesley to lunge with a fist. Bone cracked. The crowd silenced for two seconds and then a few groans echoed out, signaling what Annja suspected. The fight had finished.

Wesley had delivered the knockout punch.

"Wow," she muttered. She hadn't expected Slater would let down his guard like that. The move had been…amateur. And it made very little sense.

"You see?" Daniel clapped with cupped palms and stood, the cigar chomped at the corner of his mouth. He hooted and offered a raised fist along with the rest of the crowd.

Annja nodded in acknowledgment when Wesley's gaze found hers. He beamed and raised both his raw, bloodied fists, bouncing triumphantly to the crowd's hoots and cheers.

THE LOCKER ROOM was quiet and dark, save a bare bulb near the back. Everyone was out watching the next fight. Wesley was collecting his winnings, with Daniel standing nearby chatting up the yokels.

It fit Daniel, in Annja's mind, that he was a moneymaker

as well as money handler. He could have a career as an agent if he wanted. A fight manager, or some such. He may appear gentle, but she sensed the Irish blood running through his veins boiled.

She wanted to know if the business card was his and how he was connected with a thug who wanted Annja out of town. Or was there a connection? It could merely be coincidence. She should have asked him about it.

"Thought everyone had their eye on the winner after the fight," Slater said as she slipped around a concrete wall. The walls and floors were bare. Two rows of dented white metal lockers ran down the middle. A dark shower room sat out of view to the left of the lockers.

Slater wiped his chest dry. Standing in jeans, he turned to eye her. "You're cheering for the wrong side, sweetheart."

"I've always had a soft spot for the loser."

He splayed his arms to take the comment as if a compliment.

"Not that you are. You could have taken Wesley. You were holding back. Why?"

He smirked and tossed the towel onto a heap of used towels near the outer shower wall. His left eye was swollen but not badly, the skin hadn't been broken. By morning it would be fine. His throat was red as well as his upper chest and gut. All in all, he hadn't taken enough damage for a loser.

"Look at you, thinking you know so much. Why are you here tonight, Creed? Isn't snooping around dig sites enough for you? You need to get up close to danger, feel the spatter of blood on your face?"

"I guess being threatened with a gun to my head wasn't enough. Your charm is absolutely deadly. I can't stay away from you, Slater."

"Yeah? Well, you should. You let Pierce work his blarney and spend his winnings on you tonight. I hear there's a pub crawl going on afterward. And with Collins along, digging the cash out of his deep pockets, you can be guaranteed you won't have to buy a single drink."

Daniel's pockets were deep? She'd initially judged him not so well off, but if he was betting and buying and selling wine, then he probably wasn't too poor.

"You really want to get rid of me, Slater. Too bad your thugs weren't effective. They don't do the follow very well."

"The follow?" He tossed a sweatshirt over his shoulder and turned to face her, hands to hips. An inhale expanded his pecs and tightened his abs.

Again Annja thought he should not have lost that fight.

"Don't know what you're talking about," Slater said.

"You had me and my cameraman followed from the hospital. I don't know who else would have done so."

"Who were they?" he asked urgently. "You get a good look at them? What kind of vehicle were they driving?"

Annja stepped back and took a second to breathe through that one. He *didn't* know who had been after her? Or was he an excellent faker? He *had* thrown the match.

"Two big guys in an unmarked white van wielding guns and determined expressions. Sorry, I had to take them out."

One of Slater's brows lifted.

Annja shrugged. "Thugs are stupid. It just takes brains to defeat them."

"As you've proven with my security at the dig. Who did you say you are again? Or rather, what?"

"We've been through this. Archaeologist. Television host. In the country chasing freakin' faeries."

"Right. Good—if not oddball—cover, but for what, I'm not sure. It certainly isn't because you want to film the countryside and win a few ratings points."

"Trust me, if I could have avoided this assignment I'd be off to Africa searching for lost civilizations."

"The legitimate stuff, eh? Faeries too fanciful for you?"

She glared at him.

"I didn't send anyone after you, Annja. If I want something done, I take care of it myself."

Tugging on the sweatshirt, he reached into a locker and drew out a holster with a gun in it and fixed it across his body.

"Maybe it was your employer?" she tried.

"Maybe," Slater offered. "I'm not the man's keeper. Guy can do whatever he wants, when he wants."

"Why would he fear me?"

Slater secured the holster buckle and gave her a tight grin. "Listen, little girl, you're too smart for your own good. I meant what I said this afternoon. This has nothing to do with you. It's not personal—it's business. Just stay out of this."

"If I knew what *this* to stay out of, maybe I would. But I'm a curious little girl. I tend to end up knee-deep in the muck a lot. Even when not on a dig. Frank Neville, right?" she said, evoking the name of his employer.

Slater tugged a coat over his shoulders. "If I see you near our dig again, with the camera, I won't play nice next time."

"You going to shoot me? Or is kidnapping more your style?"

He didn't answer. When he walked past her, his shoulder slammed hers hard.

Annja rubbed her shoulder and cast a glance over it to watch him exit.

If Slater hadn't sent those men after her they had to have been sent by Neville. That meant Slater was not the highest man on the totem pole, only the one greasing the pole to keep curious parties from climbing too high.

And until she learned the truth about the disappearances of the other two archaeologists, Annja was determined to make that climb.

23

A montage of past season successes for the Shamrock Rovers, a Dublin-based soccer team, played on the plasma television above the bar. O'Shaughnessy's pub catered to the men from the fight.

They'd come to this bar because Wesley had said it offered the best *craic* around. Even though the word was pronounced like an illicit drug, Annja knew the Gaelic word meant rousing conversation, fun people and lots of it.

Wesley's split lip had reopened, and he sported the beginnings of what would be a remarkable shiner on his right eye come morning. Annja still couldn't figure out how he had won the fight. No, she knew *how* he had—Slater had thrown the fight. But she wouldn't mention her suspicion to Wesley. And she couldn't figure out *why*.

Wesley clanked his mug against a few of his buddies' mugs and settled across the table opposite Annja on a high stool. Triumph glittered in his eyes. He'd already replayed the entire fight to her on the walk over, but she suspected she might hear it again, once or twice, before the night was through.

After putting up with Slater's "security" on the dig, Wesley deserved the kudos, if only for the evening.

A waitress dropped off Annja's second pint. The creamy head spilled down the side of the frosted mug. She swallowed the dark ale. She'd told Slater she much preferred to be on a real adventure, which usually meant barren wastelands, poor sanitation and eating bugs. She'd enjoy the amenities this nonadventure offered while she could.

"So how did the two camps ever manage to come together for these Saturday night excursions?" she asked Wesley. "Did you invite Slater or was it the other way around?"

"You trying to figure who wanted to punch the other the most?" he asked.

A flash of his movie star smile made Annja glad she'd chosen to end the night in Wesley's company rather than continue to try to pry information from the uptight Slater.

Wesley raised his mug to a bunch of fellows nearby and then drank heartily. Wiping his mouth on his sleeve, he carried out a long, satisfied *ahhh*. "One of the kids on the dig—my side, that is—his brother runs the fights. He was excited telling his friends to come and check it out, but he hadn't figured that the newest people on the dig were not the friendliest. I think Slater showed up that first weekend out of curiosity. But it's all good. When we're standing toe to toe in the ring we don't necessarily want to kill each other."

"You just want to show you can take the other guy. Who's the boss?"

"You got it. And I like the workout."

Annja smirked. Not to mention the adulation that came with the win. She wasn't going to criticize him for that one.

"So do you know this guy Slater works for?" she asked. "Frank Neville?"

"Nope. And I've been on a lot of digs all over the world. I recognize most names in the industry, as I did yours. I have a weird sort of sixth sense that Neville doesn't have ties to our trade. Taking over the dig may have been a fluke. Whatever it is they think they're going to find isn't going to be riches. I got the results from the soil sample back right before I went to the fight."

"Were your guesses to the nineteenth century accurate?"

"Yep. And it's a strain of *Phytophthora infestans,* the potato pathogen I suspected. We've dug into some old farmland that once grew the crops that were annihilated in the mid-1800s."

"A lot of people died during the famine."

"For no good reason," Wesley said. "Foreign countries sent hundreds of thousands of dollars in aid to Ireland, but it never made it. Some was even stopped by England. Millions of people died during that time. It's a shame."

"Wasn't it true they still produced a lot of livestock and other field crops, yet it was owed to landowners?"

"Yes, landowners who lived in England. Irish farmers, rather than send their precious stock to the rich landowners across the channel, would sooner shoot the animals and burn the produce, than see it in their grubby hands. They sacrificed their assets, even while their starving family stood by and watched."

"The other camp has uncovered a complete female skeleton," Annja said. "It was nicely preserved in the peat bog."

"That's interesting, especially since I don't mark that site as a homestead. It's a bog. Janice uncovered a femur this morning. I think it belongs to the skull, but it's twenty feet away. It's like the body was just left on the ground. Odd, because if it's from someone who died of starvation they would have been buried. Mass graves were popular. Unless they died during the winter and not right on the homestead like this. It's hard to figure."

"So I would suspect wild animals or even an attack by thieves, the inhabitants fleeing and being shot or killed. There were a lot of wolves in Ireland in the nineteenth century. Or even, the body could have been buried in a shallow grave, then later dug up by animals," Annja said.

"Both are possible. The body at Slater's camp had to have been dragged there. It could have been marauders. Or it could have been a hard winter. Foxes were known to scavenge dead bodies."

"Have you seen indications of animal attack on the bones?"

"Nope, but we just uncovered them. Haven't had a chance to do a thorough check. Animal intrusion should be immediately obvious. Like I said, I don't know what to say."

"What about faeries?" she asked with a wink.

Wesley laughed. "I think you're ready for another pint."

Annja tilted her half-full mug of dark stout. She wanted to keep her wits about her and she'd have to drive. "I'd better call it a night. I was going to head over to Daniel's but it's getting late." She still had the curious business card she'd taken from the thug.

"You don't want to wander about this time of night, Annja. The other crowd will get you. And then maybe a hundred years in the future the archaeologists will be digging up your bones."

She shook her head, but hadn't the energy to argue. The ale was making her tired. Wesley quickly cracked a grin, and then tilted back the rest of his mug.

"Where's your puppy dog?" he asked.

"Eric is flirting with the musicians. I think he's developed a thing for flute music since we've been in the country. I'll let him chat a little longer while I go retrieve the car, which we left at the fight. This joint is really hopping this evening."

"Attribute it to the *craic*," he said. "Come on, I'll walk you to your car, then."

She followed him as he slapped a few high fives on the way out and promised to return and defend his title the next weekend. "You know I'm having some fun with you about the fair folk, Annja."

"Do I?" The night was bright and the sky filled with stars there at the edge of the city. "I expect the locals to cling to tales and myths, but you don't even live here."

"I like to assimilate the cultural beliefs wherever I go. Buddhism in Tibet. Voodoo in Savannah. Faeries in Ireland. Just have fun with it, Annja. It's not all a load of horse shite."

"I don't think what, or whoever, took the two missing men from your site would want anyone to have fun with it. Aren't you concerned?"

"They probably found some magic mushrooms like Beth did and took a boat up the river to Kinsale. I've lost a crew member a time or two. They usually come back after they're tired of experiencing the local fare, or I get a phone call a few weeks later saying archaeology wasn't for them and sorry they took off without saying goodbye."

"You don't believe either of the men did that," she stated. "And how do you know Beth found mushrooms? Did she tell you?" She couldn't reveal to him that she'd read Beth's chart.

"No. It's a guess, Annja. She was talking about seeing faeries. I may have some fun with you, but even I am educated enough to know a man's not going to see a winged woman come flying out of the forest anytime soon."

"That relieves me a little. But I'm afraid for Beth. If someone gave her a drug, why? Why not simply keep her tied up? Or even kill her?"

"Is that what you think should have happened?"

"No, but whatever she was on made her see faeries. That's odd. I'm surprised the gardai aren't all over this."

"Slater notified the police."

That explained a lot. "Slater doesn't have anyone's best interests in mind. Maybe you should give the gardai a call tomorrow and check?"

"You want me to? I will. I was hoping when Beth came around she'd have the answers. Maybe she's seen the missing men."

"He's up to something," Annja said. "Slater."

"I'm sure he is."

"But it's not your thing to get involved, am I right?"

"Something like that. Is this it?"

They climbed into the Mini and Annja pulled a U-turn to navigate back to the pub.

"Whoever Frank Neville is," Wesley continued, "will quickly learn there's nothing but bones and dirt on-site. He'll pack up camp and leave soon enough."

"But how many more will disappear before then? Do you think they saw something they weren't supposed to see?"

"I thought you were snooping about Slater's camp? What did you see?"

"The skeleton I told you about. Nothing worthy of shutting me up. I'm missing some very large piece of the puzzle, and it frustrates me. I haven't gone down to check out the river yet. I think I should take a look."

"I'll go along with you, if you like."

"Tomorrow, then. It's a date."

"Best-looking date I've had in a while. How'd I get so lucky?"

"I think it's the blarney. You're full of it."

"I do try."

24

Annja's cell phone rang. She answered without checking the caller ID—which she regretted as soon as Doug Morrell's voice rattled across the phone lines.

"Annja! Good afternoon!"

It wasn't good. And—she glanced at the bedside table—the LED clock flashed 1:00 p.m. She had slept past noon? And why did her head ache? She'd only had two pints last night.

"How are things going? Is Eric doing well?" Doug asked.

"Yes," she muttered groggily.

Sitting up on the bed, she winced at the bright daylight shining in.

"What's wrong, Annja? You don't sound so good. Is it late at night there? I thought I figured the time zones right this time. No matter. Guess what?"

"You've decided faeries don't exist and want me to come home?"

"Wrong. I'm scheduling shows for next month, and guess

who agreed to be interviewed for the Halloween special? Rob Zombie! Doesn't that rock?"

"He's a rock star, Doug, not a monster." She dropped backward across the bed, but the thud of skull to blanket flashed bright auras behind her eyes. Annja groaned. "Can we talk later? I need to take a shower and wake up."

"Annja, you sound like Kristie when I call her on location. But I expect her to be hungover."

"I'm not hungover, Doug. Just…" Not even awake yet. "I'm hanging up now. We'll talk later."

DANIEL COLLINS MET Annja on her trek to the dig site. He pulled over the Jeep and jumped out. Eric had risen early and left a note that he was heading out to film some scenery. The kid kept earning points with his initiative.

"Care for a bite?" Daniel asked.

Casting a glance at the cloudy sky, Annja agreed. "Sure. Looks like rain."

"It'll be pouring by the time we make my place," he said. "You getting a late start today?"

"I think all the residual bar smoke really played a number on me last night. Either that, or jet lag finally got the better of me."

"Come along." He gestured for her to hop in the Jeep. "I'll fix you up in no time."

Three minutes later the rain beat the land relentlessly. Annja hoped Wesley had an extra tarp to cover the excavation; otherwise, it would take at least a day to dry out and be workable enough for digging again.

"Give it five minutes," Daniel yelled as they arrived at his place. He ran and directed Annja toward the front door. "The sun will come out."

He offered her cold salmon sandwiches, which his mother

had prepared and sent home with him. Homemade pickles and deviled eggs topped off the light lunch.

"Ah! Where are my manners?" Daniel stood and tugged the napkin from his shirt. "I should have brought up some wine for the meal."

He told Annja to follow him.

Now was as good a time as any to get curious, she thought.

"Speaking of wine… Is this yours?" She pulled out the business card and handed it to Daniel. "I took it from a guy who wanted me to leave town without passing Go, without collecting two hundred dollars. You know anything about that?"

He handed the card back to her. "That's mine. But I don't know anything about collecting two hundred dollars. I barter with the discerning and often I pick up a customer by word of mouth. What was his name?"

"Didn't have a chance to ask. He was too busy shooting at me."

"Shooting?" Daniel paused and leaned a shoulder against the cedar-paneled wall. Standing so close to him, Annja noticed his scruffy dark hair was streaked with gray. And what did she really know about this man? Other than he liked to gamble, drink wine and watch fights? And seduce women under the stars upon his ritual disemboweling stone.

"Annja, what's the trouble? Someone fired a weapon at you? I don't see how that can be related to you filming a bit of the land and talking about the fair folk."

"Neither do I. But something is not kosher with Slater's camp. Though he didn't claim knowing the men after me, either. But the man whose pocket I found this in? I find it hard to believe he'd be a wine connoisseur."

"We oenophiles come in all shapes and sizes. Mustn't judge by appearance. Let me show you something," he said.

Annja followed him down a narrow hallway. He hadn't seemed nervous about the business card. She couldn't decide if he was lying. But then how could Daniel possibly be involved in sending men after her with guns? To what purpose? It wasn't as though she'd said something nasty about his mother's cooking.

"I'll look into it if you like," he called back. "But I suspect it's Slater's machismo bleeding through. As deadly as that is, I don't think the man would actually kill anyone."

"Do you know Michael Slater well?"

"No. I've only spoken to him a time or two at the dig. But you've witnessed his aggression just as much as I have."

She wasn't ready to place Slater to the business card. But he and Daniel could be allied by a common factor—Frank Neville.

They descended what felt like two stories below Daniel's modest home.

"You know Frank Neville, right?" she asked.

"Sold him some wine a time or two. He likes a good cigar, as well, but he is not from the area so I couldn't say he's a friend. What about Frank is important to you?"

"It's just a name that keeps coming up during my investigation. I like to have all the facts before making conclusions."

"Conclusions on what? How does Neville figure into a show that chases after faeries?"

"The show seeks the truth, whether or not a monster is involved. Do you actually believe faeries kidnapped the missing people?"

He shrugged. "Can't be very interesting for your viewers if the promised monster turns out to be human."

"You would be surprised."

He'd ignored her question, which troubled her in ways she couldn't quite sort out. He was just the local eccentric, right?

So why did that creeping-up-the-back-of-her-neck feeling tingle right now?

"So, what do you think?" he asked, arms splayed to encompass the room.

While upstairs it was no-nonsense, handmade wood furniture and homey touches, down here in the cellar Annja felt as if she'd entered the elite clubhouse of a true connoisseur.

She ran a palm over the varnished mahogany railing. "This is gorgeous."

Redwood wine racks grew from floor to ceiling on the two outer walls. The concrete floors were streaked with amber, which gave an old-world fade to the cellar. Gothic tin lights were suspended overhead and spaced to track the aisles. Rolling library ladders tilted against the wine racks reached to the uppermost racks. Two aisles paralleled the center counter, which was a waist-high rack that also sported goblets, corkscrews, wine journals and a computer that currently flashed what appeared to be a filing system.

"High tech," she observed. "Eric did mention you're a fanatic about wine."

"Guilty as charged. Mr. Kritz must have told him about my collection."

Right. Eric's father. The man financing this trip. And should that bother her more than it did? Why hadn't Doug mentioned that detail? Everyone was intertwined, and that raised the red flag.

Annja peered at the computer monitor. "So you have all the bottles entered in this program?"

"Yes. Any bottles I've consumed I record notes on them, as well. The bottles each have a bar code that I use to track provenance and chateau. A climate-control system monitors the temperature and keeps it at a constant fifty-seven-degree/seventy-percent-humidity ratio. The security is fierce, as well."

"Security? You get a lot of burglars out here on your little patch of green?"

"You'd be surprised at the riffraff that comes sorting about for artifacts and bits and bobs."

Like his mother?

"If they've been drinking they can be very bold," he said. "They will knock right on the door and start a ruckus. That's why I keep a 20-gauge shotgun beside the door."

"Not unwise." She eyed a huge wine bottle behind the computer screen. It was about three feet tall.

"That's called a Balthazar," he offered upon noting her wonder. "Holds twelve liters. Equal to sixteen bottles of wine. I keep it for a conversation piece."

"I bet. This is all very impressive, Daniel."

"You haven't seen anything yet."

He turned and perused a rack of bottles, drawing his long fingers down the row. He stopped at one and pulled out the bottle. "You enjoy wine, Annja?"

"On occasion."

She preferred Diet Coke and beer but she wasn't a snob. Wine would serve when appropriate.

"How long does it take to acquire a collection like this?"

Daniel uncorked the bottle he held and set it on the center counter. "I've got about twenty thousand bottles. Been collecting for fifteen years. And yes, that makes me a lot older than you."

"I wasn't aware the age difference was a concern. Is it when drinking wine and sharing conversation?"

"Not at all. But we've yet to have a scintillating conversation. Unless you consider a stolen midnight kiss?" He smiled and handed her the bottle. "Take a swig of this."

She accepted the bottle, glanced to the row of gleaming

goblets, then decided it was his character to expect her to quaff a swig directly from the bottle. So she did.

"What do you think?" Daniel walked onward, eyeing the bottles as if in search of another. He thumbed his chin. Dark ink looking like a birthmark slashed across his flesh.

The red wine was deep, pleasant and a little fruity. Annja had no clue when it came to actually discerning good wine from otherwise not. She'd once attended a tasting at New York University and had learned there were too many ways to define wine. Acid, cloying, luscious, foxy, peppery. And then to spit it out?

"It's wine," she offered. "Pretty good."

He nodded and wandered farther into the cellar depths. Taking out a bottle from a row, he displayed it to her.

Annja tucked the bottle she held to her chest and went to inspect. The label was unevenly cut around the edges, definitely not machine printed. "Old?"

"Seventeenth century. A rarity. Not many bottles survive from that long ago. The glass is so fragile. If you can find eighteenth century you should consider yourself lucky."

"Nice. French?"

"Prephylloxera Lafite. Very rare. Made before the yellow root louse infestation forever changed the vintage. It is the holy grail of wines."

He replaced the bottle. Annja lingered on the vertical row of ancient bottles that must hold so much history coded within their murky depths. A connoisseur could decipher that liquid code. But she did know that not all wine traversed the decades intact. It could very well be vinegar Daniel kept as a prized possession in some of these bottles.

"So how much does an old bottle like that cost?"

"The prephylloxera? That one put me back five hundred Gs."

"Five hundred *thousand?*" she repeated, utterly stymied.

"Yes, but that's my most expensive bottle."

And he didn't have it under lock and key? If it was her, she would put it in a safe and surround it with guards.

"People pay that much for wine?"

"Yes, and you can never know if the contents will be drinkable or reduced to vinegar."

"Then why spend so much on it?"

"It's buying history, Annja. You must be able to appreciate that."

"I do appreciate history, but not the kind that breaks the bank. I like to dig it up from the dirt. For free."

Daniel chuckled. "But you're not allowed to keep your finds."

"I can go to a museum whenever I wish and spend an entire day looking over any number of valuable artifacts."

"True. But drinking history is amazing."

"Even vinegar?"

"Even so." He pointed toward the other aisle, where he shuffled down the row and sorted through the bottles.

Annja took another swig from her bottle. History? The label was marked 1955. Old, but not surprisingly so. It was certainly before her time. "So how much did this stuff cost?"

"Five grand," he said, and turned away from her, dismissing the statement as if a mere comment of a mediocre day of sunshine.

Nearly choking, Annja swallowed hard. The wine burned now. It dropped to her belly like a stone. Suddenly the word *vigorous* came to mind to describe it. Five thousand? She inspected the bottle. A few healthy oaths tickled her tongue, but she held them back.

Daniel had handed her a five thousand dollar bottle of wine as if it were something he'd picked up at the liquor store for six bucks. What the hell?

"Ah, here." He claimed another bottle and opened it up. "A nice pinot grigio. My favorite. You bring that bottle, and I'll decant this one. We'll go up and chat a bit."

"Thanks, but I think I've had enough wine for the day. You want this one back?"

"No, you keep it, Annja. It's a gift."

Cradling the bottle carefully, for now she feared dropping it, Annja followed the man upstairs.

"I'd offer a Montecristo, but I don't believe you smoke," he said as they took the hallway back into the kitchen.

"Thanks, but I do enjoy the smell. I should probably be going. I had intended to speak to Wesley and look around the forest a bit before it gets too late. Don't want to tease the midnight hour."

"The witching hour can be very magical."

"Is that when the faeries come out?"

"They could." He winked. "They most definitely could."

25

Eric was surprised that Annja was not filming more footage for the show. Doug Morrell expected faerie stuff, and Eric was determined to get it, whether or not Annja participated.

"I should have asked to work with Kristie," he muttered as he adjusted the night-vision lens. "At least she would have been more fun. We'd probably be soaking in a hot tub right now with a bunch of leprechauns drinking a pint."

He had to admit Annja was thorough. And she was concerned for the safety of the people involved with the dig, as opposed to merely seeking a sensational story. He had learned a few things from her already, not in the least, how to maintain professionalism.

And then there was the stealth night filming and being chased by men with guns. Go figure. That was pretty exciting, he thought.

It was probably best his first assignment had been with the smart one as opposed to the sexy one. Not that Annja wasn't sexy. When he caught her unawares, just staring off at the horizon, her profile did things to him. Those full lips and that long gorgeous hair. Her body was great, too. She didn't like it when he filmed her in those private moments.

He knew he already had enough footage of screw-ups to fill a whole one-hour gag-reel special. Doug might be interested in something like that for a special segment. That would rock.

"She's going to fall for Daniel," he said, and hefted his camera to scan the land. "Dude's too old for her."

What was it about women liking older men? Eric couldn't figure it. Of course, Annja wasn't that much older than him, but she came off as older. Wise. Very smart. He respected her a lot.

That was why he'd let her sleep in and went off filming on his own earlier that day. What she was up to now, he didn't know. He hadn't been able to find her at the dig site or back at the B and B. He decided to take the initiative to start investigating, figuring Annja would be impressed.

He was eager to explore the copse of trees along the north side of the dig where Beth had emerged from the forest during the night. It was about three hundred yards from the actual work site. The river backed up to it, and he could smell the water.

"The other crowd," Eric said. "If you're out there, I will find you."

Night had fallen so quickly. Eric had started his walk to the forest when the sun was on the horizon, but now the half moon held court low in the sky. He entered the woods, picking his way slowly through the overgrown scrub and litter of dried twigs and old leaves. He recognized oaks, but had never paid attention in science class so everything else was just a tree.

His boots crunched branches and Eric realized he should

exercise more stealth, as Annja would say. If they heard him coming, they'd flee for sure.

How did one attract the other crowd?

"With rainbows and Broadway show tunes," he muttered.

This truly was a lame assignment. His father had suggested it as a means to kick-starting his career before he even graduated high school. A few credits on a major TV show would look sweet on his résumé.

Something crackled. It had sounded close. Eric swung the camera to the right. It sounded like a branch breaking. The forest flora showed in various shades of green and black though the night lens.

A blur of gray swept from the left side of the camera frame.

Eric swung to the left but did not sight the anomaly.

"Something *is* out there," he whispered.

With his heart racing, he ventured forward, stepping lightly. He liked a good fright, and knew that if he thought scary thoughts and expected the worst that his brain would follow and heighten his freak factor.

He'd seen the movies. *Blair Witch Project, Children of the Corn,* all the Halloween movies and the complete *Nightmare on Elm Street* series. Nothing good ever came to those who ventured into the woods alone. It was classic horror movie fare.

But he wasn't alone; he had the camera. It was like being alone, but not. Dude, was he starting to creep himself out?

"No way. Come out, ghosties. I'm not afraid of you," he whispered.

Something nudged his ankle. He stumbled. Eric swung the camera and scanned the ground. Leaves and branches. His Vans were darker on the toes where moisture had soaked into the leather.

If Annja was right, *people* were kidnapping workers from the dig site. But could a person sneak up on him unaware in the middle of the forest? It was impossible to walk quietly through all the branches and foliage. A person would have to be a ghost—or a faerie flying silently through the air—to get the jump on anyone.

A *snap* echoed.

Eric swung around, scanning his periphery. He had wandered quite far. He couldn't see the dim light from the enemy camp on the peat bog anymore. He could barely see ten feet in front of him. The tree canopy blocked out all moonlight and the night-vision lens distorted depth.

Close by an owl hooted. That made Eric smile.

Something was watching him, just not a human something. He wondered if owls attacked humans. He imagined their talons would hurt. He did not want to star in any part of *The Birds* alone in the woods where no one could hear him scream.

Lifting the camera to his eye, he moved slowly in a circle, taking in the narrow tree column. The wide black spaces between the trees menaced with their utter blackness. It made him feel imprisoned and yet the breeze listing at the nape of his neck only heightened his increasing anxiety.

A breeze? There was no breeze.

But wasn't this exactly like the other night? Annja had also felt a weird breeze the night they'd invaded the enemy camp, only she hadn't said anything to him. But he'd known. She had been creeped out then.

A face suddenly appeared immediately before the camera. It opened its mouth wide to reveal a gaping black maw.

Eric swore and jerked his camera hand down a few inches. Wits fled, but he clutched the camera to focus again. He'd looked away, and now he couldn't find it again.

It had been a face. And not an owl's face. It had been

human. Or something resembling human with two eyes and that big open mouth. Cripes, what had a mouth like that?

"Wasn't there," he muttered. "Couldn't have been. I didn't hear anything. Is…is anyone there?" he called out.

He turned the camera lens toward his face and spoke. "I'm hot on their trail. There's…something out there. I know I've found them. But who or *what* are they?"

Way to go, Kritz. Keep the drama level high, even when you're scared shitless.

He jerked his gaze left to right. When not looking through the camera lens his vision was poor, only picking up shadows and black foggy tree trunks.

Something fluttered near his ear. Eric swung the camera to the right, then realized the lens was still facing him—so he began to narrate.

"It's very close…whatever it is. I feel…like the temperature has dropped a few degrees. That's what happens when ghosts are around. Right? Hell, I don't want to see a ghost. There are no ghosts. Chill, Kritz. It was a stupid bird. The owl."

A branch cracked. He skipped ahead and nearly tripped, and his equilibrium faltered. Groping with his free hand, his fingers swept the chill air. His knees buckled and he fell.

The camera crunched onto a pile of leaves. Body prone, Eric dug his fingers into the cool, moist leaf cover.

Something grabbed him around the ankle. He yelled and groped for the camera but couldn't reach it. His body was dragged along the ground.

26

Annja dressed in the tiny bathroom, then peeked out the doorway down the hall before skipping over to her room. The bed and breakfast didn't offer en suite bathrooms. Four rooms shared one bathroom at the end of the hall, and two of those rooms belonged to the owner's children.

Knocking on Eric's door, she waited to hear signs of life from inside his room. Funny how she had initially been worried about keeping him out of the pubs when the only one who had been tipping back the spirits lately had been her. She had a headache from Daniel's wine this morning, which presented a sharp pain in her right temple. It didn't matter how much that bottle had cost, she'd kill for an aspirin.

Trying the knob, she opened the door a crack. The bed was made. Some of Eric's clothes were folded neatly by the pillow.

"Impressive." The sun had barely peeked above the horizon. "He must be downstairs loading up on black pudding."

Eric wasn't downstairs. He'd probably gone off filming

again, she thought. Annja filled up on fresh cinnamon rolls and then went and left a note for him in his room. Rain poured throughout the day, and she spent the better part of the time at a body shop in Cork, getting a new back window put in the Mini Cooper. Thankfully, she'd been able to slip out before Mr. Riley had noticed.

When she returned to the bed and breakfast, supper was brewing in the kitchen. Annja skipped upstairs to find her note still laying on Eric's bed right where she'd left it.

Her sense of something not being right teetered toward the orange security alert zone. She lingered in the dining room until Mrs. Riley popped in with fresh biscuits.

"Did I miss Eric?" she asked the proprietress.

"Haven't seen him all day, dear. Didn't see him last night, either. He must have tucked in early. Though you did come in rather late."

And toting a very expensive half bottle of wine. She thought about the bottle she'd stuck in the refrigerator. "Did you find the wine I left?"

"Harvey tilted it back around after midnight. I hope you weren't saving it for yourself? It's not often the mister has wine. He's a pint man, he is."

And yet just yesterday Mr. Riley had been toting a bottle of wine he'd bartered from Daniel. Some people only saw what they wanted to see, Annja figured.

Did that include faeries?

"Said it had a bit of a corky taste," Mrs. Riley continued. "Must have been a cheap bottle, eh?"

"About five thousand dollars cheap actually," Annja said. She left the woman with her mouth hanging open, the plate of biscuits tilting dangerously over the table.

The inn sat at the edge of the village. Annja just caught the tail end of a bicycle troop rolling through. They did tours across the countryside, and next time Annja was here, not on business, she fully intended to join the fun.

Daniel pulled up and jumped from the Jeep in all haste. He reached into the back of the vehicle.

"What's up?" she said.

"Mum found something this afternoon on her walk." He held up a video camera—a very familiar camera.

Annja swallowed roughly. She grasped the handheld camera. "This is Eric's. Where'd your mother find it? Where's Eric? Have you seen him?"

"You'd better take a look at what's been recorded," Daniel said. "Let's go inside, shall we?"

Confused that she held something Eric would never have left lying around to be found by a cross-country-hiking old woman, Annja let Daniel tug her inside.

Mrs. Riley stood in the kitchen examining the empty wine bottle. She flashed them a frantic gape when they entered.

"I see you shared the wine." Daniel nodded to the woman. "It's a lovely year, isn't it, Blythe?"

"Oh, Daniel, why do you do things like this?" She set the bottle on the counter and marched out of the room. "He's mad," they both heard her mutter. Stomping feet descended into the cellar, accompanied by feminine noises of reprimand.

"She's not a fan?" Annja asked, but her mirth didn't last. She sat down and powered up the camera. "Where did your mother find this?"

"In the forest edging the dig site Slater is overseeing. She was hunting for morels. Delicious this time of year, especially in a nice white wine sauce."

The digital screen flashed and the green-and-black night image appeared. It looked like trees and foliage. Eric must have been filming in the forest. But why? And alone at night? She hadn't heard him slip out last night.

On the other hand, he may have been gone by the time she'd come wandering in. He may have very well waited for her to accompany him, then gave up and went out filming on his own.

Annja turned the volume up. She heard what sounded like footsteps crushing the undergrowth. Breathing. Eric described the trees, guessing they were maple and birch. The camera angle tilted. Eric's breathing increased.

"There's something out there," warbled out the tiny sound holes. "I know I've found them," Eric narrated dramatically as he stalked forward.

Annja's heart sank. If he had been out hunting for faeries…

The image became fuzzy, then went sharp. Eric's face appeared, the green light highlighting his forehead and making his eyes eerie black. He suspected someone or something was close by. The terror in his eyes seemed real.

Then Annja got it. He was making a spoof tape to use for the show. Clever. Very *Blair Witch Project*. Doug was going to absolutely eat this stuff up. She gave Eric points for creativity, though it was more silly than frightening.

Ready to set the camera down, Annja saw that Eric had dropped the camera. His fingers scrabbled before the lens. Leaves blocked the view, and then—

She leaned forward, not sure she was seeing what it appeared to be. "He's being dragged away?"

"Appears so," Daniel said. "The other crowd doesn't like it when people poke about in their business. And they do have a penchant for the red-haired ones."

Ready to throttle the next person who mentioned the other crowd or the fair folk, Annja made fists and inhaled. Two deep breaths settled her ire.

She hadn't pinned "believer" on Daniel. In fact, she knew

he took the local myths with a huge grain of salt. So why the evasive argument now?

And why her stubborn need to disprove faeries? Perhaps she should be jumping on the bandwagon? Since when did she only see what she wanted to see?

She rewound the video to the point where the camera had been dropped.

It was difficult to make out clear shapes or determine what was foliage, tree trunks or Eric's flailing legs and arms. But she did notice what looked like a slender leg near where Eric's feet must have been lifted to drag him. A man? A mere few frames gave her good view of the attacker's feet.

"Does the other crowd often wear lace-up leather work boots?" she asked Daniel. "Eric's been taken by a human, a real person. *If* he's been taken."

She knew this could be an elaborate hoax. Eric could have recruited someone from the camp, or even one of his new musician friends, to help him pull it off. But seriously? He'd been respectful and eager to do as she'd asked him since they'd arrived. She hadn't pegged him for a practical joker.

"You haven't seen him in Ballybeag?" she asked.

Daniel shook his head. He was too calm. But then, he had no connection to Eric. This was just another disappearance to him, and he had never shown much concern for the others.

Mrs. Riley appeared at the top of the stairs with a load of laundry, neatly folded. She scowled at Daniel and turned down the hallway toward the bedrooms.

"Why did she call you mad? Do you do things like that often?"

"Things like what?"

"With the wine. Was it really that expensive?"

"It was. And no. I only offer the good stuff to the pretty girls."

Not hiding the fact that she rolled her eyes, Annja tapped

the camera. "Did your mother see anything else in the area where she found this?"

"Nope. You going to investigate?"

"Of course I am. After I've checked all the pubs to make sure Eric isn't holing up and having a laugh at my expense."

"Maybe I should go along with you?"

"Thanks, but we'll cover more ground separately. You could help by taking two of the pubs."

"Sure, I'll look into the north and south pubs.

"Thanks. I'll catch up with you later. Thanks for this."

She collected the camera and headed outside. The day was truly dreary. A fine mist grayed the sky. Annja tugged up her hood and marched toward the first pub. They hadn't seen Eric.

At O'Shanley's she was offered a pint before she could even ask a question. Annja set the video camera on the counter and took a sip. Outside, Daniel's Jeep rolled by. The horn honked twice, and the barmaid waved to him as he passed.

"I see Daniel's taken a liking to you," the woman said as she wiped the bar to the left of Annja. She'd not seen hide nor hair of Eric, when Annja had asked, though she did know him. He'd become everyone's favorite young redhead.

"Daniel's my guide," Annja said. She tapped the bar, her thoughts racing about what to do, where to go next in her search for Eric.

"Not a lot of guiding to do about here, is there?" the woman asked. "Here's the village. There's the dig. There you go. Nice as it can be."

She wasn't sure what the woman was implying, but she did catch the tone. A particular tone women used when they were sizing up the competition.

"He showed me his wine cellar last evening," Annja said, matching the challenge.

"Ah." The woman smirked and braced an elbow on the bar, leaning in. "And did he play Kiss Me Kate with you, as well?"

Annja stared at the woman's growing smirk. She felt a flush rising on her face.

Annja swallowed and clasped the camera to her chest. "So you have seen Eric?"

"Not a hair on that bright red crown of his. But you might ask Bridget." She nodded toward a shadowed corner of the pub where Annja made out a bright red-and-pink skirt slipping out from a booth. "The two are mighty close lately."

"Thank you." She slipped off the bar stool and walked across the room. Kiss Me Kate? Really? And she had fallen for it.

Bridget smiled and leaned across the table to offer a hand, which Annja shook. She drew her blue eye shadow out at the corners of her eyes in a swirl that gave her a Celtic flair. "You're the television host Eric has been telling me about. He didn't tell me you were so pretty."

"Thanks. I had no idea Eric had found himself a girlfriend so quickly."

"Oh, we're just friends. He listens to my music, or rather, tolerates it. I don't think he understands a word of what the band sings, but he's gracious about it. Where is the sweetie, by the by?"

"You haven't seen him?" Annja blew out a breath. "He's disappeared."

"Oh, no! Like the others? Taken by the fair folk? Eric told me that's why you two were here, poking about."

"I've got proof that it was a real person who took him from the forest where he was filming last night. He didn't try to contact you?"

"No. I don't have one of those fancy cell phones. He's been

kidnapped by a real person? Oh, lordy." She fanned herself
with a hand.

"Did Eric say anything to you about filming a segment
for the show and surprising me? Maybe say…making it look
like he'd been taken by faeries?"

"Och, no, he didn't. You think that's what he's up to? Well,
the boy is like to such foolery. I wouldn't expect he'd a'fooled
you, though. He looks up to you, Miss Creed. Can't stop talking about you, so much I feared the two of you were…well,
you know. But now I see you're much older than he."

"Right. I've got a few years on him, at least. Well, thank
you. If you do hear from him—"

"I'll tell him you're looking for him," Bridget said.

THE DISPATCHER for the local gardai station took the information from her about another missing person in the Ballybeag
area. She sounded disinterested, and was downright rude
when she told Annja it could be a few days before she could
get an officer back out to the dig site.

"Faeries aren't real, you know," she said. "And don't
think I'll find another officer willing to waste his time right
now."

"It's not faeries. A person, or people, have been kidnapping men and women from the dig site. Can I talk to your
supervisor?"

Annja shoved her fingers through her hair and kicked the
iron phone box post. She wondered if calling Bart could get
anyone moving, or if he even had contacts with any of the
local police organizations in the country. Probably not.

The line suddenly dropped the call. Annja slammed the
phone on the hook.

"Fine. I'll do it my way, then."

27

By nightfall, the sky had only grown darker, and the rain had no intention of stopping. Annja dressed in black and tied her hair in a ponytail before going down to the dining room to root out something to snack on. Mrs. Riley stood before the window, arms crossed.

"You skipped supper," she said, a twang of disappointment in her words.

"Eric's missing," Annja said.

"Oh, dear. You've looked in town for him? Talked to Bridget?"

"Yes, no one has seen him. It's dark, but I'm going out to walk around the dig site.

Mrs. Riley rubbed a hand along the back of her neck as if to ease out tension. "Be careful of the trucks if you're walking. They drive through every few days. So fast and loud."

"What trucks?" Annja joined her side and looked out the window, but the road before the inn was clear of vehicles.

"They head out toward your dig site, dear. I assumed they were a part of it all, hauling dirt and such."

"We don't haul dirt from a dig site, Mrs. Riley. It's all put back in place when we're finished. I'm not sure what the trucks could be for. How many?"

"One or two. Delivery trucks, they look like. Always at night, though."

"Hmm…"

"Did you notify the gardai of your missing friend?"

"I did, and they didn't sound very concerned."

"Well, it's the—"

Annja put up a palm to stop her before she could utter the words she didn't want to hear. "Thanks, Mrs. Riley. I'll be quiet when I return."

THE DAY'S HARD RAIN made picking through the forest a challenge. The tree canopy wasn't thick enough to keep the forest bed from becoming slick, and every step Annja took she had to be cautious not to fall and impale herself on one of the broken branches jutting out everywhere.

She'd brought along night-vision binoculars, borrowed from Eric's equipment. When sneaking past Slater's camp, she noticed there was a truck trail leading around the forest and likely to river's edge. There was no road, beyond the tracks that had crushed the grass. Wesley told her there were docks here and there along the river.

Annja decided to go through the woods to maintain her cover. She had trekked into the forest no more than a quarter of a mile when she saw the spotlights. A rusty delivery truck had backed up to the shore. From her position, hidden among the thick scrub, Annja couldn't determine how steep the shore was. But if there was no dock, then the drop-off couldn't be that steep.

Half a dozen men were loading something from the truck

to—she couldn't see beyond the end of the truck. The rain had softened to a mist, but it blurred her view of the activity. There must be a boat waiting below. She couldn't see a sail or hear a boat engine.

None of the men spoke, or if they did, she couldn't make out any conversation from her distance.

Whatever was going on, she couldn't figure how it would be related to the dig. They were not loading dirt from the dig and transferring it to a boat. But it seemed odd that a clandestine operation would be taking place right in the backyard of the dig.

Was Frank Neville overseeing this operation?

She would notice Slater if he were among the men. He had a distinctive walk, straight and militant. If he assumed the same role he did at the dig, his attention would not be on the men so much as scanning his surroundings.

She adjusted the binoculars and scanned the back of the truck. It looked as if large wooden trunks were being unloaded from the open truck bed. Each trunk was about five feet long and maybe three or four feet wide. It required a man on each end, gripping the rope handles, to heft them.

Kneeling on the wet grass, Annja spotted the same security guard she'd had the displeasure of meeting the other night. Instead of a dart gun, he wielded an AK-47 against one shoulder and stood near what had to be steps down to the shore.

One of the trunks dropped to the ground. The cover fell off. The men swore and the guard hustled over to bark orders. Fine stuffing tumbled out of the trunk. It looked like the shredded paper stuffing she often saw artifacts packed in. The barrel of a gun slid across the wood trunk lid and landed on the muddy ground.

She'd recognize that weapon anywhere; it was the same as the guard held—an AK-47. Though it wasn't fitted with the curved magazine, the wooden stock always gave it away. As Annja knew only too well, the AK-47 was the gun of guns, preferred by military types and terrorists worldwide. It was easy to use, easy to train others to use—sadly even twelve-year-olds—and could fire after being buried in the sand or pulling it out from a mud puddle.

A creepy feeling zeroed in on her gut, coiling tightly. Annja leaned back on her heels. She lowered the binoculars. If the trunks were full of assault rifles, there weren't many options to go with.

Was the dig a front for gunrunners? It didn't fit together—guns and skeletons—though Annja had been witness to a lot of wacky scenarios, some so bizarre even she had doubted. And if she added faeries into the equation…which she would not…

She lifted the binoculars—and choked. An arm pressed across her throat. She was dragged backward across the wet undergrowth. Her attacker wrapped his legs around and over her thighs, effectively pinning her. He clasped her left hand and slammed it against her chest, leaving her right hand free to grope for the binoculars as a weapon—but she'd use a better weapon.

Slapping the ground, she grabbed wet leaves. With a concentrated thought, she held the hilt of her sword, the blade flat across the ground.

"Shh," her captor hissed at her ear. She recognized the voice.

For the moment Annja stilled. She didn't lift the blade. Michael Slater adjusted his chokehold, releasing her, yet slapping his palm hard across her mouth.

"Out for a jog?" he muttered. "Don't answer. Be quiet, or they'll hear you."

That he cared if she was discovered surprised her, but she couldn't determine if that was a good thing or very bad.

Did he intend to save her for himself? Take her out without alerting the others?

She pulled the sword carefully across the ground so it would not make any noise.

"Whatever you think you saw," he said against her ear, his lips cool against her rain-soaked flesh, "forget it."

She nodded in agreement.

"I don't trust you, Creed."

"I…" She gasped as he slapped up the chokehold again.

"Careful," he warned. "Quiet and smart. No shouting. No screaming. Got it?"

She nodded again.

"What are you doing out here?" he asked.

"I was looking for Eric," she whispered truthfully.

"The cameraman?"

"He disappeared last night in these woods."

"And you thought the best time to look for a missing person was at night, with no moon to be seen, and a pair of night-vision binoculars?"

Stating the obvious wasn't going to win him any friendship points.

He swore softly. "I'm giving you one chance tonight, Creed. I'm going to let you go, and you're going to sneak out of here the same way you came in. I can hold off the truck for another hour, but by then you'd better be back in Ballybeag, snug in bed, yes?"

"You're running guns."

His fingers tightened across her neck, making a swallow painful. "And you are running my last nerve."

"Why are you doing this?"

"What? Snuggling with you in the mucky forest? You don't think I want to get my hands on this?" He groped her breast, but it wasn't offensive so much as awkward. A threat he'd never carry out, she felt sure of it.

"I mean, why are you not taking me in? Like you did with all the others who saw something they shouldn't have seen. You run out of LSD?"

"I had nothing to do with those disappearances. And I won't keep defending myself. Just go."

"Is this Frank Neville's operation?"

"Stop asking questions. Have you got a death wish?"

"No," she gasped.

"Then do as I say. Get the hell out of here. I don't want to see your face tomorrow, or any other day after—got that?"

She opened her fingers across the wet grass. The sword left her grip, vanishing without Slater being the wiser to its presence. "Got it."

"Head out at an angle, east," he directed as he stood and helped her to stand with a tug of his grip. "You make too much noise, Creed, and I'll be forced to fire a warning shot so the blokes at the truck don't think I'm not keeping up my end. Got it?"

She nodded.

"And Creed?"

"What?"

He gripped the collar of her shirt. "I never have to fire beyond the warning shot because I always hit my mark."

"Warning shots aren't supposed to hit, they're just supposed to…" What was she saying? The argument wouldn't matter. Slater had offered her freedom. She should take it.

Unless being captured would lead her to the others.

He released his hold on her shirt. "You're not moving, Creed."

No, she wasn't prepared to talk herself into being taken hostage. She did not purposely get involved in dealings better handled by the police. As for the weapons, he wouldn't give her a straight answer, even if she did let him have that grope he'd mentioned. But he wasn't here to rape her. He was supervising something much more covert and illegal than an innocent dig.

"I guess this is goodbye, then," she said, confused at what he was doing.

"I'm not going to miss you." he whispered.

Annja marched past him, not bothering to look back. Slater watched her retreat, gun cocked and muscles tensed to react. She couldn't shake the creepy feeling of being watched until she reached the forest edge and was out of range of the gun-running operation.

Now she knew why the people had been taken from the dig site. Somehow she had to find out where they were being kept. If the trucks ran every few nights, as Mrs. Riley had said, then there was an opportunity to move a person onto a boat and down the river to the harbor.

Kinsale was the harbor town the river opened onto. At first light, Annja intended to check out the town.

28

"Annja, I think you should come out to the site."

Wesley Pierce had called. Annja was sitting in the pub, laptop open on the bar. She hadn't wanted to bother Mrs. Riley for breakfast, and the pub opened for breakfast at six. "I'm on my way in just a bit. What's up?"

"Ah, there's something I wanted to tell you. Feel you out about a suspicion. And I found a very interesting item close to a femur that has been ravaged by animals. You'll want to take a look at it."

"What is it?"

"I'll show you when you get here."

She flipped her phone shut, then nodded to the bartender that she didn't need a refill of her coffee. Weird. Wesley hadn't been forthcoming with information, and had almost sounded a little nervous. Why not just tell her over the phone?

Annja thought about what she'd learned so far.

Annja had looked up Eric Kritz's dad online, but the only information linked to him was the QueensMark studios page.

Marvin Kritz was listed as owner. His photo was an older version of Eric, right down to his thick eyebrows and shoulder-length red hair. She could find nothing else on him, not even a Facebook page.

She admonished herself for being so suspicious, but knew it never paid to walk through life like a Pollyanna, trusting everyone. Marvin Kritz might just be a very generous father, or there could be something she'd missed on him.

On a whim, she'd dialed New York. It was late at night there, but she knew Detective Bart McGilley wouldn't mind.

"Annja? Why the late check-in? You up for a jog around Prospect Park tomorrow morning? I'm in the mood for a little forest scenery."

She wasn't keen on tromping through another forest any-time soon, especially with men like Michael Slater lurking in the depths. "Sorry, I'm out of the country at the moment."

"Ah, then that means you have work for me. There's no other reason you'd call from out of the country unless you wanted something."

"Give me some credit, Bart. I don't always call to ask a favor, do I?"

"Yep."

Okay, he had her there. Did she use her relationship with Bart to her advantage? Probably. But he was one of few people she could trust asking questions that usually involved identifying a criminal.

"I have two names I need checked out." He was accustomed to the "name calls," so she started right in. "Frank Neville, whom I believe is a British citizen, though that may or may not be true. And Michael Slater—he may be British, as well. Or not."

"I can search the databases in the United States, Annja, but if they're British citizens it might not bring up any hits."

"I thought you had contacts in the FBI and CIA?"

The phone clattered as he switched ears or hands and gruffly asked, "Annja, what are you involved in?"

"I'm in Ireland filming for *Chasing History's Monsters*. It's a segment about faeries."

"Seriously? And?"

And he knew her too well. For all the times Annja had called Bart for information on criminals or just to have her back, she wasn't about to start lying to him now. She valued his trust too much.

"I suspect the dig site is really a front for arms dealers. At least, that's the obvious conclusion after seeing a truck unloading trunks of AK-47s onto a boat last night."

"Christ. Ireland has some of the weakest arms control legislation," Bart said.

"The man running the guns isn't Irish, but I suspect British."

"A British citizen doesn't need a license to broker small arms in Ireland. Hell, Annja. If you suspect it's guns I want you to take a big step back and turn and walk away right now. No wait. Don't walk. Run. Let the big boys handle whatever it is you've stepped into."

"But who are the big boys? The local gardai have been contacted regarding three missing people and I haven't even seen them. I called them to report my missing cameraman and they hung up on me. It's as if they can't be bothered."

"Missing people? Are you talking about guns or kidnap victims?"

"Both. The dig site is riddled with all sorts of illegal activity. I know it sounds crazy, but—"

"But nothing can ever be too crazy when it's coming from your lips, Annja. You forget I've gotten these calls from you before. So you've got illegal weapons and missing people. And no sign of the local authorities. What about MI-6?"

"You think I should contact them? Yes, I suppose they would handle the weapons."

"Unless they're already involved. Annja, you have no idea the twisted channels and butt kissing that goes on between the criminals and legitimate government agencies."

"I don't suspect anything right now. I have proof of nothing. But I feel these two guys are not on the up-and-up."

"Tell me their names again."

She did and Bart wrote them down. "Could you run two other names while you're at it?"

Bart sighed, then said, "Shoot."

"Marvin Kritz and Daniel Collins. Kritz owns Queens-Mark studios in Manhattan. The latter lives here in Ballybeag and collects wine and doesn't do much else. But that could be a front. His card showed up in the wrong wallet at a weird time."

"You're filching wallets now? Annja."

"I didn't filch a thing. I just want to know what I'm dealing with here."

"Doesn't sound like you're doing much faerie chasing."

"Bart, if you even think to start teasing me we are going to meet in the ring at Eddie's when I get home."

"Sounds like a fun time to me. It's been a while since you let me kick your butt. Tell Tinkerbell hey from me."

"Not funny. Call me as soon as you have some information."

"Will do."

She hung up, but knew Bart would have her back. She'd give him a couple hours to check the names. And she looked forward to that boxing match. The only butt kicking that would commence would involve Bart's and not hers.

She packed up her gear and paid her bill. She'd better get to the site and see what Wesley was so worked up about.

No workers hunched over the dig square. The sound of tapping trowels did not echo in the still air. Not a single industrious body waved hello as Annja got out of the Mini Cooper and strode across the dirt.

"Where is everyone?"

Wesley tugged down the canvas tent tarp, letting it collect in thick billows on the ground. From the looks of the stacked buckets and folded tarps, he was in the process of packing up camp.

His smile was lackluster. Probably because the shiner on his left eye had stolen that luster. "My crew is all gone. Slater paid them off."

"I just—" Saw Slater last night, she almost said. He'd had time to pay off Wesley's coworkers since then?

"How do you know Slater did that?"

"It's a guess. But I'm sure it's a correct one."

"So you're just quitting?"

Putting on his sunglasses, Wesley stopped folding the tent. He gave the stacked tarp a kick. "Can't do much without help, you should know that. It wasn't like I didn't expect it, anyway. I was just hoping to get a little more time to dig deeper. But isn't that what any archaeologist always wants? Where's your puppy dog today?"

Too stunned that the entire camp had committed mutiny, Annja scanned the horizon and focused on the other camp. Some commotion over there caught her attention. A white delivery truck was parked behind the tent, but it wasn't the same truck as last night. She couldn't make out people's faces from this distance, but there were only three that she counted.

"Annja?"

"Huh?" What had he asked? "You haven't heard? He's gone," she said. "Eric disappeared."

"No kidding? Like the others?"

"I suspect so. But it's not the other crowd taking them. I saw the video."

"There was video?"

"Eric went filming in the forest the other night. Mrs. Collins found his camera when she was out walking. I thought he was making a joke for the show—filming a sort of spoof—but after watching the replay, I changed my mind. Looks like he was forcibly taken."

Wesley adjusted his stance and stared up toward the sun, which flashed on the metal rims of his glasses. "Sorry. I don't know what to say. I wish I had some information."

"You talk to Beth any more? Did she say anything to you?"

"Honestly, she's still kind of out of it. The doctors said, being a diabetic, she had a severe reaction to the drugs. She was mumbling about faeries the last time I visited. You said Mrs. Collins found the camera?" He scratched his head. "You ever think it's kind of odd that a little old lady spends her days bustling about our digs? And now she's the one to bring you proof of your friend's disappearance?"

"What are you implying?"

He shrugged. "Nothing. Maybe. Just don't trust that lady."

"She's probably eighty years old."

"Age shouldn't matter. Ah, sorry." He blew out a heavy breath and slapped the dust from the thigh of his cargo pants. "I'm pissed over the loss of my crew. Should have expected as much after what I found last night."

"Which is?"

"I think I've determined the reason why Frank Neville took over the camp and is forcing everyone out." Wesley dug in his breast pocket and displayed a small chunk of clear stone on his palm. "Found this while I was taking archival photographs. It's small, but a beauty."

"Quartz? Yeah, it'll make a nice necklace for your girl."

Annja dismissed the find and glanced to the enemy camp. She wanted to be over there right now. The makeshift tarp wall was no longer up. What was going on? Were they clearing out, too? Would Slater blow a gasket if he saw her again after last night?

"Annja." Wesley chuckled. "This little beauty is a rough diamond."

She took the nickel-size chunk from him and held it between two fingers. Clouds blocked the sun so the surface appeared dull. One side was rough, dirty and pocked with two smooth flat sides that resembled every piece of quartz she had ever seen. Except it also looked a lot like the rough diamond Mrs. Collins claimed to own.

"How do you know it's a diamond?"

"Took it into a jeweler in Cork last evening after I'd visited Beth. He verified as much. Offered me ten thousand on the spot."

"And you didn't take it?"

He chuckled softly. "I dated a jeweler once. She used to buy Tunisian roughs. She taught me a few things. This is worth five times that much, I'm sure. It's weird, though, because Ireland doesn't have diamond pipes or even trace indicator minerals like kimberlite."

"It didn't have to come from a mine," Annja said. "The stone could have been lost, dropped—"

"Or buried right next to the nineteenth-century skeleton we've unearthed. The same skeleton that I've verified died of starvation. So tell me how that's possible?"

She tossed him the rough and he caught it smartly. "It could have come from travelers to the area. Could have been part of a coveted stash. Whoever found the rough might not have realized it had any value, they may simply have thought it was a pretty, clear stone." Much as she had when examining

Mrs. Collin's diamond. "Are you sure you can place it with the skeletons?"

"There were traces of wool thread wrapped around it. Probably from a skirt. So my guess is the rough was sewn into the skirt."

"Interesting. Women used to do that, sew valuables like coins and jewels into their skirts before traveling. If they were robbed, the thief would rarely think to search their clothing for hidden booty."

"Exactly. Or…"

"Or?"

"The country was ravaged with wolves during the famine. If it was a woman, with roughs sewn into her skirt, she had to have traveled from someplace, well, not here."

"Like maybe she stole the stones?"

"Yes, and traveled to her family, only to arrive and find they'd been dead and buried since she left. Used to happen. A family member would go off to Liverpool in hopes of finding work, a new starting place for their family. Only problem is the English would deport the Irish as quickly as they set foot on English soil."

"So if our girl had managed to snag some diamonds and returned here to present to her family as their means to salvation, only to discover said family has died, then…you think wolves got to her? But Slater's camp is two hundred yards away, which is where Mrs. Collins claimed to have found her rough. Why the distance between the roughs?"

"You said they found a full skeleton over there? Was it missing a femur?"

Annja tracked through her memory of the video she'd seen of the skeleton filmed at night. She'd thought it was complete, but she could be mistaken.

"She could have been dragged from this site to that one," Wesley offered.

"Do you think a wolf, which may have been near starvation itself, could manage to drag a human body so far?"

"Minus one femur."

"Still. Why?"

"Either that, or the wolf attacked her here." He gestured to the site. "But she managed to run from it a ways, to over there. And after she was dead and had been gnawed on a while, scavengers carried the femur over here. It makes sense."

Annja nodded. It was a long shot, but that's what they did, pieced together the mysteries of the past. It could have happened that way. If she believed a starving woman made the trek to England, and returned home with a bounty only to find her family dead. How devastating must that have been? To have traveled so far only to find utter hopelessness upon return.

"What we need to do is match the femur we found to the other skeleton," Wesley said. "That is, if I was still working the dig. I've already put in a call to my manager. He's got a job in Machu Picchu that interests me."

"I'll do it," Annja said. "This is too fascinating to ignore. So that has to be the reason for the secrecy. Diamonds." She took the rough back, holding it high to catch the burgeoning sunlight.

"Yep." Wesley stood beside her. "And good reason to take out someone who might know too much, like Beth, Brian and Richard."

"But not Eric. What could he have discovered tromping through the woods? Certainly not diamonds."

But he could have seen the trucks filled with guns. No, the trucks hadn't gone through here the other night. However, that didn't mean Slater wouldn't keep his area clear of snoopers all the time.

"I suspect Slater's security didn't want to take any chances," Wesley confirmed.

"While the diamond find is cool, I've recently learned there's an even darker truth behind the secrecy and the splitting of the camps."

"What's that?" he asked.

"I took a walk through the forest last night. You ever see the trucks drive to the river at night?"

"I saw them one night. Didn't give them a second thought."

"Seriously?"

"Annja, I've learned when to step back and when to stand for a cause. This time stepping aside seems wise. Hell, I've called NewWorld dozens of times. I only got a return call last night from the owner. He was really strange about the find. In a creepy, urgent way."

"I suppose he wants to ensure the rough isn't stolen. The dig has finally produced something of value."

"Yes, but all the official paperwork has ceased. It's not on the up-and-up anymore. I got a bad feeling about this. I've had my share of adventure and can handle myself in about any situation. But when guys like Slater march the site with a Walther and unseen others like Frank Neville might be ordering people kidnapped…" He shook his head. "Time to head for new climes."

"So you're going to walk away? Without even knowing why?"

He snatched the diamond from her. "Not without a lovely parting gift."

"That belongs to the land owners, or the country of Ireland. What about NewWorld?"

"You tell that to Mrs. Collins." He pocketed the lump of diamond and walked off, but called over his shoulder, "You'd best clear out, as well, Annja. There's no story here worth the trouble brewing."

Hands on her hips, Annja again scanned the horizon. She saw two male figures, standing near the dig hole she and Eric had explored.

"THAT HER?"

Slater bristled at sight of Annja Creed, staring right at them from across the land that separated the digs. Obviously his message last night had not been clear. If she left, that would make his job easier. And less stressful.

"I think so," he said. "Can't be certain without a scope."

Neville's jet-black hair sprouted thickly on his head. It was short and spiked straight out. A thick black goatee and soul patch covered his narrow chin. Armani in the Irish countryside seemed out of place, and the diamond cuff links screamed "outsider," but he made it work. Slater had seen more eccentric studies walking the Russian tundra, so Neville didn't really surprise him.

Neville turned to his driver and snapped his fingers. "Hand me that rifle."

The driver handed over a Rangemaster .50 caliber.

Neville lifted the rifle before him and sighted through the scope. The rifle was heavy, but he managed it easily enough.

"Easy now, mate," Slater said when Neville fingered the trigger.

"I'm using it to see," Neville said. "Dark hair, slender body, wearing cargo pants and T-shirt like the rest of the dig slaves usually wear. You said she's a television host?"

"I didn't." Slater wasn't sure how Neville had gotten the information about Annja Creed being on-site. He hadn't reported it to him. That sort of information would have only set Neville off. As was apparent from his presence. But so far Neville hadn't mentioned the discrepancy on his part.

"It's a silly American show that talks about monsters.

They're filming an episode on faeries. She's no worry," Slater said.

"And yet she's still here. There's no dig to film now. I asked you to get rid of her."

"You wanted me to clear out the other camp. I did so. She's not officially aligned with the dig." That Neville kept the rifle sighted and ready to aim made Slater's muscles tic.

"Wesley Pierce is still there."

"He's packing up."

"Not fast enough." Neville released the safety.

"Settle down, Mr. Neville."

"Don't bloody mother me, Slater."

"You can't shoot him. The woman is standing right there."

"Yeah? Maybe the nosy bird will get the hint."

Neville pulled the trigger.

"I CAN GIVE YOU a ride into town," Wesley said as he approached Annja with a bucket in each hand. "Annja, what are you—"

She turned to see the left lens of his sunglasses shatter. Wesley's head jerked backward. He dropped the buckets. Blood poured from his eye socket. The man's knees wobbled, buckled, then he went down. His body hit the dirt.

29

Annja didn't have to press two fingers to Wesley Pierce's carotid artery to check for signs of life, but she did. No pulse.

Had he died for the rough diamond he had found?

Slater's camp couldn't have discovered a diamond mine; it was impossible in this country. Either Neville wasn't aware of those odds, or he was curious to see what more he could find—and he wasn't about to let anyone get in his way.

The rough Wesley found had to be from a long-lost cache. It was difficult, in Annja's mind, to place it to the mid-nineteenth century, as Wesley had. This area had been ravaged by the potato famine. If someone had owned diamonds, they wouldn't have stuck around to starve to death; they would have headed to Dublin or even traveled out of the country to America.

Could Wesley's theory about the rough diamond being sewn into the skirt of a nineteenth-century woman be true? It was very possible she could have died over near the peat bog. It was also possible she could have been attacked by wolves. How many more roughs were to be found?

The where and when didn't matter. But the *what* did fit into the puzzle Annja held.

If Frank Neville was trading guns for diamonds—or vice versa as diamonds were a commonly accepted currency in the world of arms dealing—then it made sense he'd be trying to obtain more diamonds. If they found one on-site, they wouldn't leave a stone unturned.

Annja slid her fingers from Wesley's neck. She avoided looking at the hole in his skull. The man was kind, and had done nothing to warrant such violence.

Without considering she could be next to take a bullet, she marched across the packed-dirt clearing toward the opposing camp.

A black SUV spun out in a cloud of dust from the enemy camp. The delivery truck she'd seen parked there daily followed close behind. Someone had rallied the troops, and after committing murder they were hightailing it out of there.

Right hand twitching wanting to hold her sword, she kept it out of sight until she needed it—if she needed it. The camp looked deserted, but she wouldn't let down her guard. Her best bet was to get as close as possible to the one who wanted her dead.

But did they want her dead? Wesley had seemed to fit the bill. He could have been used as a warning. Otherwise, she'd have a bullet hole in her head, too.

After the times Slater had threatened her to leave she should have gotten the hint. But she hadn't realized the real danger until now. This had initially been a query into missing people. Now homicide had entered the mix.

Annja jogged down the rise that edged the pitoned-off dig square. The loamy earth bounced under her fast footsteps. She eyed the excavation square; they hadn't dug down any farther than Wesley's camp. The skeleton had been lifted. Had they found diamonds near the skeleton? It was very possible. They could be from the same time period as the rough Wesley found.

She still thought it was strange, though, that the roughs were separated by such distance. But again, an animal could have easily moved the bones, as well as gotten what it thought was a rock in its maw and taken that along, too.

No one was around, that she could see. The scent of dust and engine oil hung in the air.

Stalking around the site, Annja aimed for the tents. Someone had to still be here. They wouldn't just abandon the tents and equipment, would they?

A hard impact against her shoulder clacked her jaws together. Shoved hard from the side, Annja stepped quickly to avoid stumbling. She righted herself before completely losing her balance and falling onto the spoil heap. A steely hand gripped her throat. She couldn't swallow.

"You really do have a death wish."

She shoved Slater off her with both palms to his shoulders and a heel to his shin. "You killed Wesley!"

"That was Neville." The man paced before her, flexing his fingers into fists. Trapped, or more like uncaged and ready to strike. His neck muscles were as tight as his voice. "And if you think he's going to continue to let you traipse around filming his actions, you're out of your mind. The next time you won't get a warning, Creed."

"You call a bullet through a man's brain a warning?"

"Standing in your shoes, I would call it lucky. Now take your pretty little head—the one without a bullet hole in it—away from here and get yourself on the next flight to the States."

"I'm calling the gardai."

Slater put himself right before her, his chest shoving up

hard against hers, his right hand going around behind his hip for what Annja knew was his pistol. "Did you not hear what I said?"

"Yes, you laid the blame on someone else. You're not going to get away with murder. Was Wesley's life worth a few chunks of rough diamond?"

"You think you know what's going on?"

"I can put two and two together. Rough diamonds have been found. Frank Neville is greedy to buy more guns."

Slater lifted his head, shaking it as he chuckled without mirth.

Annja matched his steps, defying him to step away from her. "If I'm wrong, then you tell me what is right."

"Can't do that."

She lunged for Slater and shoved him hard. He didn't stand down.

"Neville is an arms dealer," she said.

"Is that your guess?" He wasn't going to give her anything.

"I'm right. He's been shipping small arms down the Bandon River to the Kinsale harbor. And he thinks he can find more rough diamonds to either fund his trade or buy more weapons."

"Listen." He gripped her by the hair. She couldn't wrangle free and instead put her hands to his shoulders to loosen the pull on her scalp. "Every moment I have to deal with your idiocy, you are blowing my cover. If I have to babysit you one more day, I'd rather shoot you now and call it collateral damage."

"Like Wesley?"

"I had no idea Neville was going to shoot him. He was scanning the camp using the scope on a sniper rifle. If I'd stopped him, then the jig would have been up and the whole operation would have gone tits up."

He gave her head a shove, releasing her hair.

Sure the man wasn't going to kill her, and even more curious than her safety required, Annja did not back down. Slater had said something interesting. "What cover?"

He forced her backward a few paces with his urgent lunge. His eyes stormed. Annja stumbled until her heels connected with the finds table outside of the tent. Slater drew out his gun and pressed it under her chin. "How fast can you get out of town?"

"Apparently not fast enough for you."

"Work with me here, Creed. There's nothing for you on this particular section of land on this big island in the Irish Sea. You want some stupid television spot to impress your boss? You're not going to get it here."

Not unless the faeries were transporting AK-47s. "What cover am I causing you to risk?"

The man's narrowed eyes searched hers. Sweat beaded on his forehead and dirt was smeared on his face. He stood at the edge of some mental precipice that plunged into malice. And most people standing at the end of a Walther P99 would take a huge step back, turn and run.

Annja was not like most people. For good or for ill, she could not simply stand aside and allow whatever events Frank Neville and Michael Slater had brewed to occur. She had a young man to find. She would not return to the United States without Eric.

"Tell me," she said again. "Because I'm not going anywhere until I know the truth."

Slater chuckled sharply. He waved the gun around as he spoke, disregarding her uneasy flinches, or maybe that was the point. "If I tell you, you become the one person who can bring me down. I'd sooner shoot you than have that happen."

"You've mentioned more than a few times the threat about

shooting me, but I think when it comes down to it, you won't be able to pull the trigger."

Annja found herself staring down the imposing barrel of the Walther.

"What if I have a diamond?" she tried. If the man was greedy, he'd spare her life until she could produce the prize. If not, she'd be surprised.

"You're lying."

"Wesley found a rough diamond over in his camp. He was showing it to me before he was brutally murdered."

"Yeah? Well, I've got a handful of roughs myself. Chump change, Creed. There's no diamond mine here. I tried to tell Neville it was a coincidence. They were from some robbery or a historical cache that got lost."

"You know about the country's minerals?"

"A bit. I know Ireland has never pulled diamonds out of the ground. Gold and zinc, yes. I've been working this case for six months. This is just a sidebar to the big deal. A deal I'm never going to crack with you spooking my mark."

"Your mark? Frank Neville? Who are you?"

Now Slater pressed the gun barrel along his forehead and exhaled. The wince was either from the sun or the headache he likely labeled Annja Creed. He obviously didn't know how to react to her stubbornness. He glared at her, and for a moment Annja felt his anxiety. He was holding a secret close, and she was irritating his grip.

"You're British Intelligence," she guessed. "I thought you were military. You stick out like a sore thumb on this dig."

"I'm MI-6." The gun aimed for her forehead. "Information you will take to your grave if you've got a brain in that pretty little head."

Annja put up her palms in surrender. That he'd shared the information put her in an awkward position. But she wasn't stupid. "I won't tell, I promise."

"I believe your word is good," he said. "So now that you know, you'll leave. There are flights leaving from Dublin for the States a couple of times a day. I'll even foot the bill. See how generous I can be?"

He shoved her away and shouldered his gun. MI-6? So she'd stepped into an operation she'd be better off avoiding. Really should avoid.

But it was too late.

"I'm not going anywhere," Annja said.

Slater shook his head at her, his grimace threatening to crack his face.

"Not until I find Eric Kritz," she said. "He's my responsibility. He's only eighteen years old. He hasn't even graduated high school!"

"Bloody hell. What are you doing traveling with a kid like that?"

"It was a surprise to me. But he's a good kid. If you have any sway with Neville, if you know anything about Eric's disappearance, you have to help me."

"I don't *have* to do anything for you."

"Just like you didn't have to win that fight against Wesley?"

He cast her a hesitant stare.

"You had him beat, but you threw the fight," she said. "You're trying to hold things together, aren't you? Keeping up a facade for Neville, yet protecting the innocents to preserve your own moral code."

Sighing heavily, Slater briefly dropped the hard exterior. Annja literally felt his attitude change. Like he was being released from a prison of lies. "Check the local hospitals," he said. "Your cameraman may have gotten lost and wandered into the city."

"Is that a suggestion or do you know that for a fact?"

"Just a suggestion."

"And will I find him high on LSD like Beth was?"

"You're getting in too deep, Annja."

"Yeah? Well, there's a dead man lying not two hundred yards away from us, and the man I'm responsible for is missing. And I'm thinking if you're not going to help me, then Beth is my best bet."

"Beth doesn't know anything you don't already know. She saw the trucks delivering guns to the river one night, same as you. And don't think Neville will allow further conversation with her to happen."

"Meaning?"

"Think about it."

She started, and knew immediately Beth was in danger. If Frank Neville thought she was snooping for information, he'd be sure to cover his tracks, as he'd done with Wesley.

"Why didn't he shoot me, too?"

"I guess he thought I could handle getting you out of his hair." Slater gestured toward the dismantled camp where Wesley's body still lay. "I'll call for someone to clean up the mess."

"He's a human being, not a mess."

"Not in this game, Annja." A grimace tugged his face. "See, that's what separates you from the men. You think too much. You women, you always see with your heart."

Not always. In fact, she'd chided herself for the hard exterior that had grown around her heart since taking the sword in hand. Yet she knew a soft interior existed, or she wouldn't be so determined to rescue Eric. He had a family who loved him, and would worry should he not check in soon.

"And you can idly stand by and watch an innocent man be murdered," she volleyed back at Slater.

"Part of the job. Didn't say I liked it. And now we're getting too chatty. I intend to do what I promised Neville I'd do. I'll take you into town to collect your cameraman and then see you to the airport. Please, Annja, can you do that for me?"

The exasperation in his voice rapped against the hard shell about her heart. She didn't want to interfere in an MI-6 operation. She had no right, and was smarter than that. If she could find Eric she'd gladly leave the dirty dealings to those more qualified.

"Fine. But if Eric's not at the hospital, I'm not leaving until I find him."

30

Bit of a bustle going on about his neck of the humble woods lately, Daniel Collins thought as he scanned across the cleared dig sites. Both crews certainly did up and leave quick enough.

But his thoughts were not focused on why the camps had left, and without so much as a goodbye or thank-you for the hospitality. His focus was currently on the helicopter landing in the field where the digs had been backfilled.

The sleek white chopper looked like an alien insect as it landed between the two dig sites where once the imaginary line had been drawn. Plumes of dry dirt billowed and dispersed in the sky.

One man stepped down from the helicopter and took a look around. He gestured to the pilot and stepped out and away to avoid the upsweep of dirt as the helicopter took off, leaving the stranger standing in the center of what had only recently been a busy archaeological dig.

Even from his distance Daniel could tell the man was big,

a good half a foot taller than him. He wore a dress shirt that stretched tightly over enough muscles to make him formidable. Daniel wouldn't jump into the fight ring with that man, but he would certainly put his money on him.

As the man approached, and Daniel could make out his dark goatee and square jaw, he suddenly recognized the face. He waved, and the man nodded, not willing to wave, and reserving judgment until he got close enough to Daniel.

"Mr. Braden!" Daniel offered his hand and Garin shook it. "You do know how to make an entrance. What brings you to the land of Éire on a fine Monday afternoon?"

Garin spread his arms to encompass the empty field. "I thought I'd be landing near a dig in progress. I had no idea the field was so close to your home, Collins. Do you know what's going on here? Where is everyone?"

Daniel shook his head. "I'm as surprised as you to find it completely cleared today. They must have vacated early this morning. I didn't know you had an interest in archaeology, Mr. Braden."

With one hand resting at his hip—which inadvertently exposed the shoulder holster—Garin swept his gaze across the grounds, which had been swiftly dug back in and covered over with the sod removed weeks earlier. It was a shoddy job. Daniel was surprised the crew had not taken their time to return the land to its original condition. If not Slater, Wesley Pierce had certainly come off as more responsible.

"I own the company that is funding this dig. NewWorld," Garin said. "I got a call from Wesley Pierce last night. He's not around?"

"I haven't talked to Wesley since Saturday night. And my understanding was that Frank Neville had commandeered this dig. Pierce was hanging around to be stubborn."

"Is that so?"

"You look as though that is news to you, Mr. Braden. The

site has been under Neville's supervision for a couple of weeks now—at least, the one dig. Not sure what exactly they were looking for. Far as I know Pierce's camp found a spear shard and some bones."

"What about the other camp? They find anything?"

"Not that they'd reveal to anyone. They've kept tight security and have been causing a bit of trouble, if you ask me. People have been disappearing. Trucks running at odd hours of the night."

The imposing man ran a palm over his goatee. He looked angry and Daniel knew he was not a man to upset. In his line of business he dealt with some major players. He respected them all until they gave him reason not to.

"Did Pierce mention anything to you about diamonds?" Garin asked.

Daniel shoved his palms into his front pants pockets and shrugged. "No, sir."

"You ever hear about diamonds being found in this part of the country?"

"As a matter of fact…" Daniel knew he could trust the man with most any information, good, bad or illegal. He'd dealt with him a time or two. The man was a closed book. "Me mum found a tiny bit of rough a few weeks ago. I think it was what attracted Neville to the dig. Probably thought he could find more. I could have told him there are no diamond mines in Ireland. It was a fluke what me mum found."

"Sizable?" Garin's dark eyes squinted against the sun.

"Five carats, maybe more. But there was a noticeable crack that runs half the length. Would reduce the value by tens of thousands, I'm sure. You want to take a look at it?"

The man considered it for a few seconds. "No, Collins, let your mother keep the stone. I know she's a collector."

"She'll keep it tucked on her shelf until she dies. She's not

in the market to sell it. But I understand it would belong to
NewWorld—"

"I won't mention it to anyone if you don't."

"Deal. So, you interested in a tug of wine? My home is an
amble away."

"Always interested in what you're pouring, Collins." Garin
walked alongside Daniel as he headed north toward his land.
"How has the trade been treating you?"

"Well. Always well. I stay busy. Not a thing to complain
about."

"Good. I like to hear when a man is happy with his work.
It so rarely occurs in this day and age." He scanned over his
shoulder, taking in the dig site again. "I need to find Wesley
Pierce and learn what's gone on with the dig. This doesn't
feel right, Collins."

"If he's not on to a new job, he might be in to Cork to
visit the girl who wandered off and got lost for a few days.
She stumbled back to camp babbling about the fair folk and
looking pretty wild when they found her. I've got a Jeep you
can borrow."

"That would be excellent."

The two trod the ground at a quick pace. Daniel found he
had to increase his strides to keep up.

"You know that Michael Slater fellow supervising the other
camp?" Daniel asked.

"No, but I'll be checking him out. Anyone else in the area
you think I might like to chat with to learn what's up with
Pierce's camp?"

"Shouldn't think so. Well…there is the Creed woman.
She's a lovely duck, she is."

"Creed?" Garin stopped abruptly and Daniel had to side-
step to avoid a collision. The big man held off a grin at that
action. "Annja Creed?"

"You've heard of her? Oh, sure, it's likely you've seen her on the television. Sexy bit of thing, she is."

"You and I agree on that, Collins. How's she involved?"

"Well, I understand she was in the area to film a segment for her television show. Do you know her?"

"You could say that. Annja, eh?" Garin chuckled. "This trip won't be so dull, after all."

31

Michael Slater found a spot in the parking lot under a sycamore tree and put the Jeep in park. He pushed his sunglasses to the top of his head and glanced at Annja. He had the cool, calm, double-agent act down pat, but she wasn't buying his friendly demeanor. He had no reason to suddenly be nice to her.

"I trust you can look around without bringing too much attention to yourself?" he asked.

"Why the sneak? I'm looking for a friend," she said. "For once I have a legitimate reason to be in the hospital."

"Neville's got men guarding Beth. And if he's taken Eric, the situation will be the same."

"Thanks for the heads-up. If you are in on this, why not tell whoever is in charge of guarding the captives to let Eric go?"

"It's out of my hands, Annja. Actually, your friend was never in my hands in the first place."

That made her wonder. If Slater was working for Neville

had he lost control of his part of the operation? The gunrunning part? If he was MI-6 shouldn't he have Frank Neville under surveillance at all times, and know exactly where the missing men were?

"Do you—"

"The less you know," he cut her off abruptly, "the better. Right?"

She nodded. "As long as you're not holding back information about Eric."

His wince didn't speak well to that one. "Just stay away from Beth Gwillym. Promise me, Annja. You don't have time for that trouble."

She eyed his cell phone. He held it ready to dial. Would he report her to Neville the moment she stepped out of the car? A means to dispose of the nosy TV reporter.

She trusted him. Because she'd run out of options. And part of her believed he just wanted to get her and Eric out of the country and off his back.

"I'll stay out here," he said. "I'm calling the airport and booking a flight for you. You've got ten minutes. After that, I'm coming in after you."

SLATER DIALED REGGIE Marks, the barge captain. Everything was on time. The barge had pulled away from the shore near the dig site and would be at the Kinsale harbor in a few hours. The river was tidal and the high tide came along twice a day. They'd timed this perfectly.

The captain also confirmed the camp was completely vacated after Slater left with Annja. All tents were packed up and the site backfilled. Wesley's body had been picked up and put someplace where a dead body would not raise a lot of questions.

Slater didn't want to know, so he didn't ask.

A call to Neville was answered by one of his bodyguards.

Slater did not like talking to the riffraff. He was given the excuse Neville was indisposed.

Indisposed was such a big word for the IQ-lacking thugs who tailed Neville like a puppy dog.

"We on schedule?" Slater asked gruffly. The bodyguards weren't privy to schedules and time frames, but they liked to think they knew everything.

"Had a dely. The last truck has been detained somewhere north of Kinsale. We'll be tracking that soon as Mr. Neville gets…"

Yeah, whatever. Soon as Neville gets his act together. The man was a small-time arms dealer who had delusions of grandeur and a bad case of ADD. He simply could not stick to the task at hand without seeking other projects. Though Slater had to admit the idea to raid the defunct arms dumps across Ireland had been genius. Neville had arranged a gray deal with a Pakistani contact that MI-6 was also keeping tabs on.

"I'll check in again to ensure the truck is back on track." Slater slapped the phone shut and shoved it in his shirt pocket. He tipped the sunglasses down from his forehead to block the sun.

"Babysitting an arms dealer. Chauffeuring some idiot television host. Who the hell did I piss off to get this bollocks assignment?" he muttered.

But honestly, he didn't mind chasing after Creed. She was nice to look at, yet too smart for *his* own good. She was the type he could work with, and enjoy it. Moral, smart and determined. Focused, too. He sensed she wasn't eager to step on MI-6's toes, but as well, she wasn't about to leave the country without her cameraman. The boy would appreciate her dedication.

When she finally got around to finding him. Which, if

Slater had his way, would take just long enough for the camp back at the river to clear out.

ANNJA ALWAYS STOOD a little taller when in the presence of a nun. She attributed that to growing up in a Catholic orphanage. But if any nun ever heard that she'd once used a rosary to choke a man intent on stabbing her, they'd whip out the ruler and wield it over her knuckles.

She hadn't killed the man, just choked him long enough to knock him out so she could escape whatever dire situation she'd been in at the time. Dire situations were commonplace in her life.

She couldn't deny she thrived on the adrenaline rush.

"You don't have a John Doe?" she asked.

Annja waited, fingers silently tapping the laminate counter, while the woman checked the computer screen. She was nice enough and understood Annja was worried about her friend. She'd described Eric to her and said he'd gotten lost in the forest during an overnight hiking excursion.

"We do have an unidentified man in intensive care, but he's sixty," the nun said. "Have you checked with the gardai? Missing persons are usually reported to them."

"I have." She cringed inwardly. She would, as soon as she got Slater off her tail. The man was intent on getting her out of the country, and he wasn't going to take his eye off her until he did.

Didn't he have better things to do? Like taking down an arms dealer?

He'd said he'd been on the case for six months. It seemed an inordinate amount of time to collect intelligence and arrest an arms dealer. But she hadn't a clue how the operations were done, so she wouldn't question it.

Collecting Eric and hightailing it out of there seemed the best, and safest, bet. Maybe Slater had contacts with the local police force? She hadn't thought of that. That would be her first question when she got back to the Jeep.

"Thanks for looking for me. I'll check the other hospitals in the city," she said, and turned to wander toward the reception lounge.

When Slater had mentioned calling in someone to *clean up* Wesley, Annja knew that didn't mean delivering him to a funeral home for a proper burial. The bad guys never did go in for funeral expenses. She should have stuck around to ensure his body was handled properly. But it would have upset her more, and wasted valuable time.

She wondered now if Wesley had a family, and how they would eventually learn of their son's death. She should make an effort to find them and—what would she explain?

Right now she wasn't sure what she could say to whom. Not without the risk of blowing Slater's cover. She did not want to do that. She'd been admonished more than a few times by Bart for getting too deeply involved in criminal cases that a layman had no right sticking her nose into.

NewWorld would be notified, and they could handle contacting Wesley's next of kin.

A big man in a dark sweatsuit shoved past her so hard, she was slammed palms-first into the wall. The sound of an alarm stopped her from shouting at him. Annja looked down the hallway in the direction he'd come from. Nurses and a few others in white coats rushed into the room she knew was Beth's.

"She's crashing!" someone called.

Crashing?

Tempted to rush toward the room, but sensing her best bet was following the fleeing man with the wide shoulders and an urgent need to be gone from the scene, she took off after him. Down the stairwell she raced but didn't catch him as he opened the door to the first floor.

He charged through a side door marked Patient Drop-off. Dodging a parked red Ferrari with a well-dressed man helping his mother from the car, the thug ran across the street and jumped into the passenger side of a black SUV.

The flash of a gun in the front seat, and the look from the man riding in the backseat, flipped on Annja's intuition switch.

"Neville." It had to be. Who else would want Beth dead? Slater had intimated as much.

Keeping from glancing about for the parking lot where Slater waited, Annja stopped in front of the Ferrari. The SUV didn't pull away from the curb. Whoever sat in the backseat saw her through the blackened window screen.

When the window rolled down, she stepped quickly up to the SUV and leaned down.

"Annja Creed?" the man in the backseat asked.

"You must be Frank Neville." He tilted his head in acknowledgment.

He had dark features and hair, and a goatee framed his narrow face. Menacing dark eyes belied his calm expression. A crisp white business shirt topped off dark trousers. The glint of a diamond cuff link flashed at his wrist. On the seat beside him sat an open laptop computer connected to a cell phone.

"I have been wondering when I'd get to meet the infamous Annja Creed," Neville said. "We need to talk."

"Yes, we do," she replied.

"Get inside."

The window rolled up and the door lock on the opposite side of the SUV popped up. Annja walked around behind the SUV and gripped the door, pausing to consider her options. Slater wasn't going to like this. But he was on the other side of the building, and wouldn't have a clue.

Besides, she didn't need to let Neville know she knew who

Slater was. She wouldn't blow his cover. She just wanted to find Eric. She climbed in the car

The scent of sweet tobacco lingered in the car's interior. Annja impulsively tabbed the window button, but it didn't move down. The driver must have her side locked.

"Drive," Neville said, closing the laptop and shoving it in a leather pocket on the back of the seat before him. The glass partition in the center of the front seat slid noiselessly up to fit against the ceiling. "What are you doing at County General, Miss Creed?"

"I had hoped to find a friend there."

"Did you find him?"

She noted his guess wasn't female. "No. Then I thought I'd look in on another friend. Beth Gwillym."

"She's not your friend." Neville shifted, bracing an elbow on the back of the seat. He was gaunt, yet strapped with muscle like a junkie who did daily crunches in between fixes. "Beth disappeared days before you arrived in Ireland. It's not possible you could have been friends."

"We've chatted online."

"I don't believe that." A tilt of his head stretched the thick muscles bulging at his neck. "You want an honest conversation? Tell me the truth."

"I *am* being honest. I had hoped to find my friend in West County General. The man I traveled here with—Eric Kritz— went missing during a hike through the forest the other night. I thought I'd check the same hospital Beth was in since the manner of their disappearance was similar."

"Is that so? Wandering about the forest popping magic mushrooms?"

"So you've heard about her condition?"

"I make it a point to know certain things. Like things about you. I understand you're with a television program. You should consider gathering a more intelligent crew. Or is that how the Americans operate? Get stoned and party all night?"

"He was forcibly taken," Annja said sharply. She cautioned herself to maintain control of her voice. She wanted to show she wasn't intimidated by Neville's presumed power and presence, but she also couldn't come off as cocky. "If you know so much about everyone, I suspect you may have an idea where I can find Eric. Once I know he's safe, we'll pack our bags and leave the country."

"If I believed that, I'd put you on a flight to the States myself."

"A generous offer."

The SUV turned onto a gravel road. Annja hadn't realized they'd left the city limits. Green pastures and rolling landscape zoomed by the windows. "Where are we headed?"

"I'm checking on items lost in transit. Now, back to this truthful conversation. I don't believe you," Neville said. "So I intend to handle matters using a more tried-and-true method."

"Would that be the same method you used on Wesley Pierce?"

He studied her with emotionless black eyes, his head bobbing slightly as the car rolled over the country road. Annja felt the proverbial spiders crawling up her spine. This was not a man to joke with.

"Just tell me about the LSD," she said. "Why?"

He shrugged. "It wasn't something I'd originally ordered, but it did work well. The barge captain had some lying around and injected the men so they wouldn't be so boisterous. When they started seeing faeries, well…"

"You thought that was a perfect cover."

"Silly, but effective, especially in this part of the country. Ah," he said, glancing ahead, yet not dropping the chill demeanor. "We're here."

Annja looked out the window. A field of sheep grazed to the north and a brisk green hedgerow walled a portion of the south view. Another white delivery truck—no, it was an armored truck—was parked fifty yards beyond the SUV, straddling the makeshift gravel road.

"Get out," Neville ordered.

32

Two bodyguards exited the front of the SUV. Neville waited until Annja got out of the back, then he did so.

The unexpected roadblock sat idling. Neville directed one of his men to check it out.

She'd come this far, and expected she wouldn't get any answers about Eric. But if she could take out the thugs, then she could even the playing field. She knew they weren't going to let her walk away from this. The bullet hole in Wesley's forehead pretty much ensured that.

Neville spat on the ground, then said to the thug standing near him, "Murphy, get rid of her."

Murphy approached her, pushing aside his suit coat to reveal a gun in the shoulder holster. He had no intention of being nice about this, so she wouldn't be, either.

Interestingly enough, the gun was just for show. It appeared he was in the mood for a tussle before the final game. He bent to elbow her aside the hip. Elbowing an opponent was a slick move, but it put the elbower in a vulnerable position, opening him to a counterattack.

Annja dodged a swing from him as he anticipated her move. Jumping high, she cleared his left arm and landed steadily. She summoned the sword to her right hand. The solid weight of it landed her grip. She owned it as much as it owned her.

Swinging wide and putting her weight into it, she slashed the battle sword's blade across the thug's shoulder. He wasn't close enough for the blade to do more than slice the fabric.

Gunfire dispersed the dirt near her feet. Pebbles spattered, pinging Annja's ankles. The thug who had returned to Neville's side prepared to shoot again, but Annja saw Neville gesture for his man to hold off.

"A bloody sword?" the thug facing her down grunted. "Where in the hell?"

"I keep it in my pocket," she said. "I never know when the big boys will want to play."

Annja spun and swung out her right leg, aiming to hit the thug low behind the knee. Bone cracked and he landed on the other knee screaming. Standing over him she swept her sword hand down across the back of Murphy's skull with the hilt. The connection of sword and fist to skull reverberated up her arm and clattered her teeth. She felt like she'd whacked a bowling ball with a stick.

The thug dropped onto hands and knees, but wasn't out. He grabbed her ankle and pulled, upsetting her balance. Swinging, she cut through the back of his coat. Blood misted the air.

She stood over him, an executioner wielding swift death. *You claim power with your sword…It is not your power to own.*

The dream haunted her suddenly, but she would not allow it to alter her focus.

She wasn't about to behead anyone. Annja valued human life. If she could put the thug out of order, that was her first choice. But if he attempted to take her life, she'd do what she had to do. She didn't feel threatened right now. And knowing that Neville held his other dog at bay increased that certainty.

The man wanted her alive. He'd had plenty of opportunities to kill her if he'd wanted to.

A swipe of her blade cut through Murphy's forearm. Flesh and muscle parted and blood oozed from the deep cut. That stopped him from pulling out his gun. The man yowled and cursed her in Gaelic.

Stepping wide and wielding the sword with both hands high at her shoulder, Annja defied him to approach her. From the corner of her eye, she saw Neville on his cell phone. The thug next to him stood with his arms crossed high over his chest.

Murphy kicked the ground, but the dust and dirt didn't spume high enough for her to breathe it in. She swung low, slicing across his shin. That brought him down, begging for her to stop.

"Gun out," she demanded, holding the sword on him.

He gingerly reached in for the gun, and tugged it out by the grip. He set it on the ground before him. She told him to give it a shove. He did, sending it under the SUV.

"Score one for Annja Creed!" Neville shouted. He clapped dramatically and even whistled.

The thug standing next to Neville put his hands to hips to expose his hardware. Annja approached, but he didn't go for the draw. Well-trained thugs were always appreciated.

That didn't mean she was going to drop the sword. She was nowhere near safe standing before the man who had shot Wesley Pierce in cold blood. And after his ridiculous cheering stopped, his grin dropped and his dark brows drew together.

"You're quite an interesting woman," Neville said. "While

you're not smiling for the camera and posing for celebrity skin shots on the internet—"

She would never live that photo down. It was not her photograph. It had been her head Photoshopped onto someone else's body. But now she knew where the man had researched her.

"Annja." Neville rubbed his tattooed wrist. She couldn't get a good look at the tattoo. "You're sticking your nose into the business of people you don't even know."

"And here I thought our conversation on the way here indicated friendship," she said sarcastically. "Where's the other guy?" she asked. "Slater?" No sense in letting Slater take the fall for her actions. Was he still waiting outside the hospital for her? He'd given her ten minutes. He should be swearing a blue streak.

"Slater should be watching you right now instead of leaving the task for me," Neville said. "I believe you've been warned once or twice to leave us alone. I have been beyond tolerant, Annja."

"I noticed your lacking manners when you shot Wesley."

"You see what a hazard you are to me?" He thrust out a hand and the thug put a pistol into his palm. Neville checked the cartridge, slapped it sharply into place, but didn't aim it at Annja. "I can't have you running about telling that information to anyone."

"If you wanted me dead you would have shot me by now."

"Perceptive."

Yes, and she'd done this stand-down against the villain with the gun enough times to know when she had time and when she had best run for her life.

"Tell me, where does a fashionable young television host come by such a big bad sword? You're skilled with it, but is it so practical to get through customs?"

"It's something I picked up at a souvenir shop."

Neville actually grinned. The lift of his dark brows added a devilish effect to his facade.

"Where's Eric Kritz?" she demanded. "He wasn't doing anything wrong. Just out for some silly forest shots. He probably didn't even set foot on your dig."

"The redhead? You don't know? The other crowd got him. I understand they're thick in that forest. People wander in. Some are never seen again. Some are found days later, wandering, babbling about seeing faeries."

"Eric was taken by a man. I have the video proof."

Neville sucked in his cheek, producing a nasty slurping noise. "I'll need that camera, you understand."

"We can trade. Eric for the camera."

"I don't make bargains."

"Then you'll have to shoot me and hope I haven't already passed the video along to the authorities. Or for that matter, reported Wesley Pierce's death."

"Go ahead. I have the gardai on my payroll."

"I thought we were being honest with each other?"

"I am. You haven't seen the police wandering the site, looking as if they're interested in solving any cases, have you?"

Annja didn't allow her jaw to drop, though mentally, it was hanging on the ground. Judging from the rude treatment she received during her phone call to the police the other evening, it was very possible. Corrupt government and city officials were a dime a dozen.

But he didn't have MI-6 on his payroll. She hoped. There was the slightest chance Neville was aware he had a government spook shadowing him. That would keep his actions guarded. He wouldn't risk innocent lives under Slater's watch, would he?

Where *was* Slater? He must have realized by now that she wasn't coming out of the hospital, and had to have gone inside looking for her. He would have seen Beth in cardiac arrest—and then what?

Neville's cell phone rang and he flipped it open to answer.

Annja gripped the sword and eyed the thug flanking Neville. Though he wore dark sunglasses she could feel his gaze slither over her shoulders.

"Yes, we've located the truck just out of Kinsale. You take care of the woman?" Neville eyed her.

He was talking to Slater.

"You lost her?" Neville eyed her and smirked.

If Slater had lied and told Neville he'd put her on a flight, Neville would have immediately known Slater was up to something.

"Yes, check the hospital. She may have stopped there looking for that nosy cameraman. We'll talk later." Neville snapped the cell shut and tucked it in a pocket.

"You're a popular gal, Annja. Everyone wants you." He eyed the truck. "But here's the thing. I need you to do a little job for me. You ever drive an armored truck?"

"Nope."

"It's easy. Just a few more gears than you're used to. You'll pick it up."

"Boss." The bleeding thug leaning against the SUV trunk pointed toward the truck.

Annja spied a man step around the front of the armored vehicle. He exercised the long, rangy stride of confidence. Dressed from head to toe in black, he cradled an AK-47 across his shoulder, the long barrel tilted toward the sky.

In her peripheral vision, more men appeared, spreading ranks out from their leader. She spun and counted ten men total before she turned a complete circle and caught Neville's tense expression.

"Friends of yours?" Annja asked, hoping he'd nod evilly.

"Bandits," Neville hissed under his breath. "Shit."

33

One of the men, obviously the leader, stepped forward from the ranks that had surrounded Annja and Neville and his men. He approached with the rifle barrel held up against his shoulder, displayed as a means to show who had the most firepower. Black pants and a ragged black T-shirt fit a stout, muscular build. A knit, multicolored beret capped scruffy dark hair. Dirt darkened his round face. He looked as if he'd been camping in the bogs for weeks.

Before he got close enough, Annja swept her right hand out and threw the sword under the SUV. She then released it into the otherwhere. She couldn't fight all of them.

"Uniquely entertaining show," the man called. Ten feet from where Annja stood next to Neville, he stopped, hooking the gun over his forearm, barrel pointed at Annja and Neville. He glanced at her. "Hello, luv." To Neville he said, "The bird is talented with the fancy sword. And I suspect none too pleased with her situation if she is having a go at one of your own?"

From his pause, Annja guessed he waited for her to reply that indeed she was looking for new companions. Much as she did not trust Neville, and knew his only intent was to get rid of her, the ragtag crew surrounding them appealed even less. She was better off sticking with three men who wanted her dead as opposed to joining a dozen who may also wish her dead, if not battered and abused before that imminent death.

"Just a little play," she said carefully, keeping her spine straight and legs planted but her knees slightly bent. Ready. "All in good fun."

The leader laughed and cast a glance over his shoulder. Some of the men standing in a defensive chain about their leader chuckled. Each held a rifle or AK-47 aimed on them.

"I see you've located my truck," Neville said.

"Lots of weapons inside that vehicle," the leader said. "Plenty valuable."

"I'm willing to sell if you can pay the price," Neville offered. He stepped forward, beside Annja. The brush of his shirtsleeve across her bare arm unnerved her, and she had to force herself to remain calm before the leader's discerning gaze. "I'll let you have it for ten thousand."

More laughter echoed across the still grounds. Annja's shoulder muscles were knotted tighter than a steel spring. Plotting offense was foremost in her mind. If any one of the men opened fire, she'd head for the SUV where she knew the keys hung in the ignition.

"Feck me, but you've got it wrong." The leader gestured toward the truck. "That. Is my truck." A proud smile beamed at them, cracking the dusty coating at the corners of his eyes. "You cannot sell a man what is already his."

Neville bowed his head and swallowed, fighting aggression, Annja knew. One of his thugs stood by the SUV and was guarded by a gunman wielding an AK-47. The one on the ground was surrounded by three gunmen sporting the same. There wasn't much leverage Neville could command.

Annja wondered what he'd done with the pistol he'd been holding earlier. Knowing the positions of all weapons on the playing field was important. And why hadn't these bandits searched them for weapons?

Finally Neville asked, "And how much are you selling *your* truck for?"

"The truck?" The leader glanced over the dusty white vehicle. An old armored truck painted white and rusting along the wielded seams. "I can let you drive away with it for five thousand." Neville grimaced. The leader stepped forward, closing his distance to Neville by three paces. "But the contents will cost you thirty thousand quid."

"The weapons are barely worth ten thousand," Neville argued. "I'll give you twenty thousand euros for the arms and vehicle."

Bargaining with a dozen armed men? Annja clenched her fingers in a grip but did not call out the sword. If she took out the leader, his men would riddle her body with bullet holes faster than she could shove Neville in front of her as futile cover.

"Are you fat in the head? You're offering euros?" the leader asked. "Have you looked at the currency exchange lately?"

Annja couldn't believe this.

"What kind of businessman do you take me for?" the bandit continued. "You're duping me seventeen percent, mate. I don't like those terms. Do we like those terms, boys?"

A clatter of weapons prepared to fire.

"Do you believe this?" The leader directed at Annja, "Is that how he treats you, luv? Does he take you to the cheap pubs and treat you like you're second class?"

"Okay!" Neville snapped. "I'll pay the thirty thousand. Pounds."

"Ah!" The leader bent forward in exclamation. "The price just went up to fifty thousand. And the bird included." The leader winked at Annja. "You can come along with us, luv. No second-class treatment from me and me boys. Nothing but the best for you. I have jewels. You like jewels?"

"I'm not much into the sparkly stuff. But thanks, anyway," Annja said.

She would not begin to imagine what a man like him would do with her. Any female, for that matter. Just standing close enough to smell him gave her a bone-clattering shiver.

Annja caught Neville's sneer. Was he considering handing her over? She conveyed her most serious "I got you out of trouble" look, but suspected it would do little good.

"I can't let her go," Neville said. "She's my driver."

"Then you'll have to cover the difference in price," the leader said cheerily. "What do you think she's worth? Ten, twenty quid?"

Annja bristled, but remained silent.

"You get your whores rather cheap," Neville said.

"I'm talking thousands, you bastard."

Neville held up his hands near his shoulders. "Your price is too rich for my blood. The weapons are old. They've been sitting in storage for almost a decade. You can have them."

"That is what I had intended from the beginning," the leader replied. He gestured to a man at his side, but then stopped him. Annja followed his gaze across the horizon.

Neville turned to eye the oncoming vehicle. Slater advanced slowly in the Jeep. He couldn't be aware of what was going down, and yet if the man were at all trained in conflict he wouldn't be stupid.

The entire crew of bandits raised their weapons and aimed at the vehicle. Slater stopped and exited slowly, arms held high to show compliance. The sun flashed on his amber sunglasses lenses.

"He's my man," Neville said.

"The man who was supposed to keep an eye on your truck?" The leader snorted out another belly-bending fit of laughter.

A gunman met Slater and with a shove of his assault rifle into Slater's side escorted him to stand beside Annja. Slater played along and did not retaliate for the abuse.

"What's going on?" Slater said to Neville, loud enough so all could hear. "I got your call. These men don't look like the receivers we hired."

Good play, Annja thought.

"They've taken control of the truck," Neville said, "and want to sell it back to me for fifty thousand."

"Don't forget the bird," the leader said with a wink at Annja.

She inched closer to Slater until her arm nudged his. It wasn't a signal; it was merely a means of connecting with the one side she felt a little safer standing next to. Not that either side had her best interest in mind.

"Fifty thousand is steep," Slater said. He glanced to his boss. "You buying?"

"Forgot my checkbook," Neville said. "I don't need this batch. They're substandard and rusty. Half are riddled with sand and dirt."

"Well, now." Slater spoke loudly at the leader's rallying signal to his men. "We shouldn't be so hasty. A little sand never interfered with the operation of a Kalashnikov. Give it a shake and clean it once in a while, and you've got a fine weapon. And just so you know, I *did* bring the checkbook."

Annja caught the narrow look Neville cast at Slater. He hadn't a clue what his right-hand man was up to. Nor did he appear amused. So why was Slater taking the reins?

"You want me to sign the check?" Slater's question was directed toward the leader. "Like the man said, the guns are probably dirty. It'll be difficult to sell them."

"Then how will you sell them?"

"We've got established partners who are willing to take less-than-desirable weapons on occasion because they know we'll deliver the top goods when requested. So, is it a sale or not?"

The leader glowered at Annja.

"She's not included," Slater said quickly. "I'll put in an extra five thousand pounds to cover the loss to you."

Five? Annja clenched her fist.

The leader, noticing her umbrage, laughed. Then he sobered quickly. "No checks." He spat on the ground at Slater's feet. "I'm not much for financial institutions."

"I imagine not. So let me show you what I'm willing to offer instead of paper."

Taking command of the show, Slater slowly lowered his right hand. Annja counted the pairs of eyes leveled on his action—too many for her to take out single-handedly, and even if Neville were to grow a spine and Slater backed her up, they'd be roadkill in a matter of seconds.

"It's in my pocket. I'm just going to take it out slowly," he cautioned. He lowered his tone and muttered, "Trust me." Annja sensed that was more for her benefit than anyone else.

At that moment, her opinion of Michael Slater altered. It moved from the dirt beneath her boots to right around her ankles. He was trying to keep it all together, with as little collateral damage as possible. And doing so surrounded by a band of bloodthirsty bandits would test any man's courage.

Reaching into his left breast pocket, Slater drew out something that produced a big grin on the leader's face. His men

chattered and nodded approval. The rough diamond caught
the sun as Slater held it between two fingers.

"Where the hell—" Neville said.

"Not from our cache," Slater muttered out the corner of
his mouth. "Found it on Pierce's body."

Annja tightened her jaw to keep from wincing. The man
had ransacked a dead man's body?

"Nice size, yes? Estimated cut will yield up to ten carats.
Worth a hundred Gs easily," Slater said. "It's grade A,
flawless."

The leader held out his hand and Slater slowly placed the
stone in his palm.

When he'd had the time to assess the diamond's value, and
when he'd gained those particular skills, was news to Annja.
On the other had, if MI-6 was really involved, he could have
met with an expert and had the stone appraised.

"It's a pretty stone," Slater said as the sunlight flashed
in pink and blue on the surface of the smooth sides. "Much
easier to sell than a truckload of weapons. Hell, you can go
buy yourself six truckloads with that rock."

The bandit leader nodded once. He tossed the stone in the
air and caught it smartly. "You would pay six times the price
I am asking for a truckload of rusty old guns?"

Slater glanced to Neville. "My boss has a client waiting
for a shipment. You're forcing us to make the sacrifice."

"Heh. That is what I do best."

The leader studied the diamond again. It would be easy for
a lowlife like him to sell a rough diamond. Unless he owned
a suit and had connections with the rich and famous, it was
the cut stones he'd have trouble unloading, Annja knew.

In the diamond trade, it mattered little where the rough
had come from, only that it could produce a valuable cut
stone. The moment it passed from a thief's hands to someone
licensed to deal in diamonds the stone became legitimate.

Diamond dealers rarely traced the pedigree of a stone. She knew that was the reason blood diamonds funded a staggering portion of the warfare in the world.

The leader cast a look at her, waggling his brow.

Annja shook her head, refusing a worse fate than being left with Neville.

"We have a deal," the bandit said. "But I do not like to walk away without a bonus."

"Bonus?" Neville asked sharply.

The leader aimed his weapon at the truck. One bullet deflated the rear tire. He nodded and hooked his gun over a shoulder. Turning, he walked off without another word.

The surrounding bandits maintained position until their leader had descended behind the rise of low blue gorse, then they left in shifts, until finally the last disappeared as stealthily as they had appeared.

"Seriously?" Annja asked Slater. "You stole a diamond off a dead man?"

He cast her a droll look. "He wasn't going to use it."

"Nice timing, Slater." Neville slapped him on the shoulder. "But we didn't need those arms." Still, Neville nodded, apparently pleased the situation had been solved without his blood being shed.

Slater gripped Annja's wrist. "Now, what are we going to do with the woman?"

"Like I said, she's my driver." Neville nodded at his thug, silently commanding him to take Annja by the arm. Slater handed her over, giving no indication her recent decision to trust him had been valid.

"You're going to let her drive to the warehouse?" Slater shook his head fiercely. "We don't need another piece of collateral damage. Leave her here. She can walk to wherever it was she came from."

Neville stepped up to Slater. Though he was half a foot

shorter the man commanded Slater's attention. "You were supposed to get rid of her."

Annja caught Slater's angry glare. He was trying to keep her out of this, but she had forced his hand.

"I don't snuff women," Slater said. "And she's a television personality. People know where she is and they will know if she goes missing. It'll be bad for business. You ask me, whoever thought nabbing the cameraman was a good idea should have been thinking more clearly."

All of the men exchanged steely glances. Annja couldn't determine who had been the actual kidnapper. Then she recalled Neville had mentioned the barge captain.

"Then she comes along," Neville said. "We need someone to drive the truck."

"I'll drive—"

Neville stepped in front of Slater as he headed toward the truck. "No, you help the lady up into the driver's seat. I want you to bring up the rear in the Jeep."

Neville exerted his power and Slater was forced to concede or raise questions from his boss he'd rather not answer.

Annja did not want to get into the truck. Whatever waited at the end of the drive might not include her, breathing. But what if Eric was there?

"I need to know for certain Eric will be released if I do this," she said.

"He's…out of it right now," Neville said. "Unable to talk."

"High on LSD, just like Beth?"

Neville shook his head. "Beth was a mistake."

"Why didn't you kill her right away?"

"I am not a cruel man, like you want to believe, Annja."

She mentally rolled her eyes. Why did the bad guys always think by not pulling the trigger they were doing good, or at the very least, a favor?

"There are others missing, as well," she prompted.

"A few people got in the way. I took measures into hand. Now, I do love this chat. It's so rare an intelligent woman intrigues me. But I want to get rolling before the sun sets."

"You think this truck will get far with a flat tire?"

"Got it under control." Neville gestured to his uninjured thugs, who shuffled toward the back of the truck and began to release the spare tire from the undercarriage. "Slater, why don't you get Murphy and Miss Creed situated while we wait."

Slater slapped a hand on Annja's shoulder. She kicked his shin, setting him off balance, and managed to swing under his bulk before he landed on the ground.

A gun barrel stabbed her under the chin. Neville helped her to stand. "Play nice, Annja. You won't do your friend any good if you're dead."

She nodded and put up her hands in placation. A shove from the pistol pointed her toward the truck cab. Slater slapped a hand on her shoulder and shoved her forward, but didn't release her.

"Drive," he muttered, so others could not hear. "Follow Neville to the warehouse. Whatever you do, don't get out of the cab. These vehicles have been outfitted specially. The windshield should be bulletproof."

"Should be?"

"You are a bloody pest," he hissed. One final shove put her beside the truck cab, "Open it!"

Annja stepped and opened the door. A body fell from the driver's seat. She jumped to the side to avoid getting plowed to the ground by the dead weight.

"Martin," Slater directed. "Get this thing out of the way."

Martin, who had put the spare tire in position, walked over and gripped the driver's body under both arms. Half the skull was gone. Annja guessed he'd taken a high-caliber shot at close range.

"Hop in, Miss Creed," Slater said.

Steeling herself to put the dead man out of her thoughts worked only so long as it took to look over the spray of blood across the back of the beaded wooden seat cover. Small chunks of skull bone and flesh glinted with sunlight.

Slater invaded her space so quickly Annja didn't realize he'd cuffed her left wrist to the steering wheel with a plastic zip tie until it was too late.

"I can't sit in here with this…" She swallowed.

He pressed his bulk along the length of her body and leaned in to wipe across the seat back with his sleeve.

"You are far too comfortable with dead bodies and their parts," she muttered.

"Comes with the territory. Now play nice if you want to get out of this alive, got that?"

"Is that offer still good to put me on a flight out of the country?"

"Expired when you decided to become a royal pain in my arse."

"Get away from me," she snapped. "That's good enough."

He jumped down and Annja settled onto the seat. It was so large she didn't need to sit all the way back against the wet beads.

She wrestled with the zip tie. "I'm not going to jump out of a moving vehicle," she said.

"I certainly hope not." Slater shrugged off his suit coat, the sleeve thick with human remains, and tossed it to the ground.

She didn't understand why Neville needed her to do this when his thug could easily drive the truck. And there'd be no body count that way. Though it was a great way to keep her under thumb, as he'd explained. And the bad guys were always less rational than they believed themselves to be. He probably thought this was a grand plan.

"The directions are programmed in the GPS. But the SUV will drive ahead of you so you won't get lost," Neville explained as he approached the truck. "Don't need you diverting off course. Now I'll let Martin give you a little instruction on driving a truck and then we'll send you off. Good day, Miss Creed. Happy to have you on board."

34

Neville and his entourage drove a quarter mile ahead of Annja. The SUV didn't push beyond thirty kilometers an hour. She knew passing them on this narrow road and taking off for freedom was out of the question.

Annja wanted to follow Neville to the warehouse, or wherever it was he was leading her. If the slightest chance existed that she'd find Eric at their destination, she couldn't pass it up.

She'd gotten the hang of the ride, and could manage steering without twisting her wrist. But a sharp turn caused the thin plastic zip tie to bite into her flesh.

Summoning the sword into her grip, she carefully clasped the blade and worked it under the plastic band. The zip tie severed and she dropped the blade into the otherwhere. Freedom obtained.

Now, to follow the bad guys to their lair.

Ten minutes into the drive, Annja's cell phone rang.

She tugged it from her pocket and checked the caller ID. "Garin?"

Sucking in her upper lip, she vacillated on whether to answer. Whatever the man wanted was never a simple "Want to do lunch?"

On the other hand, sometimes it was an invite to dine, in a country at least two thousand miles from her current location. She appreciated his intent to seduce her—because that is what it was, a drawn-out seduction. But just because *she* knew it would never happen didn't mean she had to shatter the man's hopes.

The front of the truck swerved dangerously close to the gravel shoulder. Gripping the wheel, she realigned the truck on the road with a squeal of the tires.

She checked the side mirror. Slater, behind her, hadn't reacted. The Jeep remained four car lengths away.

"No time for chatting." She tossed the phone onto the passenger seat. He could leave a message.

Though she could handle the stick shift on the gravel roads, she had to keep a keen eye out for bumps and stray turtles. And sheep. And keep far enough behind Neville. The SUV stirred up the dust.

Her phone jingled again.

"No time for this, Garin. Not unless you can swoop in and—"

The man *was* skilled at rescue operations. He'd had a hand in helping her out of a few tight spots. Not that Annja felt she needed to be rescued at this very moment. Slater was close in her wake. Bringing another person into the mix might only spook Neville, and ultimately, she may never learn where Eric was being kept.

She let the call go to voice messaging.

The green fields segued to city grays and tarmac as their cavalcade entered the outskirts of Kinsale. The delivery truck bumped across a railroad track, the warning horn from the engine announcing an oncoming train.

Moments later, Annja's phone rang and, thinking it was Garin again, she ignored it. It rang unceasingly and she finally slapped it open. "Yes?"

"Annja, I've been cut off."

"Slater?" She checked the side mirror. No sign of his Jeep. "What's up? How'd you get my number?"

"Never mind. I wasn't able to beat the train. I think it'll put me about five, ten minutes behind you. There's a harbor in Kinsale that Neville has been accessing for the river drop-offs. First, you'll stop at a warehouse to load more weapons."

"If Eric is there—"

"I know, you intend to save the day. Don't be stupid, Annja. The man shot Wesley in cold blood. You think he's going to let you live after you arrive at your destination?"

"No. And I'm not being stupid. I just wasn't given the 'run now and seek freedom' option."

"Annja, listen to me. Follow Neville to the warehouse, but don't drive inside. Once he's got you inside, your number is up. Stay outside, you hear me?"

She nodded.

"I can't hear you."

"Okay. Stay inside the truck. Dangerous inside the warehouse. Windows are bulletproof. What are you going to do? You can't blow your cover."

"I don't intend to. I'll figure something out."

"Figure something out? You don't have a plan?"

"Trust me, Annja."

Since no one else was making the same offer, she accepted. "I'll meet you in the city."

THE SUV PULLED into a warehouse at the edge of the small harbor town. Annja suspected it wasn't large enough to be a major shipping port and probably catered to fishing boats, maybe the odd yacht or two. That was a lot more convenient for running guns than a larger port, which would employ a port authority to check all incoming and outgoing shipments.

She noted the warehouse was set apart from what looked like the city proper. It was private, and there were no residential houses in the immediate vicinity.

The warehouse sat at the bottom of a hill that blocked direct view of the sea. The harbor was ahead, flocks of white seagulls her clue. The clear blue sky looked too perfect for this moment.

She slowed the truck to a stop before the corrugated steel warehouse door that slowly rose on pulleys. Neville's vehicle drove inside and parked. The man got out and shook hands with a waiting man.

A couple of men who were already in the warehouse rushed to the SUV to assist. Murphy, clutching his injured arm, was helped out. He flipped off Annja, and unstrapped his gun.

Neville signaled with a wave of his hand for her to drive forward and park to the right next to the steel loading ramp. Normally a truck such as she drove would back inside to be loaded. She was facing forward.

And she didn't intend to drive any farther into the lion's den. Shifting into park, Annja scanned the side mirrors for the cavalry. It had been five minutes; Slater had to be close behind.

An angry bark accompanied a rap on the truck's steel door. Annja waved the thug off and locked the door.

She knew it was a risk to consider leaving the vehicle. "I didn't exactly promise to sit tight," she muttered.

Slater was a trained professional. He had been working with Neville for months, and knew the man's foibles and modus operandi. He obviously knew when to do exactly as he'd been commanded, or when to wing it to save the day, even when Neville would sooner jump ship and abandon his profits to bandits.

A quick count tallied four men besides the wounded Murphy and Neville. All were armed. Neville didn't appear to be one to get his hands dirty. He just pulled out a gun and shot anyone who pissed him off. And he had no reason to keep her alive from this point on.

Could Eric be somewhere inside the warehouse?

She surveyed the loading ramp that angled up to a wooden dock. It was stacked with the same wooden boxes she'd seen being hauled to the river the other night. Weapons and ammunition set to be loaded into the truck she sat in—along with the guns already inside—and then driven to the harbor, was her guess.

She did not want to participate in transporting illegal arms to be shipped off to some war zone.

Could this shipment be legal? There were so many variations and fine print to the arms-dealing trade. Annja knew there were three types of deals. White, gray and black. White deals, dominated by governments and weapons manufacturers, were considered above the table, completely legit. The black deals, freelancer central, were strictly under-the-table and illegal.

It was the appropriately named gray trades that were the most confusing and hardest to label good or bad. They involved clandestine deals made by freelancers on behalf of governments.

The windshield cracked. Annja jumped. The glass did not shatter but the crackling continued out from the initial hit, spidering to all corners of the window.

Neville stood in front of the delivery truck, his pistol aimed for a second shot. Bulletproof generally meant no cracks, at least not as much as this windshield was cracking. The vehicle was old. She had maybe two or three more shots before the bullets pierced the window.

"I can't just sit here," she said.

Unlocking the door and opening it, Annja gave it a kick. The thug standing outside took the steel door in the jaw and stumbled backward. Arms splaying, he didn't drop his weapon, but it clattered as he hit the concrete.

Annja summoned the sword to hand. In the compact truck cab it stretched out over the passenger seat. She knew what she was doing. And she had been given this power; she was not assuming a thing. The dream could not have been portentous. This was her fight to own.

Annja leaped out into the fray.

35

Thug number one lay sprawled on the loading-dock floor. He was out cold after Annja had clocked him in the jaw with the truck door. He still held the pistol in hand, which she had time to kick across the floor. It landed under the left front tire of the truck.

She now only had three thugs to deal with. Murphy was standing, but she wasn't too worried about his ability to fight with his wounds. And Neville remained an amused bystander.

Slashing the sword before her soughed the air crisply. The battle sword was nothing fancy, but it did hold a fine edge and could cut through flesh with ease. She had no compunctions about doing just that if any approaching attacker threatened her life.

From the back of the warehouse where the loading platform stood four feet high, two men in sandy-colored overalls charged at her. They didn't pull out guns. As they got closer to Annja, they synchronized their moves. Arms stretched out, they clasped the forearm of the other to form a bar between them.

Sword blade upright, Annja pumped her arms and ran toward the men. Three feet from the oncoming battering ram, she leaped, did a summersault in the air and came down on bended knee behind the two surprised thugs. As possessor of the sword she'd learned a few impressive moves.

Lunging up to stand and swinging the sword in warning toward the thugs, she turned, bringing her sword arm down and behind her as she faced Neville.

He crossed his arms high on his chest, his gun tucked in his waistband. A shrug silently conveyed the message "I'm watching. Show me your best."

At the moment, Annja detected no danger from him and so focused on the three remaining deterrents to her continued breathing. Behind Neville the loading platform stretched along the wall; one end was connected to a steel roller ramp used to slide boxes into a waiting truck, the other end stopped at the wall. On the second floor, at the top of a stairway that hugged the brick wall, an office door caught her eye.

Annja made a run for it and jumped onto the platform. If Eric was here, he was behind that second-floor door. She spun to sight her opponents as a pistol cracked. The sound was off. The weapon hadn't fired correctly. And it hadn't come from Neville.

The third thug who hadn't yet approached her yelped and dropped a pistol near his feet. Gripping his bloody hand he swore in Gaelic. The gun must have misfired, which was virtually impossible with a well-made weapon. If those were the kinds of arms Neville was selling, Annja wondered how he could keep up the business and not bring countless unsatisfied customers after him with blood in their eyes.

She didn't have time to struggle with the right and wrong of the quality of product offered in illicit arms sales. The two thugs who had failed to corral her earlier moved to opposite ends of the platform. The dock thundered under her feet as they clambered up in pursuit.

She met the first, but the clatter of the steel platform distracted her and she lost her timing. He charged into her body with a grunt, fearless of the sword. The impact loosened her grip on the sword. Even with it she couldn't fight effectively when the man was so close. He punched her in the gut. Her shoulders hit the corrugated steel wall. The wall clattered like close thunder.

Releasing the sword into the otherwhere, Annja used the fact she was pinned by the shoulders to lift her knees and jam her heels into the thug's shins. The hard rubber soles of her boots scraped down his shins, but his heavy overalls protected his skin from damage.

A forehead to his chin reverberated in Annja's skull. Her opponent released her long enough to receive an open-palmed smack aside his jaw. Following quickly with another palm-heel jab to his ribs, she kept the punches coming, keeping her elbows in and close, and head down.

She pressed her opponent backward against the wall— and was grabbed from behind. Two iron-strong arms banded about her shoulders and upper chest. Sucking in a breath, Annja kicked from her standing position, pushing backward, but she couldn't topple her aggressor.

Calling the sword to hand, she slashed it across the other thug's chest. A diagonal red line stained his overalls. He gripped his chest, not believing that he'd been cut.

Suddenly Annja's equilibrium altered. The thug holding her lifted her off the ground. Her body tilted too far off balance. Wrapped in her opponent's grasp, together they teased gravity—then fell.

The thug shouted. They both landed hard on the floor. Jaws clacking, Annja struggled against the sudden blackness that grasped at her consciousness. Wheezing in a breath of oxygen, she countered the near-blackout.

Thankful for the padded landing, she pushed off from the thug's barrel chest. He was out cold. Standing, she turned, sword in hand, just in time to catch the other man as he leaped from the platform and into her embrace.

With no time to swing, she sent the sword clattering across the floor while she wrangled with the man who was bleeding profusely from his chest. Bending her knees would center her gravity and make the catch easier, but the man was too big for it to matter. Her muscles gave way and Annja dropped, twisting, so the man would be beneath her when they landed on the floor.

Not allowing him time to think through his next move, Annja gripped his head on both sides, grabbing hair, and slammed the back of his skull into the floor. The first hit made him blink and groan. With the second he stopped moving at all.

She sensed someone rush toward her as she knelt over the fallen man. It was Murphy, and he was injured, but determined. She wouldn't have time to stand and meet his attack with the sword, so Annja rolled off the man's body and looked up to find Murphy's feet swept out from under him.

Slater locked his arm across the man's neck. Just when it looked like he'd snap his neck, he instead applied pressure to both sides of his neck, focusing on the carotid, reducing the man to unconsciousness.

The subtle *snick* of a gun safety sliding off alerted Annja. It wasn't a Walther P99.

"God, I love a woman who can fight," Neville said. His aim was squarely for her forehead. "It really turns me on."

Annja scrambled to her feet. Unsure of whose side Slater would stand on, she backed toward the truck, keeping herself in the middle between Slater and Neville.

"Whoa, Frank!" Slater stepped before Annja in a protective stance. That answered her question. "What's going on?"

"I can ask you the same." Neville waved his gun at Slater. "What's with the hero stuff? Fighting on the wrong side?"

"I'm trying to keep down the casualty count."

"You weren't hired for that."

"No, but I was hired for discretion. And if you had kept the barge captain out of the land operation, we wouldn't even have this problem right now because no one would have been kidnapped to get them out of the way."

"I'm disappointed in you, Slater. Taking the woman's side?"

"You know whose side I'm on." Slater avoided eye contact with Annja. He shrugged his shoulders and touched the gun at his side, but didn't take it out of the holster. "Can't be murdering innocent women now, can we?"

"I can, and I will, if that is what is required from one with a spine. Christ, no wonder this operation is going tits up. But I will admit, you're right. Miss Creed is far too interesting to dispose of in such an unoriginal manner. Bullets are so passé."

Neville paced the floor in front of the loading platform, surveying his fallen men. "I'll say it again, she's quite the talent. Amusing to watch her take out my men so easily. I won't even ask about the sword. I have a feeling that falls somewhere along the lines between mysterious caches of diamonds and the other crowd."

Annja breathed in, lifting her chest. Hands at her hips, she maintained a ready stance. Slater was not breaking his cover, which could put her at the disadvantage. But he had protected her so far; she wasn't willing to give up on him yet.

"Where is Eric?" she asked.

"You—" Neville pointed the gun at her while he spoke

"—don't get to talk. You," he said, switching his focus to Slater, "had better do some fast talking."

"Just preventing collateral damage," Slater said.

"You always have my back, Slater. You've been a valuable asset to my team. But we can't let her stroll out of here now. She's seen everything."

"Miss Creed can keep her mouth shut."

"Are you going to see to that?"

"If I have to." Slater looked at her, but she didn't react.

"You've done a lousy job of it so far." Neville cocked the trigger. "I think you and the woman have a thing going on."

"That is ridiculous," Slater said.

"You don't say that very convincingly." Neville eyed Annja up and down, his reaction more disgust than interest. "The only reason you would protect her is if you're involved with her. Honestly, I don't care who you screw on your own time, Slater. But in this situation, your extracurricular shagging has caused me one hell of a headache."

"We are not—" Annja began.

"Shut up," Neville barked at Annja. "I know how to handle this. We're going for a ride, the three of us. I'm tired of you shadowing me, Slater. I should have done this days ago."

Neville nudged one groaning thug with his foot. The man managed to pull himself up to stand. He was the least damaged of the men, and quickly retrieved a rifle and magazine from a nearby box. He directed Annja and Slater to the SUV Neville had arrived in.

"Annja," Slater whispered as they approached the car, "you were supposed to wait inside the cab until the cavalry arrived."

"Did you take a look at my final resting place?"

He glanced over at the damaged windshield. "Bloody hell. Sorry. You okay?"

"Sure. Did you blow your cover?"

"Let's hope not."

36

Neville did the honors. He handcuffed Annja to a rusty length of chain with links so thick they looked designed to securely hold tugboats. It would definitely keep her in place. Slater, too.

The chain ran through an iron loop, attached to a five-hundred-pound iron anchor. On the other side of the loop, Slater grimaced as Neville's man secured his wrists. He hadn't struggled since Neville had taken them in hand. Nor had he given any clue to Annja that the cavalry might be on their way. But she could hope. Wouldn't MI-6 protect its own?

What was going on in Slater's brain? And why did she need to know so desperately? It wasn't going to help her escape this situation. Focus was required.

"You've been nothing but trouble since day one," Slater said to Annja, loud enough for all to hear. It would serve him to keep up the act. MI-6 did not need one of their own revealed, even if he was two steps and a forced leap away from death. "Should have put a bullet in your brain when I first had the thought."

Neville patted the iron anchor that two thugs had dragged down the wooden dock from its perch on a concrete platform. "The pretty ones always are the most difficult to kill. More fun to shag, though, eh?"

Slater did not react to Neville's prodding.

"You had potential, Slater. Your work was appreciated. Until you tried to screw me over. Any last words?" He patted Slater's chest and drew out the folded sunglasses from his chest pocket.

"Not the Ray-Ban's, mate," Slater protested. "Those are my best pair."

"You think it's going to be bright where you're going, Slater?"

"I can hope."

With a chuckle, Neville returned the sunglasses to Slater's pocket and slapped his cheek. "Any brightness will be from the flames, mate. Drop them!" he said.

Slater lunged near Annja's cheek, making it look as if he'd lost his balance. "Don't panic," he whispered.

A thug shoved him aside and put all his weight into pushing on the heavy iron anchor.

Not panic? Piece of cake. A gang of gunrunners were going to push them off the dock and into the harbor. The drop may not be deep this close to shore—in fact, Annja hoped it was a nice long sloping incline—but it wasn't the depth that would kill her, it would be the lack of air and her inability to breathe like a fish.

Annja was an above average to excellent diver. She could hold her breath a long time. No world record breaker, though. Slater, military trained, should be able to outlast her.

But it wouldn't matter with the handcuffs binding them together.

Another thug joined in and the anchor wobbled. It wasn't going to slide easily across the warped wood dock, and while they rocked on it to get momentum, Annja teased the idea of kicking one of them into the water. It wouldn't help her plight. If the drowning plan didn't go over, she suspected a couple bullets to the backs of their heads would serve, much as Neville thought it passé.

She gave Neville the evil eye. "Don't hurt Eric. He's an innocent."

"Like you are innocent of snooping and putting yourself in my way? You know too much about our operation, as does your friend."

"He's just a kid. If you've kept him drugged, he'll never remember a thing." Appealing to the man's lacking compassion was a losing battle. But his sense of freedom was another thing. "Eric's father financed our trip here. You'll have him on your ass if you don't send his son home in pristine condition. If you don't go to jail for arms dealing, then kidnapping and murder tend to alter a man's choice of Armani to prison orange."

"I'll take that into consideration. See you around, Miss Creed. Mr. Slater."

Her wrists were jerked roughly. The anchor wobbled onto its curved base and the eye of the iron weight tilted toward the sky.

Annja sucked in her breath. Her heartbeats thudded heavily. She'd been in worse situations. She'd once survived a tsunami in India. She'd been buried under tons of sand while hiding in an Egyptian tomb. She'd battled monsters, run away from natural disasters, fought bloodthirsty machine-gun-wielding pirates, and somehow she always managed to walk away.

She could do this.

The heavy weight rolled over the end of the dock, splintering the wood. Annja stumbled on a piece of serrated wood as she was literally dragged forward. Airborne, she tugged on the chain, but realized it would only pull Slater closer to the anchor.

"Hold your breath," he said.

The anchor broke the impact as it crashed into the water's surface. But it also served to suck down the water and created a sort of cup of air. Not good.

Annja swung her legs forward. Slater did the same. Her hiking boots hit an arm of the anchor, and her entire skeleton felt as if it was jerked inside its skin, as if she were being skinned alive. A sharp wave of cold water hit her lower back and shoved her forward. She collided with Slater's chest, but he shoved her away. It had been an instinctive reaction; his body had been jerked from hers without volition.

It was difficult to inhale air as she was being sucked down in a gush of bubbles and rapidly moving water. The dark water and millions of air bubbles trilling about like champagne distorted her vision. She lost all concept of where Slater was until his foot kicked her shin. The stinging connection almost made her release her air.

Her right fingers clasped, wanting to hold the sword, but with her wrists cuffed, it would only be an impediment.

Then she realized what he was doing—Slater was tangling his leg in hers.

So he could keep her close? The chain would do that. Or to wrangle her into some kind of death grip to make it all go faster? Whatever he had planned, she let it happen. If he harbored one final iota of malice against her, now was a bad time to try for revenge.

And then he grabbed her shoulders—with both hands. He was free. Pulled downward, arms first and body following Annja, Slater clung to her. He shoved the chain into her hands.

She grabbed a twist of links. Though wet, the built-up rust

on the iron cut into her palms. They had stopped descending. The anchor must have landed on the bottom, but it could still slide down the incline. Looking up, the surface glittered silver; they were no more than twenty feet under.

Slater fussed at her wrists, wrenching the cuffs painfully across her bones. He must be picking the handcuff locks. It was the only thing that made sense. Annja held the chain that would keep them weighted and prevent them from floating to the surface.

Air rapidly soughed from her lungs. A burn sizzled at the top of her lungs, clambering up her throat. Her temples pounded, as did her heart. The water wanted to cave in her skull and suck down her insides.

In the next instant, her right hand was free. Slater wrapped his legs about her waist to keep them together. With a tug at the chain, she took his signal and dropped the heavy metal links. They floated upward. Her left hand was still cuffed and she dragged the length of heavy chain with her.

Grabbing her hand, Slater tugged her sideways. They kicked through the murky water. He aimed for under the dock. It wouldn't be wise to surface out in the open if Neville and his gang were still around.

As her head broke the surface, Slater shoved a palm over her mouth. Vision blurred by water droplets, she focused on his shaking head. He put a finger to his lips. *Don't make noise.* He pointed upward.

Careful not to sputter and gulp in air, Annja treaded water. The heavy chain pulled her down until Slater grabbed the links, reducing the weight. Overhead, she eyed the shadows moving over the slatted dock boards. They'd stuck around to make sure their quarry didn't surface. She could only be relieved they hadn't fired a couple of rounds into the water to ensure their dirty deed had been successful.

Water spilling from her mouth in dribbles, Annja inhaled

too quickly and sputtered. Slater pressed his hand hard over her mouth. She understood he was trying to protect them both, but this wasn't helping. Wrenching his hand away from her mouth, she gasped as quietly as she could manage.

He made the okay sign, and questioned her with his eyes. She nodded affirmatively.

Slater put a sure hand to her back and tugged the chain. It helped her to stay above water. Together they moved toward the shore slowly, riding the residual waves from the anchor drop.

They followed the overhead footsteps. Voices spoke, but Annja only picked up parts of the conversation for the slap of water against the seaweed-slimed moorings cracked like fire blazing in a pit.

"…the warehouse…"

"…destroy it, and those inside. Let's clear out."

"…out of this country by…"

"Pick up the EUCs, and get out of here."

Annja's face went underwater. Slater lifted her by the arm. She hadn't realized how tired she'd become. Her legs felt like jelly. Her gut ached. The shore was still thirty feet away.

"You're not okay," he whispered. "Put your arms around my neck."

A car engine purred into gear and took off.

"I can make it to shore." Annja renewed her kicks but slung her free right arm about his shoulders. "But I'm not keen on drowning."

"You were calm and focused," he said, hooking an arm around her waist and leading the way toward shore. "I'm impressed. I thought I might have to drag a body up to the surface."

The shore was steep and slick with algae, but they managed to climb to the mossy bank. Before they summited, Slater scanned the periphery. The dock was situated in a recreational park that had been closed for flora restoration.

"Clear," he said. "Unfortunately."

Annja rolled to her back and stretched out her arms. The handcuff dug into her wrist but she could not complain. A glimmer of the setting sun flashed orange on the horizon. The scent of motor oil and seaweed hung in the air. Overhead a seagull tilted dangerously close, then swooped off over the water.

"They said something about going to the warehouse," she said. "I'm sure that was Neville's voice."

"They're going to destroy the evidence."

"Can you get your MI-6 guys on it?"

Slater coughed up water and spat to the side. "I can't call the operation off, Annja. And bringing in more men would shut it down fast."

"So you're going to maintain your cover? Isn't the gig up? He tried to kill you."

"Just breathe, Annja. Christ, we've both risen from Davy Jones's locker. Give me a few minutes to think, will you?"

A few minutes could mean the difference between them picking up Neville's trail—and ultimately finding Eric—or never seeing them again.

"But they have weapons somewhere in the area?"

"In the warehouse where you drove the truck. They'll move them to the harbor. Fast. Neville is disgusted with all the meddling, namely by you."

It had never been her intention to meddle. It was completely bizarre that a quest for faeries had turned up arms dealers digging in the dirt for diamonds. On the other hand, it was par for the course for her.

"But what about the dig?" Annja insisted. "Were more diamonds found?"

"Two more roughs. Enough to satisfy Neville's need for finances."

"Wait a minute." She crawled up onto her elbows. "You *knew* Eric was in the warehouse?"

"I…"

"Is he there now?"

He dropped his head onto the ground and exhaled. "It's very likely."

"Then why did you take me to the hospital this morning?"

"I thought I could get you to chase all over Cork looking in every hospital while we cleared out the dig site and the river drop. I didn't anticipate you'd go for a ride with my boss, or that bandits would decide to go shopping in our stash."

"You bastard. Eric could have been harmed or killed in that time. Just who are your alliances to?"

"Eric is not a detriment to Neville's mission. Though, now that you've made it clear to Neville the kid is on your team, I'm not so sure." Slater coughed and rolled to his side. Fine sand and moss coated his cheek. "We should go. Right now."

He helped Annja to stand. She shook off the shivers but the chill air worked relentlessly at her bare arms and wet skin. She shoved a hand in her buttoned pocket and pulled out her cell phone and gave it a flick.

"Let me get that handcuff off for you." Slater lifted her wrist, holding it gently. "Don't tell me that thing still works?"

"Waterproof to thirty feet," she said, and hoped it was really true. She'd not tested it until now. "I like your underwater lock-picking skills. What did you use?"

"The bow from my sunglasses. I was sweating when Neville took them from me."

He stuck the end of the wire bow into the handcuff and

worked his magic. The heavy chain dropped and Annja clasped her wrist. "Quite the MacGyver."

"Who's that?"

"A guy on—forget it. What was that about EUCs?"

He stared at her as if he could see into the gears turning in her brain, determining if she was trustworthy.

"I already know too much," she offered. "May as well tell me the rest."

"That's the worst argument I've heard in a long time."

"Have you got a rebuttal?"

"Why does that sound more sexy than you obviously think it does?" He smirked and said, "End user certificates. Neville's not my ultimate goal, Annja. Someone has been forging EUCs."

"I've heard of them. For shipping purposes?"

"When weapons and ammunition are shipped, flown or transferred to another country they must be accompanied by a signed and notarized end user certificate. The certificate guarantees that the guns will be used in the receiving country and not be rerouted somewhere else to be used as a means of terror. It's meant to restrict the flow of materials to embargoed states. Neville's forger does a bang-up job. But he's not on our payroll."

"So MI-6 wants this forger?"

"If he's not on our team, then we can't control him."

Made sense. In one of those underhanded, shouldn't-this-be-legit ways. The arms deals Neville was making were obviously gray, overseen by the British government, whether or not Neville was aware of it.

"Wait." Annja flipped long wet strands of hair from her face. She wished for a blanket and dry shoes. But if Slater wasn't shivering, she wasn't about to pull the wuss card. "You said they were going to destroy evidence at the warehouse?

Would that include something like people who have gone missing from the dig site? Including Eric?"

Slater sighed. "Probably."

"We have to get back to that warehouse."

"We're out at city's edge, with no vehicle or weapons. We'll never make it in time to stop the destruction."

"I just want to get there before they kill anyone."

"Even after the man tried to drown you?"

"And shoot me, don't forget that."

"And sell you to a bandit as his new girlfriend."

She'd forgotten about that one. "Eric is my responsibility. I won't let him down."

"Guess that means we're going for a walk. I don't have my wallet or ID. It won't be easy to rent a car."

"Are you telling me MI-6 didn't teach you how to hot-wire a vehicle?"

"Annja, grand theft auto is against the law." He said it with a grin. "But I like the way you think."

They scanned the area. On the way to the dock, they'd driven about ten minutes from the warehouse; they were still within city limits.

"West. It's a quiet part of town. Mostly warehouses and old machinery shops," Slater said.

They climbed the moss-padded embankment and slopped their way across the gravel. Wringing out her T-shirt, Annja would have liked to stop and empty her boots of water, but she didn't want to risk losing time. She'd walk off the water.

Five minutes later they'd entered a neighborhood that reminded her of a medieval village with its cobbled, narrow streets and terraced houses fit tight against one another. It was the kind of neighborhood she could live in.

A pimped-out white van pulled up alongside Annja and Slater with an abrupt squeal of the tires. Slater gripped her arm. She allowed him to pull her back so he stood in front of her.

"Who is it?" Annja asked.

"Oh, this day just gets better and better." Slater slapped at his shoulder holster but Neville's man had removed his gun. "It's the bandits who hijacked our truck."

The van doors opened. Out jumped two men, followed by the familiar leader in the knit beret. This time he held his AK-47 ready to fire. "Hello, luv. We meet again. Got yer boyfriend with you this time, I see. What are the two of you selling today, if you will?"

"Sorry, fresh out of contraband weapons," Slater said. He raised his hands slowly to his shoulders.

The leader's brows narrowed and he chewed a cigar stuffed at the corner of his mouth. He gestured with his rifle as he spoke. "I have a bone to pick with you."

"Get in line."

Annja winced at Slater's casual dismissal of real danger. The two men flanking the leader cradled their AK-47s like cherished children.

"That diamond you traded for the weapons was flawed."

"You're fashin' me," Slater said, assuming the dialect. "That's a risk you take when you—"

"You said it was grade A! I know me rocks, and that stone was bloody grade nothing! The thing shattered when I tapped the crown with me pistol."

"What the hell did you do that for? Diamonds are not forever," Slater argued calmly. "The diamond industry only wants you to believe that Valentine's crap so you'll shell out the big bucks for your woman."

"Shut up!"

Slater took a step back when both AK-47s aimed for his chest. "Let's talk about this, mate."

"I am not your mate. You duped me out of fifty thousand

pounds and this prime bit of bird." The leader looked Annja's wet body up and down. She held eye contact with him. She wasn't about to show fear. "Now you and the bird are going to bleed."

"You wouldn't kill an MI-6 agent," she blurted out.

Slater dropped his head down and he huffed out a breath. "She's lying."

"MI-6?" The leader locked gazes with her and she nodded. She wasn't willing to risk another death match, not when Eric's life was on the line. "Show me your ID," he said to Slater.

"I don't carry ID," Slater said, "because I'm not MI-6. Don't listen to the woman. She's been chasing faeries all day."

The leader jerked back a shoulder as if offended by that remark. He gestured for his men to lower their weapons. Approaching Annja, he tilted the AK-47 against his shoulder. A strong whiff of marijuana surrounded him. "The other crowd, eh?"

She shrugged. "Why the hell not? They've been stealing crew members from an archaeological dig."

"You see?" Slater said.

Studied as intently as any man with glassy eyes and a gun could possibly do, Annja defied his insolence with a sure stance. Finally he nodded and stepped back. "I believe the woman before I believe the man who tried to sell me worthless glass."

"It was diamond."

"Is that the kind of diamonds your Mr. Neville deals in?" The leader chuckled. "And he's got an MI-6 agent attached to him? Ha! I think I will leave the poor bastard to his own troubles. Leave them," he directed his men.

And that was it. The men piled into the van with intention of driving away.

"Are you headed into town?" Annja yelled after the leader. She didn't flinch as Slater slid her a razor-sharp condemnation in a glance. "We need a ride."

The leader's brows raised as he considered the nerve of the woman he'd just threatened to kill. "Faeries, eh?"

"Yes. Maybe. I'm sure they're out there somewhere." Feeling absent of good sense, and a trifle lost, Annja ran a palm up and down her arm. The shivers would not leave her alone. She hadn't a better plan, and really, how dangerous could a bunch of stoned bandits prove? "I felt their presence," she said.

A decisive nod preceded the bandit's gesture. "Hop in, luv. Where you headed?"

"To White Street." Slater gave the address.

"Will I be delivering you to the man with the glass diamonds?"

"No, he's too far ahead of us," Annja said. "It's a matter of life or death, though. A friend of mine." She winced and gave the leader a sincere face. Playing up to his compassion was working so far. "He's in trouble."

Rolling his eyes, and swinging his weapon, the leader gestured he was in compliance.

Annja was allowed to sit in the front seat and grabbed hold of the door for support as the van pealed into motion. Slater fit himself into the back among the other bandits, of which Annja hadn't managed a proper head count. Slater was a big boy; he could handle himself, she thought.

A small glass bong suspended by a black ribbon bobbed from the rearview mirror and various empty shells and AK-47 magazines littered the floor. The whole vehicle stunk like week-old athletic socks left out to dry in the sun.

"You best be careful if you're tracking the fair folk," the leader said to her. "Me cousin went for a five-day walk last summer all in his own backyard. He didn't escape the fair folk's clutches until he turned his clothing inside out."

All righty, then. Annja refrained from asking if the cousin had been eating magic mushrooms. She glanced at the bong.

Her eye fell upon a business card stuck in the open ashtray.

She grabbed it and winced as she read the single word and a phone number. She flicked it at the leader. "Wine?"

"Oh, aye. If you want some bloody good wine you go to that man. He likes to barter."

She would bet he did. And she wouldn't even ask what kind of barter he took. It wasn't as though the cavalcade of bandits had much to offer beyond weapons and illicit drugs.

"You keep it," the leader said. "Tell him the Handy Man sent you."

She nodded. "Will do."

37

Annja still wasn't answering her phone. Yet it was ringing, so that meant she had to be aware someone was calling. Garin Braden knew the woman had a talent for getting herself into trouble. She also had an incredible knack for getting out of said trouble. Most of the time, skill was all she required. Sometimes she needed help. Sometimes she amazed him with her luck.

But he did like to know if that luck was holding out now. He was in the area. Why not lend a hand?

He left another voice message. He was in County Cork looking for Wesley Pierce, and was aware she'd been filming on the dig.

Where was Pierce? Spending NewWorld's profits from the sale of the rough diamond?

That both digs had cleared out so swiftly did not sit well with him. And while the name Frank Neville meant nothing to Garin, he suspected if Neville was powerful enough to wrest a dig out from under NewWorld's control, then he must have a particular reason for it.

Could there have been more diamonds? He'd done some internet research. There were no diamond pipes in Ireland. But there had been a heist in the nineteenth century that Garin placed to the area where the dig was located. It had been a sensational case, kept under wraps by the burgeoning diamond industry. A find related to that case would yield a handful of roughs—worth a fortune nowadays.

Yet how did that tie in with Collins?

People who associated with Daniel Collins were more than mere treasure seekers. Ruthless cutthroats was a term that came to Garin's mind. And because of that, he was even more determined to find Annja and make sure she was safe.

THE ARMORED TRUCK RACED away from the warehouse as the bandits' van chauffeuring Annja and Slater arrived. Slater swore, grabbed the driver's shirt collar and demanded he follow the truck.

"Wait!" Annja opened her door to keep him from driving off. "Don't you see that smoke? Eric could be in there."

"I have to track them," Slater argued. "They'll lead me to the harbor where Neville may have a contact waiting. It's imperative."

"You think the forger could be waiting there?" Annja asked.

He nodded.

"Then leave me behind." He grabbed her arm as she attempted to slide from the passenger seat. "Let go, Slater! It's just smoke right now. I can still get inside to look for him."

"You're going to inhale smoke and never make it out. Give it up, Annja, he's dead."

"No." She tugged out of his unrelenting grip.

"Let her go!" the leader of the bandits said. "And you, too, mate. Get out. We're not a taxi service."

Slamming the door behind her, Annja stalked toward the warehouse. She eyed a wooden barrel below a water drainpipe slinking down the side of the building, and headed toward it.

The van drove away slowly, braked—she heard a loud curse—and it veered backward to the door beside her.

Slater stepped out of the van, running, and peeling off his shirt as he did so. He tore it in two as he approached her. Annja grabbed the shirt sections and dunked them in the water barrel.

"Are you always this stubborn?" he asked as he squeezed the water from his half of the shirt. "What does hosting a television show have to do with running into a burning building? They don't give medals to idiots, you know."

She smirked and tied the wet shirt over her mouth and nose. Tugging it down she said, "I thought you had a forger to catch."

"I'm giving you fifteen minutes. We can't be inside this building any more than five or ten, as it is. It may be smoking now but it can become an inferno in a heartbeat. Stay close to me."

"You stay close to me," she said.

She turned and kicked in the front door. Smoke billowed out, and Annja squinted against the burning fog. He was right, more than ten minutes in this death trap and no one would be walking out alive. Fortunately, the warehouse was wide-open, which dispersed the smoke, yet it also provided more oxygen to fuel the fire.

She scanned the warehouse floor. Not one wooden crate had been left behind on the bare concrete. The office was located on the upper floor that overlooked the loading dock.

Flames licked around the door, but hadn't yet crept to the walls.

"This way!" she shouted. She pressed the shirt over her nose and mouth as she ran.

Annja took the steel staircase hugging the wall two steps at a time. Rushing to the end of the landing, she kicked down the door she suspected was an office, sending flame sparks flying into the smoke-filled room.

Fire roared behind and below her. Its beastly growl warned her she had to be quick. She wasn't keen on fire. She'd had nightmares about fire. She thought it had something to do with Joan of Arc and the sword.

Ducking low and inside the office, she heard coughing. Near the door, someone grabbed her ankle.

It wasn't Eric.

"I got him!" Slater dragged the bound man out. "It's Brian Ford," he yelled. "He's alive."

The admittance of air into the room fanned a burgeoning flame licking in the office corner near the window. Annja heard a man's muffled shout.

She raced to the wall and beneath a boarded-up window she found Eric. His hands were bound before him, but his ankles were free. He could have walked out—unless he was drugged. Head tucked down toward his chest, he hacked and choked. Flames ate at his shirt.

She slapped the flames out. He shouted and cursed.

"Eric, it's Annja Creed." She tugged his arm but he wouldn't move. Instead, he gazed up at her. His face was black from the smoke, and sweat runneled streaks in it.

"So beautiful," he moaned. "Your wings…"

"I'm not a faerie," she said.

"Yes, the faeries."

"Hell, he's high on LSD. Slater!"

The MI-6 agent crouched on the floor next to her and

assessed the situation. "I can lift him over a shoulder if you help me get his head and shoulders up. The smoke has already zapped my strength. We have to hurry."

The wall behind them exploded, shooting splinters and sparks into the room. A splinter seared across Annja's cheek. She slapped at it and sucked at the wet shirt. But it was no longer wet, and she was now inhaling smoke.

Heaving up Eric's head, she shoved him toward Slater, who managed to wrangle him onto a shoulder and stand. Slater stumbled and faltered.

"You're going to make it!" Annja shouted.

"It's too smoky in here!" he called.

Tugging up the shirt over his face, she gave the loosened knot at the back of his head a tug to secure it. "Just follow me!" She grabbed him by the belt loop and led him toward the door.

Outside, the other man sat in a daze against the stair railing. "Can you move on your own?" she asked him. He nodded when he saw Annja. "Get down the stairs now!"

He shuffled forward on his butt and took the last two steps in a leap, landing on the concrete in a belly flop. He might have broken something, but he wasn't yelling in pain.

Slater used the railing for support, sliding against it as he stepped down, and made it to the ground. He stumbled once he reached the bottom step. Annja lunged to catch Eric's body and he sort of rolled over her and she bent to make sure he landed more gently than Brian.

"Sorry." Slater coughed.

"No apologies. Let's get out of here. I've got Eric. You grab Brian."

They raced to the door and outside into the gray evening sky.

Clean air infused Annja's lungs. Slater collapsed near the water barrel, Brian's body splayed out beside him. She tugged the shirt from Slater's face and gave his cheek a smack with her palm.

He gasped in a breath and heaved in rapid breaths.

Annja turned to Eric to assess his condition. He was breathing and moaning about faeries. He'd be okay, but she had to get him emergency care. Brian, too. He'd passed out near the doorway.

Raindrops spattered her head and shoulders. For once, she was thankful for the weather. And yet...

"Where's the other guy? I thought there was another one?" She gripped Brian's shirt and shook him. "Was there another man with you?"

"Richard," he muttered. "Think...he ran off..."

Annja could only hope it was an escape to freedom, and ultimately a local hospital.

"Five minutes to spare," she said to Slater, who checked his watch. "Time enough for you to drop us off at the emergency room before heading to the docks."

"Deal. I'll find us a vehicle." He touched his cheek and winced. "Was the slap necessary?"

"You were flirting with unconsciousness."

"I never flirt, Annja."

"And that's a good thing?"

His relieved grin accompanied a shake of his head. So the man was human underneath that stoic countenance. Any other time, and any other place...

"What will you do when you find the boat?" she asked.

"I'll take care of it, Annja. It's not the shipment I'm worried about, as I've explained."

"But after you've arrested the forger, you have to stop the boat, right? Can you get to Neville once he's taken to open water? What if they've already departed?"

"Annja, leave things to me. All right? I've got it under control."

She looked over his sooted face and chest and noted that he eased himself up slowly to a stand as if his back muscles ached. He had no weapon, no shirt, no contact with his superiors, not even a car.

"Do you think the Handy Man went after them?"

"Doubt it. The bandit knows MI-6 is involved now. That'll keep him away, and ensure he alerts every criminal in Ireland of my identity. Thanks for that, Annja."

"I was trying to keep us alive. I know it was stupid. I *am* sorry."

He clapped a hand on her shoulder. "You're good at staying alive. I like that about you." He winked and nodded. "Let's find us a vehicle and get these men to the hospital. Hell, a phone to call an ambulance would be good right now."

She tugged out her cell phone. "What's the emergency number in this country?"

THEY WEREN'T COVERT; that was sure. Four men loaded heavy wooden trunks onto a yacht moored at the end of the Kinsale dock. They did work efficiently. They'd done this before, Garin assumed. He liked experience and always sought to work with men of a certain talent in his own endeavors.

He lowered the binoculars. He wasn't sure he wanted a piece of this action, though. If MI-6 was involved the deal was gray. He preferred things to be either black or white, no fuzzy middle stuff. And he liked to stay as far from any organized government as possible.

So long as Annja Creed didn't show up he would let them go about their business.

38

Annja answered her cell phone on the first ring. Eric slept peacefully in the hospital bed to her right; he didn't wake from the noise.

"How many times does a man have to leave a message to get your attention?"

"I never realized how desperate you were for attention from me, Garin. What's up? You've called half a dozen times."

"Where are you?"

"Where are *you?*"

"In the same damned country as you. I'm looking for Wesley Pierce. Are you okay, Annja?"

"I am. How do you know Wesley? You're in Ireland?"

"He was managing a dig my company NewWorld was supervising."

"You own NewWorld?" She knew the man owned corporations and companies like some people owned pets, but this was a surprise. "Why didn't you ever tell me you owned an archeological dig management company?"

He sighed. "Is it so important right now? Where can I find Pierce?"

"In a cooler." She winced at the awful remark. "He was shot this morning by an arms dealer named Frank Neville."

"And you are investigating? Sticking your nose into places it probably shouldn't be stuck?"

"It's been stuck since before Wesley's death. I'm here in the country, officially, to chase faeries."

"You know, I believe that."

Delivered with such deadpan sincerity, she had to smile.

"Neville's running guns, and I got stuck in the middle when he decided to kidnap Eric, my cameraman. Eric's okay now. In the hospital, recovering. Thanks for asking. Did you know about the diamonds found on-site?"

"I got the phone call from Pierce last night. Diamonds? I thought it was singular, just one. How many?"

"Besides the one Wesley found? Neville had a rough but it turned out to be flawed. I'm not sure of any others found, though I suspect it was a treasure cache that may have yielded a couple prizes. But it couldn't have come from the ground. This area isn't conducive to diamond mining. The mystery of the diamonds confounds me."

"Annja, there are some things you're better off not knowing about."

"Gotcha. So that means I won't get any help from you unless I jump through your hoops?" Ready to hang up, she stopped when he pleaded for her to listen.

"Can you give me a location on Wesley Pierce?" Garin asked. "NewWorld should contact his family."

Surprised at what sounded like genuine compassion, Annja said she wasn't sure, but a local mortuary would be a good place to start looking. "Michael Slater might know. He was directing half of your dig. And he's MI-6. Did you know that?"

"MI-6 is involved?" Garin exhaled gruffly, one of those sounds a man makes when he's had enough of life's surprises. "Then I'm out. I'm not treading on their walk. And you shouldn't, either, Annja."

"Don't worry, I'm done. As soon as Eric is well enough, we're hopping a flight back to New York."

"What's his condition?"

"Whoever took him gave him LSD to make him think he was seeing faeries. That's how the local rumor got started. The doctor said he should be fine with rest."

"And this was done to him by someone I employ?"

"I'm not sure. Do you employ Frank Neville to run guns for you when he's not digging for diamonds?"

"I'm having the name checked out, but I haven't heard of him before. You're in such a mess, Annja, and still you didn't answer my call. Didn't you think I would offer to help you if you asked?"

"Your help always comes with conditions. I'm fine, Garin, really. Though I am still curious about the origin of those diamonds."

"They're from a nineteenth-century heist."

"What? How did you—?"

"It's called the internet, Annja. People use it when they want to find out things and do research on obscure facts."

"Or surf for porn."

"Let's not bring your private habits into play, sweetie. After Pierce called me about finding the rough, I did some research at Ireland's National Archives website because I am also aware the country does not spit up diamonds from its soil. And if you've been looking over the dig, you could verify my theory."

"All right. Shoot."

"Seems in 1850, one Elizabeth Price, daughter of an impoverished land owner in your area there, decided to take her chances and hop a ship to Liverpool during the height of the potato famine. How am I doing so far?"

"Potato famine. Yep, we found evidence of the pathogen that destroyed the potato crops at the same level I suspect Wesley found the rough diamond. Continue."

"Seems Price was only in Liverpool three days before the police grabbed her and deported her to Cork. The English were very keen on keeping the Irish out of their country. Let them starve and keep their diseases to themselves. Miss Price, though, was a crafty sort, and hooked up with one Harvel Kilmer of Kilmer Gemstone Acquisitions one night. I assume he thought he was picking up a whore. He woke in the morning absent half a million in rough diamonds he'd been carrying in packets in his valise. It was kept very low-key. The police pursued Miss Price onto the ship, but never found her. Kilmer put a bravo on her tail to follow her home."

Annja nodded, loving this story. That it made a lot of sense always put the cherry to the top of any archaeological question she muddled over.

"The company never reclaimed the diamonds. The bravo was discovered dead on a Cork dock a week later. Seems he had syphilis and was in a bad way even before embarking after Miss Price. My research places the Price family land in the dig area, very close to the Bandon River. You didn't know that?"

"I hadn't gotten that far. Wesley told me about the diamond, and then he was shot. As I was standing beside him."

"Neville?"

"Yes. But don't worry—"

"Right, MI-6 is on the case. Want to make a bet your gunrunner walks free?"

"That's ridiculous. He's murdered two people that I know of, and I'm sure they're not his first. Michael Slater knows what he's doing. I trust him."

"Sure. So I guess I walk away empty-handed. No diamonds. Not even a date with the prettiest woman on TV."

"Kristie isn't working this segment with me. Sorry."

"Kristie is far from pretty, Annja. She's more the cheerleader persuasion, which encompasses a whole different scale of beauty, and trust me, it's a shallow beauty."

"Whatever." Though she didn't mind the clarification. She wasn't hung up on looks, and knew Kristie's ratings surpassed her own segments on the show, but the occasional "you're not so bad" was appreciated.

"You're tough and smart," Garin continued, "but you're not keen on taking compliments. That bothers me about you."

"Don't lose any sleep over little ol' me."

"I don't, actually. But I do wish you'd embrace your beauty more freely. Then again, your lacking vanity is refreshing. So few women are like that, Annja. That aside, you need anything else?"

"No, I think I'm good here. Thanks, Garin. And thanks for the history lesson. It helps to fill in some holes."

"Talk to you soon."

No sooner had she hung up when the phone rang a second time. It wasn't Garin again, which made her a little sad. Talking to him had managed to lift her spirits. Despite the fact he was more of an adversary than friend, Garin's brand of nemesis often took a more nuisance form. And she did enjoy talking to a man who had walked through five centuries of life.

"Yes, Doug?"

"Annja, how's it going? Haven't heard from you for days. I was beginning to wonder if the faeries got you, too?"

His snicker didn't twang her funny bone like it usually did. Some faeries—kidnapping people and overdosing them on LSD.

"I'm fine, Doug, thanks for asking."

"And Eric? How's he enjoying the Irish beer?"

"That's Guinness, and he's…sleeping right now."

"At this hour? I know it's, like, eight in the evening there, Annja. I did the math."

"Yeah, well, Eric spent the night in the forest filming. He's been working very hard. I'm impressed with his work ethic. I hope his teacher appreciates what he's doing for this report. He's kicking back for a much-needed rest."

She needed the lie for the moment. But it wouldn't be right to conceal from Eric's father that his son been kidnapped and drugged. There could be complications in his future that would require his father having that knowledge.

Of course, Eric was a big boy; he would have to tell his family that himself. Thinking of his father, there was one piece to this puzzle that still made her wonder. She'd yet to hear back from Bart.

"Doug, what does Eric's father do for a living?"

"I told you he owns a film company, and I think he does notary stuff on the side. He financed the trip there."

"Yes, funny you didn't mention that to me before I left New York."

"Didn't think it was necessary. Why? What's up?"

"I didn't say anything was up. So how does Eric's father know Daniel Collins?"

"Not sure. Maybe he sold him some wine?"

"Could be. What do you mean by notary stuff?"

"You know, he officiates important papers and stuff. What do you call it? Notary public, that's it. Why?"

"Just curious. Eric and I haven't had much time for personal chat, we've been so busy filming."

"So you got good footage? Actual faeries?"

"What do you think, Doug?"

"Just remember, I am the Photoshop master. Any clues on the missing people?"

"They were found and they're doing well. The two men are currently hospitalized. Unfortunately the girl died in the hospital. Drug overdose. "

Annja swallowed the lump in her throat to think that if she had been ten minutes earlier, she could have prevented Beth's death. Beth had probably stumbled onto the enemy dig and had seen something they didn't want her to see—like trucks hauling weapons. That was it. She'd been volunteering, for Christ's sake.

It always hurt when innocents were hurt or killed. And it did happen around Annja more than she cared for. Wielding the sword accompanied some fantastic yet fearsome adventures. She killed those who would kill her first. And she protected those who could not protect themselves.

But not all the time.

Did that mean her dream held truth? Perhaps she wasn't capable of wielding the sword?

No, she wasn't going to have this inner argument again. She'd come to terms with what must be done if she continued to follow the sword's command.

"Annja?"

"Give us another day here, will you? Eric and I will bring home a great feature for the show. Promise. Bye, Doug."

She hung up in the middle of his goodbye, and leaned against the hospital wall, closing her eyes. It was never easy when innocents were harmed or murdered because they "got in the way."

But she could handle this and all that accompanied wielding the sword. Because if she did not, then who would?

Eric's father was not going to like hearing that his son had spent a day in the hospital. Could they convince him his son had stumbled onto some magic mushrooms? She hated the lie, and decided she'd leave it to Eric to decide if he was going to be truthful or lie to his father.

A notary public? That was interesting. Especially after all she'd learned from Slater. Someone was forging EUCs and selling them to gunrunners. She figured a person could sell one of those certificates for an impressive amount. The certificates were an absolute necessity to transport arms into a foreign country.

Could Marvin Kritz possibly be involved with this case? It didn't fit together as neatly as she hoped, but it was certainly worth checking out.

She hoped Slater had the means to arrest Neville and put him away for a long time. The man had ordered Beth's death. Annja couldn't know how many others had died because they had gotten in his way over the years.

Both Brian and Eric were going to be all right. The nurse had said Eric needed a day of rest, and he could be discharged tomorrow evening.

That left Annja to film some segments on her own. Because she wasn't in the mood, nor did she have the inclination, to interfere in MI-6's business.

Walking out the emergency entrance, Annja scanned the horizon. The harbor opened to the sea a dash to the east, and she walked, following the fresh lure of the salted sea breeze. She'd known this trip was not a vacation, but right now it felt good to steal a few minutes to relax and get her head together.

An iron-railed parking lot overlooked the neat harbor. It was picture perfect, almost as if someone had arranged the boats because they knew *National Geographic* was going to take pictures.

Annja counted eight boats and figured the ratio of seabirds to boats was about a hundred to one. She smiled at the cloud of flapping white that moved as a group from one end of the dock to the other.

It was small as far as harbors went. Mostly local boats and

skiffs. But also very little supervision. A gunrunner's perfect foil to a larger port like at Cork.

A cruiser yacht was moored at the far west end. It must be eighty feet long and its white mainsail hanging slack. Annja recognized the wooden boxes being loaded onto it. There must be dozens of the boxes.

"Neville? No freaking way. I thought Slater was going to…"

She hustled along the railing toward the end of the docks. Where was MI-6? They were not going to let Neville sail away.

"Annja Creed."

She swung about. A familiar man in sunglasses and wearing a wry smile sat in a black sedan parked within surveillance range of Neville's operation.

"Slater? What's going on? Aren't you going to—"

He put a finger to his lips to silence her. "Thought you'd be on a flight to the States by now."

Calming her frantic need to punch him or grab him by the shoulders and shake some sense into him, she approached the driver's side.

"Eric won't be discharged until tomorrow," she said. "I thought you'd have Neville in cuffs."

"And I thought you were going to leave this to the proper authorities?"

"Yes, but I don't see any proper ones taking action."

"Annja." He shook his head and tilted it back against the headrest. The sun flashed on his mirrored shades. "You seem to have forgotten I am a dead man."

"You're a—"

"And so are you," he chastised. "So I'd keep out of the yacht's line of vision if I were you. We don't want to spook them with a ghost."

She leaned against the car door, crossing her arms and

slinking down so her hip nudged the door handle. "So you're going to let the man transport the weapons? Is there a ship waiting out of the harbor somewhere?"

He nodded.

"But after he murdered Beth and Wesley, and tried to kill you and me—"

"Succeeded, Annja. Neville believes both of us are lying at the bottom of the Bandon River. So speak more softly, will you?"

"Yet you're sitting here, still keeping an eye on him?"

"My replacement is on the way. I never leave a job until I'm sure it's being covered. I suspect an agent has already insinuated himself into the loading crew."

"But he's not here to make an arrest," Annja decided. Slater shook his head. "So MI-6 lets the murderer go?"

He tipped up his sunglasses and eyed her through narrowed lids. He offered no apologies. And much as it frustrated her, Annja realized he was doing his job. She hated government agencies.

"Arms sales promote peace, Annja. Think about it."

"I'd rather not."

"It's the truth, as ridiculous as it sounds. Sometimes you have to join the fray to learn the enemy's secrets. It's not a perfect system, but it does work. Just be thankful you're alive. How *are* you alive? You're one tough woman. Ever think about working for your government?"

She laughed nervously. "Never. I couldn't live with the moral ambiguity."

"You'll stick with sensational television, then." He dropped his shades onto his nose, concealing the wicked glee Annja had glimpsed in his eyes. "Nice knowing you, Creed. Walk east, away from me. If I see you go near that boat—"

"Don't worry. I'm heading to the forest to stir up some faeries. Gotta bring something home to the boss man."

"Good luck with that. Don't worry, Pierce's family has been notified he was killed during a tragic cave-in offshore of the Clonakilty Bay, scavenging for buried treasure. His body has already been prepared for the flight home. His family took it well. They knew their son was an adventurer."

"You called them?"

"No, we've got people to make calls like that. People with compassion."

He said it without a flinch. The man possessed compassion, much as he'd like to deny it. An exterior armor of indifference was a necessity to do his job well.

"Thanks." She offered her hand, and Slater shook it.

She didn't have to like him for his morals, but she did respect him for his integrity.

"Hey, I have something for you," she said.

"For me? A gift? You shouldn't have."

She propped an elbow on the driver's door and shuffled her suspicions about Eric's father around in her brain. It didn't feel right, but she was very intuitive. And yet…he must be connected somehow. Why would a father pay for a trip to send his son to Ireland if he weren't the one behind the forgeries? What was she missing?

"The cigars," she said.

"I love a good smoke. Where is it?"

"No. The cigars. A box of Montecristos. It was a gift to Daniel from Eric's father, Marvin Kritz. And Daniel is big on bartering with less-than-savory sorts. I wonder…" She took out Daniel's business card and handed it to him. "I think he may be your forger."

"What proof do you have?"

"Nothing, beyond the fact that the quiet man is always the most suspicious. He's got ink stains on his hands, and I can't imagine he spends a lot of time composing love letters. And I've learned that Eric Kritz's father is a notary public. He's a friend of Daniel's. He sent a gift with Eric to give to Daniel. Looked like a box of cigars. I wonder if MI-6 wouldn't like to take a look at those smokes?"

"I bet they would. You figured this all out on your own?"

"Hey, sometimes I'm good."

"You're always good, Creed." He flicked the card between his fingers. "Don't know why I didn't suspect him in the weeks I was on the dig. But it makes sense. Neville did have dinner at Collins's mother's one night, which was the catalyst to our misadventures digging in the dirt. I wonder about that old lady."

"I think she's harmless."

"She'll be checked out thoroughly. I'll rally a couple of agents and send them over to Collins's house right now. Thanks, Annja."

"No problem."

"Hey, Annja? I'm never in one place for very long, but if you're ever in London—Albany Road—why don't you look me up?"

"I may do that. Good luck, Slater."

39

Daniel Collins opened the door to two men who wore lack-luster black business suits. They flashed badges that he had no time to read, but he guessed they were from some idiot government department and had seen one too many slick spy movies.

"Gentleman." He stepped aside so they could enter his house, and they did. Their eyes took in everything from stone floor, up the whitewashed walls, to the tin ceiling. "What can I do for you today? A bit sunny for the dour clothes. You lose your direction on the way to tip back a parting glass?"

"We've got a warrant to search your home, Mr. Collins," one of the men said.

"Aye? What would that be for?"

"Here's the warrant. You can read it while we take a look around. Do you mind?"

Daniel snatched the folded document. He didn't have to read it. Why bother? He tucked it in his front shirt pocket and stepped aside. "Don't mind at all. Fancy a cigar while you're snooping about?"

THE NURSE WAS GOING over Eric's discharge papers with him, so Annja left them in the room and found a table near a window in the hospital visitors' lounge. She twisted the cap off a soda bottle and tipped back the root beer. Eric's father had been notified of his hospital stay for insurance purposes, but Eric gave no indication of whether or not his father knew the truth about his reason for being admitted, or if he was angry with him.

As far as family was concerned, Annja didn't know anything about having the standard nuclear family. Her childhood had been fun and she'd survived it well enough. So why she allowed comments about family to poke her nerves sometimes was beyond her.

It was nearing supper, and the day promised a few good hours of sunlight still. Eric was eager to go out and film a final segment for the show. He was feeling fine, he said, and was glad to be getting out of the scratchy hospital bedsheets. He had suggested they catch a midnight flight.

They would only be able to allude to the existence of faeries in County Cork, Ireland. But Annja knew belief tended to be strong without actual evidence. With little proof of the winged creatures they had come to pursue, Annja still knew how to make the show work. Hell, she could claim to have administered a little fairy dust in some of her past segments. Plus, Eric had filmed a couple of interviews with locals in the Ballybeag pub and had gotten some great sound bites.

Just because you couldn't see something didn't mean it didn't exist, whether it be a tangible entity or something found, more often than not, in the hearts of the locals.

The notion to ring Daniel before she left town seemed more cruel than wise. The man had been nice enough to her, but if he was supplying Frank Neville, and others of the same criminal ilk, with forged EUCs, then she wasn't going to stand back and allow him to continue.

Rachel Collins would never invite her to dinner again. The old lady was capable, though; she could take care of herself. Heck, if she ever thought to cash in the diamond among her ephemera collection, she'd be set for life.

Someone sat across the table from her and stretched out his legs. A man. The slightest hint of cologne tickled Annja's nose. It was familiar and spicy. Daring a glance at him and a tired yet friendly smile—she dropped the smile.

"Long time no talk, Annja." A dark goatee framed Garin Braden's smug grin. Dark eyes the color of rich peat twinkled.

"Are you visiting someone here," she asked, "or do you just like to follow me?"

"Actually, I did get a chance to visit with an old friend."

She looked at him with a suspicious expression.

"I picked up a couple bottles of Lafite—prephylloxera, the grail of Lafites—for a party I'm hosting this weekend," he said. "Want to come along for a night or two? It's in Berlin on the river Spree. I think you'd like my apartment there. I just had it redecorated by some hot young designer in Louis XV style."

"Rococo. Groovy," Annja said. She'd heard the term *prephylloxera* recently.

In a cozy wine cellar.

She leaned across the table, ignoring the mischievous twinkle in Garin's eyes. "Would your wine dealer happen to be Daniel Collins?"

"None other."

"And he was actually home?"

"Of course." His smile turned mysterious and Annja felt her heart sink. "Why do you suspect he'd not be in residence?"

"I just…"

Garin delivered the coup de grâce of smug smiles. "You can't expect that I would allow a friend—and good source of Lafite—to be detained by the authorities, do you?"

"You stopped the arrest?"

"Annja, you wound me. I would never dream of obstructing justice. And I had no idea an actual arrest was intended. But I may have suggested that Collins take inventory of any stock he might have and that he should relocate it while he did so."

"Oh, you are too rich."

"I am, as a matter of fact." He sat back, running a hand down the front of a suit that likely had cost him thousands, without his checkbook breaking a sweat.

"I meant it facetiously," she said. "How could you do that?"

"Annja, do you really want an explanation? I like to remain an enigma to you. It keeps the mystery and makes for a fascinating relationship."

"We do not have a relationship."

"Annja, you wound me. Here I thought we were family."

"Family? We are the farthest—"

"There are many definitions of the term. One mustn't be related by blood to feel a familial connection to another."

The idea of family had been bothering her lately. And now here Garin Braden sat beside her, offering something she wasn't sure she wanted, and yet couldn't resist considering.

"Is there any more?" he asked, with a gesture to her root beer. She shoved the bottle toward him. He tipped back the remainder in a swallow. "So how did the faerie hunt go?"

That he generally knew everything she was involved in, sometimes down to her every footstep, had ceased to startle her. The man had his ways. He had people. He was a five-hundred-year-old immortal who manipulated the world to his whim. What more could she say?

And he considered her family.

In a mystical way, she probably was.

Annja sighed. "Faeries don't exist, Garin. Or did I just spoil a childhood belief of yours? Did your mommy read you fairy tales when you were little?"

"We didn't have books, Annja. None that my family could afford. And our fairy tales in the fifteenth century were more about dragons and virgin princesses. Why is it so difficult for you to believe in faeries? Why can't you allow a little whimsy into your life?"

She stared at him. "Who *are* you?"

Garin flashed a million-dollar playboy smile. "If you're not keen on the designation of family, then I'll have to go with friend."

"Try enemy."

"Ally."

"Nemesis."

"Harsh. But not always unwarranted." He shoved the empty bottle her way, dismissing the topic as easily. "So what plans have you got for your next adventure? Sea monster fishing off the coast of Wales? Chupacabra in Mexico?"

"We did the chupacabra last season."

"Nice. So, what's the verdict? Will you come to the party?"

"I don't know... I don't think I can swing it. I have to see Eric back to New York—"

"He's a big boy. I'm sure he can handle the flight by himself. Might even meet a sexy young college student desperate for conversation."

True. And Annja didn't relish the long flight. "I didn't pack for a party," she said.

"You forget I know your dress size as well as your—"

"All right," she replied, cutting him off before he'd mention that her bra size was also in his knowledge. "One day in Berlin, partying like a rock star."

"I've some great wine for the occasion."

She rolled her eyes. If the bottle she'd consumed had been worth five thousand, she didn't want to know how much this Lafite cost. In Garin's case he'd likely bartered. Such was his nefarious world of living large. She also did not want to know if he had gained illegal paperwork from Daniel. She just did not need to deal with that.

"Come on." Garin stood and offered his wide, strong hand. "We'll put the kid on a plane, then we'll fly in my private jet to Germany."

"We've got some filming to do before the flight leaves at midnight."

"Fine. I'll hold the jet while you two poke about in the woods. Deal? I do love spending time with you, Annja."

Annja was looking forward to a little rest and relaxation. And sure, she could admit to curiosity about Garin's party. If you couldn't put the enemy away from you, it was always wise to keep them close to you.

THE BOG GLITTERED under the setting sun. For the first time since Annja had set foot on Irish soil she could fully buy into the idea of mystical or magical beings. Even the air felt lighter, as if she could float as she walked across the blanket of spongy soil.

She approached Eric slowly, speaking as he recorded the final segment for the show.

"As the wind moves through your hair, and the rich, fragrant air invades your pores, the centuries past come alive. It's possible that mighty warriors with mystical powers once tracked this land. Ancient rituals, some still practiced today by believers, have firmly cemented the supernatural to this realm. So close your eyes, and open your heart to the magic of the enchanted land of Éire."

"That's perfect, Annja."

It did feel right. She ran her fingers through her hair, then let it fall loose as she tilted her head to the darkening sky. Already the stars twinkled faintly. The moon promised to be full in less than a week. This evening the air was so still, not even a cricket chirped.

"That's beautiful," Eric commented. And Annja realized he was still filming. "I got your silhouette against the dark sky and the moon. We wrapping?"

"Yes." She twirled a finger as signal to cut and stop filming. "I think we got what we need. How are you feeling?" she asked.

"Not so bad. The fresh air is incredible. I can finally breathe again."

"We'd better head into Cork." She offered to carry his equipment to the Mini and they packed it up and drove toward Ballybeag, where they'd exchange Mr. Riley's car for a taxi to Cork.

"I seriously thought it was faeries that took me," Eric said from the passenger side. "Man, that was some crazy stuff. LSD? You know I've never done drugs before, Annja. I feel kinda lousy about that."

"Don't dwell on it, Eric. It wasn't your fault. And, as the doctor explained, you will not become addicted. What are you going to tell your father?"

"The truth." He shrugged. "But I don't want Doug or you to get in trouble."

"Whatever your father has to say to us, we can handle. I should have kept a closer watch on you."

"I'm a big boy. My father knows that, too. I don't think he'll huff too loudly after I explain it was necessary to obtain the information for our story."

She wasn't sure what to say to him about the fact that his father could be involved in sending notary supplies to Daniel Collins. MI-6 hadn't found proof, because Garin had tipped Daniel off. It was something father and son could work out together.

Family. It was never easy.

Berlin

"GARIN." ROUX NODDED as Garin entered the study. The old man had been examining his latest find displayed on a wood stand—the Concubine's Jade. "This one must have set you back a pretty penny."

"Pennies are worthless nowadays. That chunk of jade was all about the Ben Franklins," Garin replied.

"Sixteenth century?"

"Rumored to possess untold powers of joy when the planets align just so and the moonlight flashes through the center of the stone."

"As usual, joy remains elusive." The old man chuckled and accepted the tumbler of Scotch Garin offered. "It's odd when we find ourselves consuming hundred-year-old Scotch, isn't it?" He tilted back a swallow and nodded satisfaction to its smooth texture.

"Only odd because we walked the world long before it was created."

"Indeed. So about those charges on my credit card... Five hundred thousand to the Heifer Organization—a worthy cause—but really."

"It'll provide livestock to those in need. I personally buy a few arks of animals every year," Garin said.

"Yes, but the other half million." Roux narrowed his pale blue gaze on Garin, but such a look wasn't capable of making him flinch. Garin had mastered indifference toward his once-master centuries ago. "The Infinity Life Cryogenics Society?"

Garin smiled. That had been Ruth Banyon's dying wish. She'd wanted to be preserved cryogenically, until such a time when she could be defrosted, and well, after that it was all a bunch of nonsense to Garin.

Who was he to deny her?

Before he could explain, Roux's attention was diverted behind him to the stairway. "Annja!"

"ROUX, I DIDN'T KNOW you'd be here." Annja stepped off the bottom step and glanced around. The reception hall was vast and marble sparkled and gold accents glittered everywhere, but it was strangely quiet. "Where is everyone else?"

"The actual party doesn't begin for another hour," Garin, who wore a black tuxedo, the same as Roux, said. "Roux and I wanted to share a drink with you first. That dress fits you perfectly."

She smoothed her palms down the white silk. It was fitted from shoulder to knee and clung to all her curves. Garin had left it in a guest room for her and allowed her to shower and relax a while. The dress was a nice change from tromping about in loose cargo pants or layered T-shirts and hiking boots.

The maid had helped her to sweep her chestnut hair into a chignon and said it called attention her brilliant hazel eyes. Taking compliments was never easy for Annja, but the change of clothing and location worked to release her inhibitions. She was in the mood for a party.

"You don't mind, do you?" Roux asked. "That we keep you to ourselves a bit?"

She shrugged. "Not at all. Where's the booze? I've got a nasty case of faeries I need to get over."

"Did you find any?" Roux asked as Garin prepared a tumbler of Scotch for Annja.

"I found belief," she said. "That seems to be more than enough for some folk." She lifted her glass to them. "So, what shall we toast to?"

"To you, Annja," Roux declared. "Happy birthday!"

She paused, midsip. Utterly flummoxed, she merely stared at Garin and Roux. For a moment she thought she might tear up, but then she gasped and said, "My birthday?"

"Don't tell me you forgot?" Roux said. "I marked it in my calendar. I know I have the right day."

"Yes. No, I didn't—well, yes, I did. I just never think about it all that much. Seriously? So this party is…"

"For you," both men offered. Roux lifted his chest proudly. The old man displayed much affection toward Annja, which she accepted as a sort of father to daughter relationship. While she suspected Garin's feelings of desire and pride for her conflicted. "We've got a gift for you."

"I…haven't been given a birthday gift for ages. What is it?"

Garin stepped back and swept a hand before an easel standing beside a white marble hearth.

Annja stepped over and tugged the black cloth away from the painting. "Oh, it's a…well, the style looks a lot like Jean Fouquet." Medieval studies were her forte, and she admired many renaissance painters. Fouquet was fifteenth century. "But no. It's not Fouquet. It can't be. I've never seen this painting before."

The painting was a subject that had become very much her own. It featured Joan of Arc tied to the stake with the flames at her feet and a disturbed crowd looking on.

"The colors are beautiful. My gosh, this is so…generous." She turned to both men. "Thank you. I love it. It'll add some much-needed color above the couch in my living room."

"What makes you believe it's not by Fouquet?" Roux asked. "Take a good look."

Roux winked at Garin as Annja bent to closely examine the painting. She almost touched it, but then jerked her fingers away. "This is an original."

"It is," Garin said. "It was listed at auction as in the style of Jean Fouquet."

"But it *is* Fouquet," Roux said.

"The style is most definitely his, but..." She searched her memory for what she knew of Jean Fouquet. "He didn't actually start painting until around 1445. So he couldn't have possibly witnessed this scene."

"What makes you think the man wasn't sketching the events he witnessed as he journeyed toward becoming a painter?" Roux asked.

"Really? Do you think he actually witnessed Joan's burning? It's so sad to consider now."

Though she wielded Joan's sword, Annja was ever aware what the sainted warrior had gone through in her quest to accomplish what she believed must be done. And to be punished so cruelly was unthinkable.

"Wait a second." She bent closer to inspect the face of one of the soldiers in the crowd. Utter horror stretched his face as he looked up the flames that licked at Joan's feet. "Is that—? It can't be."

"It could be." Roux stood beside the painting and assumed the tilted head pose of the man in the picture.

"That's you! And the other guy is—" The soldier standing shoulder to shoulder with the horrified one looked away from it all, unwilling to witness the tragic event. She turned on Garin. "You?"

He nodded and shrugged. "It was not a good day."

"This is absolutely incredible. That Fouquet sketched

this and then later rendered it—but it's not in his gallery of work."

"It was lost after a fire obliterated his workshop in Tours. We've been aware of its existence but have never quite been able to put our hands to it until it showed up at auction recently," Roux explained.

"We thought you'd like something from both of us," Garin said over her shoulder. "Deny it all you like, but we three are a sort of family. In a roundabout way."

So that was the reason behind his reference to family earlier. If she had known he'd been planning this surprise she might have been nicer to him. On the other hand, probably not.

"This is amazing. It's perfect. Thank you." She turned and hugged Garin, which surprised the hell out of him. But before he could settle into the warmth of her embrace, she pulled away and went to hug Roux. "Family? I can see that. In a roundabout way."

"Families can never claim to be perfect, or even nice to one another all the time," Roux said.

Garin lifted his tumbler. "To family."

RACHEL COLLINS STOMPED out the back door of her house to the scrubby plot where forest met the field. She spotted the gray rabbit immediately. It disregarded her. She was just the old lady who tended the garden and made it full of carrots and cabbage every summer.

Lifting the spear of Lugh over her head, Rachel thrust it forward. She wasn't strong, but the spear left her grip with an unnatural speed and found a sure path.

Upon impact, the rabbit flipped into the air, its hind legs twitching and flailing. The spear cut through its gut and moved clean out the other side.

Holding her arm out straight, fingers curled to catch, Rachel caught the spear as it returned.

"Handy piece of work, this old spear." She trudged toward the rabbit, but a glint on the ground caught her eye. She bent and nabbed the small, cold nugget. "Coo, what's this? Looks like gold."

The Executioner®

Don Pendleton's

ENEMY AGENTS

American extremists plan a terror strike....

When California's Mojave Desert becomes the training ground for a homegrown militia group with a deadly scheme to "take back" America, Mack Bolan is sent in to unleash his own form of destruction. But first he'll have to infiltrate the unit and unravel their plot before it's too late.

Available in June wherever books are sold.

GOLD EAGLE®

www.readgoldeagle.blogspot.com

GEX391R

TAKE 'EM FREE

2 action-packed novels plus a mystery bonus

NO RISK
NO OBLIGATION TO BUY

SPECIAL LIMITED-TIME OFFER
Mail to: The Reader Service

IN U.S.A.: P.O. Box 1867, Buffalo, NY 14240-1867
IN CANADA: P.O. Box 609, Fort Erie, Ontario L2A 5X3

YEAH! Rush me 2 FREE Gold Eagle® novels and my FREE mystery bonus (bonus is worth about $5). If I don't cancel, I will receive 6 hot-off-the-press novels every other month. Bill me at the low price of just $31.94 for each shipment.* That's a savings of at least 18% off the combined cover prices and there is NO extra charge for shipping and handling! There is no minimum number of books I must buy. I can always cancel at any time simply by returning a shipment at your cost or by returning any shipping statement marked "cancel." Even if I never buy another book, the 2 free books and mystery bonus are mine to keep forever.

166/366 ADN FDAH

Name	(PLEASE PRINT)	

Address		Apt. #

City	State/Prov.	Zip/Postal Code

Signature (if under 18, parent or guardian must sign)

Not valid to current subscribers of Gold Eagle books.
Want to try two free books from another series?
Call 1-800-873-8635 or visit www.ReaderService.com.

* Terms and prices subject to change without notice. Prices do not include applicable taxes. Sales tax applicable in N.Y. Canadian residents will be charged applicable taxes. Offer not valid in Quebec. This offer is limited to one order per household. All orders subject to credit approval. Credit or debit balances in a customer's account(s) may be offset by any other outstanding balance owed by or to the customer. Please allow 4 to 6 weeks for delivery. Offer available while quantities last.

Your Privacy—The Reader Service is committed to protecting your privacy. Our Privacy Policy is available online at www.ReaderService.com or upon request from the Reader Service.

We make a portion of our mailing list available to reputable third parties that offer products we believe may interest you. If you prefer that we not exchange your name with third parties, or if you wish to clarify or modify your communication preferences, please visit us at www.ReaderService.com/consumerschoice or write to us at Reader Service Preference Service, P.O. Box 9062, Buffalo, NY 14269. Include your complete name and address.

GE11

James Axler
Outlanders®

TRUTH ENGINE

An exiled God prince acts out his violent vengeance…

Cerberus Redoubt, the rebel base of operations, has fallen under attack. The enemy, Ullikummis, is at the gates and Kane and the others are his prisoners. The stone god demands Kane lead his advancing armies as he retakes Earth in the ultimate act of revenge. For he is determined to be the ultimate god of the machine, infinite and unstoppable.

Available August wherever books are sold.

Or order your copy now by sending your name, address, zip or postal code, along with a check or money order (please do not send cash) for $6.99 for each book ordered ($7.99 in Canada), plus 75¢ postage and handling ($1.00 in Canada), payable to Gold Eagle Books, to:

In the U.S.
Gold Eagle Books
3010 Walden Avenue
P.O. Box 9077
Buffalo, NY 14269-9077

In Canada
Gold Eagle Books
P.O. Box 636
Fort Erie, Ontario
L2A 5X3

Please specify book title with your order.
Canadian residents add applicable federal and provincial taxes.

GOLD EAGLE®

www.readgoldeagle.blogspot.com

GOUT58

THE GODDESS TEST

In a modern retelling of the Persephone myth, Kate Winters's mother is dying and Kate will soon be alone. Then she is offered a deal by Hades, lord of the Underworld—pass seven tests and become his wife, and her mother will live and Kate will become immortal. There's one catch—no one who has attempted the Goddess Test has ever survived.

AVAILABLE WHEREVER BOOKS ARE SOLD!

www.HarlequinTEEN.com

HTGT2011MM

JAMES AXLER

DEATH LANDS®

Perception Fault

From the rubble of the future comes potential…and peril!

In Denver, Ryan Cawdor and his companions are offered a glimmer of hope: a power plant, electricity, food and freedom. But the city is caught in a civil war between two would-be leaders and their civilian armies… and Ryan is caught in the middle, challenged by both sides to do their bidding. Tomorrow is never just a brand-new day in the Deathlands.

Available July wherever books are sold.

Or order your copy now by sending your name, address, zip or postal code, along with a check or money order (please do not send cash) for $6.99 for each book ordered ($7.99 in Canada), plus 75¢ postage and handling ($1.00 in Canada), payable to Gold Eagle Books, to:

In the U.S.
Gold Eagle Books
3010 Walden Avenue
P.O. Box 9077
Buffalo, NY 14269-9077

In Canada
Gold Eagle Books
P.O. Box 636
Fort Erie, Ontario
L2A 5X3

Please specify book title with your order.
Canadian residents add applicable federal and provincial taxes.

GOLD EAGLE®

www.readgoldeagle.blogspot.com

GDL99

Don Pendleton's Mack Bolan®

Kill Shot

**Homegrown radicals
seek global domination!**

The terror begins with ruthless precision
when the clock strikes noon, gunfire
ringing out in major cities along the East
Coast. At the heart of the conspiracy,
sworn enemies have joined for the nuclear
devastation of the Middle East. As blood
spills across the country, Bolan sights his
crosshairs on their nightmare agenda.

*Available June
wherever books are sold.*

Or order your copy now by sending your name, address, zip or postal code, along with a check or
money order (please do not send cash) for $6.99 for each book ordered ($7.99 in Canada), plus
75¢ postage and handling ($1.00 in Canada), payable to Gold Eagle Books, to:

In the U.S.	**In Canada**
Gold Eagle Books	Gold Eagle Books
3010 Walden Avenue	P.O. Box 636
P.O. Box 9077	Fort Erie, Ontario
Buffalo, NY 14269-9077	L2A 5X3

Please specify book title with your order.
Canadian residents add applicable federal and provincial taxes.

**GOLD
EAGLE®**

www.readgoldeagle.blogspot.com

GSB142

Don Pendleton
POWER GRAB

The balance of global power is threatened....

An explosion at a New York shopping mall
launches an all-out Stony Man effort against the
new face of terror. A brilliant and brutal warlord
turned dictator is poised to destabilize the entire
Middle East through blood politics, and several
planned attacks are about to lead to desperate
chaos. But the enemy isn't just targeting American
soil—he's poised to savage the world.

STONY
MAN®

*Available June
wherever books are sold.*

Or order your copy now by sending your name, address, zip or postal code, along with a check or
money order (please do not send cash) for $6.99 for each book ordered ($7.99 in Canada), plus
75¢ postage and handling ($1.00 in Canada), payable to Gold Eagle Books, to:

In the U.S.	In Canada
Gold Eagle Books	Gold Eagle Books
3010 Walden Avenue	P.O. Box 636
P.O. Box 9077	Fort Erie, Ontario
Buffalo, NY 14269-9077	L2A 5X3

Please specify book title with your order.
Canadian residents add applicable federal and provincial taxes.

**GOLD
EAGLE** ®

www.readgoldeagle.blogspot.com

GSM113